I0593625

ABOUT THE AUTHOR

Lexie Winston has been an astronaut, rock star, princess and time traveller. In her dreams. But none of the dreams have lived up to what becoming an author has been like. She gets to live in a world of pure imagination, and her heroines get to do the things she's always wished she could.

When not writing books, Lexie is a mother of two gorgeous teenagers and the wife to a patient and understanding man. They live in Western Australia and are lorded over by a black toy poodle. She loves camping, reading and if her iPad was stolen, her world would explode. (It has the kindle app on it.) And you can find all links at

www.lexiewinston.com

RINGMASTER

LEXIE WINSTON

NEIGHPALM PUBLISHING

ALSO BY LEXIE WINSTON

The Collectors Division

(Paranormal Reverse Harem Series)

Guardian

Guardian's Blood

Guardian Ascending

Collector's Division Omnibus

Neighpalm Industries Collective

(Enemies to Lovers Reverse Harem)

Abandoned Girl

Broken Girl

Tormented Girl

Wanted Girl

Cherished Girl

Loved Girl

Superficial Girl - Jacinta's Story Part 1

Superficial Girl - Jacinta's Story Part 2

Neighpalm Industries Collective 1-3

Neighpalm Industries Collective 4-6

First published by Neighpalm Publishing in 2023

Copyright © Neighpalm Publishing 2023
The moral right of the author has been asserted.
All rights reserved. This publication (or any part of it) may not
be reproduced or transmitted, copied, stored, distributed or
otherwise made available by any person or entity, in any form
(electronic, digital, optical, mechanical) or by any means
(photocopying, recording, scanning or otherwise) without prior
written permission from the publisher.
This is a work of fiction. Names, characters, businesses, places,
events and incidents are either the products of the author's
imagination or used in a fictitious manner. Any resemblance to
actual persons, living or dead, or actual events is purely
coincidental.

Ringmaster - Galaxy Circus series

Mobi format: 978-0-6455262-8-8
Print: 978-0-6455262-9-5

Cover design by Raven Ink Covers
Editing by Elemental Editing

AUTHORS NOTE

Ringmaster is the sixth Galaxy Circus
novel, a fast-burn RH series that contains
some adult situations which may be
triggering, such as dub-con.

Galaxy Circus will also contain MM and
male appendages of a somewhat interesting
nature.

**THIS IS NOT THE LAST BOOK IN THE
SERIES**

GALAXY CIRCUS GLOSSARY

PLANET ICEEN

Lightning Cats

They are a shifter race that has two forms—a bipedal human form and their cat form. Their bipedal form is humanoid in shape, but they are covered in a soft downy fur except for the front of their torso and genital area. They have sharp teeth, big ears, and long tails in this form. Their animal form is similar to a saber-toothed tiger from Earth. They can shoot lightning from their tails, and it can be used for defense and attack.

They are a matriarchal society and live in family groups called streaks. They have alpha, beta, and omega distinctions, but there is always a female alpha who acts as head of the family.

Alphas have a rut and omegas have a heat. Only alpha and omegas can breed with one another, and betas can only breed with their own designation. There are male and female omegas. Both have breeding capabilities, but male omegas are rare. Most are killed once their designation is discovered to prevent competition with females for coveted positions within the streak.

The planet Iceen is a frozen tundra of caves and outcroppings, and the streaks usually have two dwellings—a cave for their animal form, and a dome-like, insulated glass building which they live in with their streaks.

Maxsim (Alpha Lightning Cat)

The leader of the streak of lightning cats that performs in the circus, despite it being a matriarchal society. Maxsim is a dark aqua blue that ombres out to snowy white in the legs, with black, tribal style markings across shoulders, chest, and arms. He has high cheekbones, cat ears, feline eyes, a tail, and fangs, which are bigger when in animal form, as well as a broad chest and well-defined arms. Fur covers his body when in humanoid form, except for a patch across his chest and down to his groin.

Maxsim keeps the rest of the streak safe from an aggressive Natalia.

Natalia (Beta Lightning Cat)

Only female in the group that performs in the circus. She is heir to her matriarchal streak, but is a beta designation. Natalia has pale blue fur all over, with long black hair, high cheekbones, cat ears, feline eyes, a tail, and fangs. She has small breasts, a slender, toned body, and a lean backside and legs. She has naked patch across her breasts and down to groin.

She wants to form a streak with Maxsim, Trace, Fuse, and Sim, but they are alphas and cannot breed with her. She took her omega sister's place, who was supposed to be the one performing with the circus.

Echo (Omega Lightning Cat)

He is a pure white lightning cat, with a smaller frame than Maxsim's, and built much more delicately. His designation is omega, and he has survived because he comes from a rare streak with a male omega. The streak, with help from the warlocks, protected him while growing up. They hid it, and he presents himself to the world as beta. He wants to form a streak with Maxsim, but not Natalia. She discovered he is an omega and keeps trying to kill him.

Other cats in the group
    Trace (Alpha Lightning Cat)
    Fuse (Alpha Lightning Cat)
    Sim (Alpha Lightning Cat)

Mazlan Natalia's mother and Matriarch of the Lightning cats (Omega)

Sky blue fur

Minx Natalia's sister (Omega)

Shoshi Natalia's younger sister 10 yrs old (omega)

Jalin Echo's mother (Alpha)

Astrea Maxsim's mother (Omega)

Yalani

An abominable snowman type creature with shaggy white and gray fur. They are good at blending into their surroundings. It is a hunter-gatherer species that lives in caves on Iceen. Eight to nine feet tall, they are an aggressive species that will attack if they feel threatened. They live solitary lives unless mated and raising a family.

PLANET SKARR

This planet is the birthplace of the human race. The original humans were exploring Skarrians who crashed on Earth, and because they no longer had access to the magical waters, lost all their supernatural abilities.

Skarr looks much like Earth from above though the land masses are unfamiliar and the sea has a slight pink tint to it. I'm pretty sure that's got something to do with the two pink moons that shine brightly in the sky orbiting the planet

Skarrians are mostly polyamorous and have attraction marks that show up on both parties' bodies. If attraction wanes on either side, the marks disappear. Skarrians find themselves bonded to others after five rounds of sex, which requires them to orgasm simultaneously. Skarr is basically a sister planet to Earth in that it is made up of ten different land masses surrounded by pink oceans, but it has different species of plants and animals.

When reproducing, all bonded members of the family must participate to produce a child.

Lila Jenson (Liliana Adams) mimic and whisperer power

Orphaned at a young age, she moved from foster family to foster family, never really fitting in anywhere, though nothing terrible happened to her. One family put her into gymnastic lessons and self-defense courses to keep her out of trouble. She has no real goal in life, but has always thought there must be something more than working in a bar and having the occasional one-night stand.

She is average height, with a curvy figure, long chestnut hair with turquoise streaks, golden skin, and green eyes.

Lila discovered she has grandparents who are still alive, and they invited her to learn their family business.

Her mimic forms so far include Celestian, Warlock, Barcoa, Aquilian, Fire and Earth Elementi, Necro and Rilunese

John Adams, William Adams, and Eric Adams

Triplet brothers who appear to be in their late

forties, they possess chestnut hair, tall, slender builds, and emerald green eyes.

They have been searching for Liliana, also known as Lila, for years, and are thrilled to have finally found her. They are also the CEOs of the Galaxy Circus and guardians of the power orb.

William has a buzz cut and is gruff.

Eric has long hair, which he wears in a man bun, and is the joker and tease in the family.

John has short, tousled hair and is the kind and loving brother, but he is subject to spirals of depression.

Liliana Adams (Missing)

Lila's grandmother and namesake. She disappeared just before Lila's parents were killed. The Adams brothers haven't moved on because they haven't felt their bond break and they hope she's out there somewhere in the galaxy

Alina and Marcus Adams (Dec.)

Lila's parents moved to Earth in order to raise her in relative safety, but they were killed in a car accident. Alina had blonde hair and green eyes, and Marcus had brown eyes and the same chestnut hair as the grandpas and Lila.

Magenta

She is a performer in the circus. When on

Earth, she uses the circus silks, but on other planets, she uses her levitation powers. Magenta has bright pink hair and pale skin. She is mid height with a slim build and light blue, almost gray, eyes. She has been a lifeline for Lila when it comes to all things alien.

Broderick Potter (Bubby)

Captain of the mothership and Marcus Adams' best friend. He has red hair and a red beard with crystal blue eyes. He's rugged and well-built and thrilled to meet Lila.

Phillip and Fiona

They are Lila's twin cousins, but not on the Adams' side of the family.

Fiona has long, curly red hair, brown eyes, and freckles with a tall, slim build.

Phillip's red hair is cropped short, and he has brown eyes and freckles with a tall, slim build.

They oversee the dinosaur act. The dinosaurs were hand raised in the zoo on Skarr.

Captain Lester

Captain Lester is an alternate captain for the mothership and circus pod. He has an abrasive personality and a voice like he smokes two packs of cigarettes a day.

Terrans

Security officer for the circus pod and brother to Ferrans.

Ferrans

Security officer for the main ship and brother to Terrans.

Susie (A Night Most Wicked)

She is Lila's best friend, with dark, mahogany skin, melted chocolate colored eyes, and black corkscrew curls. She's a nurse and previously lived with Lila. Recently drank the waters from Skarr activating a dormant spark of power.

Vivian

The Adam's brothers sister in law. She is a member of the Skarrian council and a widow. Her own bond group died in a mysterious shuttle accident. She is Phillip and Fiona's grandmother and raised them when their own parents died. Detecting lies is one of her Skarrian abilities.

Oshan (mimic) The last known Skarrian mimic. He wears a glamor that has him looking like Dumbledore from Harry Potter complete with robes. In reality he is a blonde haired blue eyed man who looks about the same age of her Grandpas. He's hundreds of years old and has a large family.

Mimic's are immortal and their mates and partners also become immortal but any children from the pairings don't. Mimics can assume male or female form of whatever race is in their database.

Caspian and Lila's babies

Cordelia - purple when in kraken form, has pale blue skin and bright purple hair in her human form.

Jack - blue when in kraken form has pale blue skin and blue hair in human form.

Calypso - mottle blue, purple and pink in kraken form and in human form her skin is mottled blue and purple and she has longish pink hair.

PLANET FLUXX

Fluxx is a sister planet to Skarr, and its waters have magical properties too, but it gives its inhabitants the ability to shift into another creature. Fluxxians are animal shifters with three forms—humanoid while retaining coloration and some features of their animal, half form, and beast form. Fluxxians can use glamor to blend in and must do this when on Earth and in public. Fluxxians have fated mates, and their animal will dictate how they reproduce.

Caspian (Kraken Shifter, Lila's First Mate)

Caspian performs in the first act in the circus, shifting into half form and juggling multiple items with his tentacles.

He has mottled blue and purple skin, piercing stormy blue eyes, nipple rings, and vivid purple hair shaved on either side with a long section on top the drapes over one eye. His tentacles are purple and blue when in half form. Caspian's beast form is large. Male krakens implant their parents with their eggs via an ovipositor, and the womb then fertilizes the eggs, basically doing the opposite of a human. Fertilized eggs can lie dormant inside the female for a long time until she is ready to give birth. Drinking a large amount of the male kraken's cum tells the eggs that you are ready for babies. Four weeks later, they are born in kraken form. Two weeks after that, they are able to shift into their human form for the first time. Krakens can have anywhere between one and six babies at a time. Non-kraken mates will have their biology changed when given the mating bite. This allows them to carry a kraken's eggs for their partner.

Dylan (Dragon Shifter)

Dylan is in the first act of the show, which is a fire breathing act where he actually breathes fire.

He has ebony skin, wings, a metallic black shimmer to his scales, yellow and green reptilian eyes, and fangs. He also has sharp cheekbones, and his nose flattens slightly in half form.

Dylan is the man whore of the circus. He befriends Lila early on, only to betray her later and get kicked out of the circus for his act of aggression.

Silac (Naga Shifter)

Silac is one of the shifters who replaced Dylan in the first act. A Naga shifter, he has tousled emerald green hair in his humanoid form, with long, lean muscles and nipple rings. His eyes are orange and black. When he is in half form, he has a snake body from the waist down, with emerald green scales covered in horizontal orange stripes and black diamonds. Naga males have a hemipenis that hooks in to hold their partner close during copulation, and their mates give birth to live young.

Tirrian (Dragon Shifter)

Tirrian is the dragon shifter who replaced Dylan in the first act. Where Dylan was pitch black, he is more like an oil slick black. He has a shimmer to his skin that flickers from green and gold to pink and blue. He appears holographic depending on what angle you look at him from. In half form, his wings are the same color and his scales are holographic pink. He is tall, broad, and muscular. His hair is black with pink streaks in it, and his eyes are black with lines of pink in them. He's an asshole.

Dragons can only have young with female dragons or their mates. Once again, a mating bite will change a non-dragon shifter mate to allow them to lay eggs. Eggs are incubated by the couple for two months before being born. They must be kept at a certain temperature to ensure a live birth. Homosexual dragons can hire surrogates to help them with reproduction if they wish, and it is common practice for young dragons to offer this service as a way to start their own hoard before they wish to begin their own family. There is a website that can help facilitate this.

Caspian's family

    Mother - Mira (kraken shifter)

    Father - Murphy (kraken shifter)

    Sisters - all kraken shifters

Naia

Marin

Ocean

Neri

Marilla

Brothers - all kraken shifters

Morgan

 Malik

 Neptune

 Fisher

Sister in laws

Saleny (dragon shifter) married to Morgan

Luxsim (Unisci shifter) married to Neptune

Brothers in law

Felix (wolf shifter) married to Neri

Unisci: Big cat shifter. Large like a saber tooth tiger, but has pitch black fur like a jaguar but it is long like a persian cat.

Sissolic - head of the Bravalana Basilisks.

Kinga - his daughter and Silac's fiancee.

PLANET CYBERTRONIA

A technologically advanced planet inhabited by life forms that are half organic, half nanobot technology, allowing them to change their features at will. Reproduction occurs through intercourse, but parents program their respective organic matter with the traits and features they wish their babies to have. Once the baby is born, their source code is imprinted on a microchip, which is then deposited into a secret storage facility for safe keeping.

Pleasure Bot Industries is one of the main sources of employment for Cybertronia. They produce lifelike robots for sexual pleasure and are one of the galaxy's most popular purchases. Pleasure Bots are not like cyborgs, in that they are incapable of thoughts, feelings, or responses that have not been programmed into them.

Link Tesla/Digicon(Cyborg)

Link is the ship doctor for the Galaxy Circus and is one of Lila's boyfriends. His skin tone is peach with a shimmer. He has silver hair and eyes. He is built like a swimmer, with long, lean lines, a tapered waist, broad shoulders, and he is able to change his body parts at will. Cyborgs can't lie.

Josa Spears (Cyborg Nurse)

Josa is the nurse to Link's doctor, but he was hired by Link's mom to spy on him and the circus. He was promised Link's hand in marriage and a share of the Pleasure Bot Industries fortune if he complied. He has the same shimmery skin tone as Link, with metallic green hair and eyes. He has a slender, feminine frame and a dirty attitude.

Deianira Digicon(Cyborg A Night Most Wicked)

CEO to Pleasure Bot Industries and Link's mother. She doesn't like to be told no.

Ricky (Cyborg A Night Most Wicked)

Sent to Aura as a gift from Deianira. Blonde hair, tanned skin and gorgeous body.

PLANET VILAX

Vilax is home to a race of blood drinkers, the sanguinistas. Much like Earth's legend of vampires, this race is strong, fast, and has heightened senses. They can fly, and are very hard to kill. Their bodies will regenerate as long as their body parts are close to one another. To kill them, you need to burn both of their hearts. They are a warrior race and one of the fiercest in the galaxy. Military service is mandatory for all Vilaxians.

Vilax only gets five hours of sunlight a day, so while they are not allergic to the sun, they do prefer the dark. Sanguinistas drink blood because their bodies cannot process their own red blood cells. They have a fated mate called a blood rose, but not everyone finds them. They live in family clans, and blood sharing can be a sexual thing, but with children, it isn't.

Saxon (Sanguinista)

Saxon is part of the aerial troupe in the circus. He has magenta-colored eyes and thick, short black hair that's long enough to run your fingers through. His body is muscular and broad, and he has pale skin and fangs.

Hale (Sanguinista)

He is in the same troupe as Saxon and is Saxon's best friend. He has blond hair, teal eyes, and fangs.

Radella (Sanguinista)

Estrella (Sanguinista)

Velorina (Sanguinista)

Xenos (Sanguinista)

Saxon's twin brother, his hair is longer and worn tied back.

Dante (Sanguinista)

Chocolate brown hair that falls in floppy curls over his forehead and lavender colored eyes. Tall and athletic.

Kavita (Sanguinista)

Pin straight long red hair that falls to her ass

and dark eyes with red flecks in them and ruby red lips. Tall and athletic.

Crimson (Sanguinista) A Night Most Wicked

Long red curly hair, tall, toned and lean. Crimson is antisocial and could never fit in with a sanguinista clan so once she finished her compulsory public service for Vilax, she got a job working at the Pleasure Inn so she would have a variety of options for feeding. Clients like being bitten during sexual relations. She was in a relationship with Savannah prior to Xane and Aura taking over the brothel. Aura bestowed a mating bite on her, permanently joining her in their group and she stopped seeing clients.

PLANET WESTALIN

This is the warlocks' home planet. Warlock powers include, but are not limited to, mind manipulation and control, teleporting, and manifestation. Powerful warlocks have harems to feed from because they are psychic feeders who feed from strong emotions. Weaker warlocks and other creatures make up these harems. Weaker warlocks benefit from it, as they are able to feed off the stronger warlock at the same time and get a temporary boost in power. Members of the harem receive a wage and a comfortable position within the warlock's household. Powerful warlocks are able to absorb powers and life force, but it is frowned upon and is only used as a punishment. Warlocks have soulmates they call intimates. When a warlock finds their intimate, they no longer need a harem to feed from.

Xavier Colest (Crown Prince)

Xavier is one of the most powerful beings in the galaxy, only second to his parents. He is mostly with the circus because he gets bored easily. He helps with glamor to confuse the humans. He has purple/blue eyes and long indigo hair. His body is lean and muscular, and he has piercings in his ears, nose, and eyebrow. His ears are pointed, and he has lavender-colored skin with silver markings.

Xylene Colest

Queen of the Westalins and Xavier's mother. She was best friends with Alina and Marcus Adams, Lila's parents.

Cronus Colest

King of the Westalins and Xavier's father. He was best friends with Alina and Marcus Adams.

Xane Colest (A night Most Wicked)

Nephew of the King and Queen and former Strike team commander. Mate to Aura Gasm, master of the Pleasure Inn and powerful warlock. He has long indigo hair, shaved at the sides exposing more silver tribal like tattoos on his skull, and is tied back and there's a top hat covering it. Silver rings line both ears, as well as in his eyebrow and his bottom lip. Sharp cheekbones with eyes that look to be purple and pouty lips. Rescued

Aura when they were enslaved on an illegal brothel ship.

Elyan (Warlock, Head Harem Girl in Xavier's Harem)

Nambra (Warlock, Harem Member)
She has red hair and a voluptuous figure.

Lexus (Warlock, Harem Member)
She has short dark hair and a petite frame.

Ara (Warlock, Harem Member)
Ara has pale pink hair, eyes, and skin.

Jastia (Warlock, Harem Member)
Jastia possesses buttercup yellow hair, eyes, and skin.

Sinath (Rasque, Harem Member)
The Rasque is a humanoid race that looks like an Earth grasshopper. They have segmented arms and legs with plated body structure. Their penis is covered by plated sections, which retract when manipulated. Once the penis extends, claspers lock the copulating couple together.

Mithus (Milobar, Harem Member)
He has a stingray-shaped head and body, with

arms, legs, and a barbed tail. Mithus has two penises, which both have barbs that activate during intercourse, locking them within their partner.

Zanorn (Morpheian, Harem Member)

A race of metamorphs, they are able to take any shape they desire. In natural form, they are like a blank slate with limited features and gray skin.

Topirey (Dionall, Harem Member)

Dionalls are plant creatures with two forms— one is an upright humanoid sentient form, and the other is a stationary plant form which is similar to the Earth's Venus flytrap, only a lot larger and it feeds on flesh. They have leafy foliage on their head and sharp teeth, and are able to grow their body parts at will.

Aryan

Elyan's brother and secretary to the King and Queen of Warlock.

PLANET AQUILIA

Aquilia is seventy-five percent water, and the Aquilians are an aquatic species with three forms—humanoid, mer, and beast form. In beast form, they resemble an Earth dolphin, but are scaled and have sharp teeth. They come in a variety of pastel colors. In half form and on two legs, they retain the pastel colors and cannot glamor. They require a glamor spell if they want to tour Earth. Family groups are called pods. Aquilians rarely leave their home planet, and if they do, they will return once they form a pod so that their young are born in their home waters.

Nikos (Aquilian Prince)

Nikos is one of the performers in the dolphin show in the circus. He is a member of the Aquilian royal family, but not in line to inherit. He is arrogant and horny. He has pastel green skin, and his scales are pastel green and gold. His hair and eyes are metallic gold.

Nixie (Aquilian princess)

Nixie is Nikos's sister and also a performer in the circus. She's friendly and fun and is interested in exploring the galaxy. She does not want to get trapped by being mated on Aquilia. Nixie is also open to trying relationships with other species. Her colors are pastel blue and gold, with metallic gold hair and eyes.

Galaxy Circus Pod Members
Joaquin
Nolani
Marin
Dorado

King Marlin - large overweight King of Aquilia. (think manatee) Is an asshole

Raen - Nikos half brother. Dark hair soulless eyes, black and silver scales.

Queen Nerissa - Nikos and Nixie's mother.

Molastay trench. - a trench in the middle of Aquilia that is so deep nothing has ever reached the bottom. Inhabited with a variety of sea monsters.

PLANET RILU

Rilu is a desert-like planet with small green oases dotted across its land surfaces. There are no above ground oceans or seas, but there are large underground ones which provide fresh water for the inhabitants of the planet. At each of the oases, which usually center around a small lake, are wells which provide fresh drinking water for travelers. Some of the larger lakes have permanent villages established for trade. The people of Rilu are nomadic tribes. They raise larnuks and are miners. Under the surface of Rilu are extensive gem mines, and the people of Rilu mine the gems for trade and to feed their larnuks.

Larnuks

These are creatures much like Earth's Pegasus, possessing both wings and a horn. They come in the same colors as the gems that are mined on their planet—emerald, ruby, sapphire, gold, and amethyst. They eat gems and spout fire, and they have sharp, vicious teeth. They are bred and raised by a larnuk mistress or master who will bond with their herd. The larnuk will bite them, and a lock of their hair will turn the same color as the larnuk's. The more streaks a master or mistress has, the more larnuks they control.

Rilax

Rilax are berries that grow in the mines alongside the gems. The berries are used to make rilaxious, a pink alcoholic beverage popular across the galaxy. It is slightly bubbly with a thick, creamy consistency.

Zala (Larnuk Mistress)

Zala is the larnuk mistress for the circus and is in charge of that portion of the show. She has exotic, Middle Eastern looks with darker skin and wavy, pitch-black hair with streaks of color in it from her horses. Her eyes are a pale blue, almost white, rimmed in kohl, and framed with long black lashes. She is tall and slim, and her body is covered in silvery scars from bonding with her horses. Five appear in the show, but she has more.

Chief Zana

Zala's father and reigning head Chief of Rilu.

Zilla

Zala's sister and has a crush on Tirrian.

Zamala

Zala's Grandmother and seer.

PLANET MORLASH

Home of Morpheian race. They are shape shifters who can merge into any form, metamorphs. They are hermaphrodites and all members of the race have breeding capabilities. They usual assume a preferred form which is either male or female, Aura prefers to be both.

Morpheians are polyamorous and bestow a mating bite in their natural form to seal their mate to them. It is quite a painful process ensuring that the mate is genuine.

Aura Gasm Proprietor Pleasure Inn (A Night Most Wicked)

Aura was kidnapped by alien sex traffickers as a teenager and forced into an illegal brothel where they was regularly abused to keep them in line.

Developed Stockholm syndrome and tried to defend their captors when the ship was raided by a warlock strike force led by Xane. Xane, besotted by Aura nursed them back to health and have been together ever since.

PLANET CELESTIA

Celestian are what humans would call angels. All Celestians have wings and powers. Powers tend to be emotive in nature, healing is one of the powers, as is being able to manipulate emotions. Celestians glow with heightened emotions, the color their glowing tells what emotion they are feeling. Lavender is horny.

Celestians are also polyamorous and reproduction involves a magical process that combines everyone's DNA ensuring the child is a part of all mates before depositing the embryo into the chosen carrier.

Savannah (A Night Most Wicked)

Tall and voluptuous with a long mane of blonde curls, and silver eyes. Savannah is a product of rape and forced breeding which should be impossible with the way Celestians breed. She was cast out by her mother as a baby, never fitting in anywhere, teased and ridiculed. She made her home the Pleasure Inn as a way to make herself feel good. Crimson taught her she didn't need to have sex with someone to be loved.

Mark (Marcus Aurelias) (A Night Most Wicked)

Stolen from his parents by unknown assailants. Needs to go through an activation ceremony. Mark is Susie's boyfriend. He has black hair and gray eyes, and worked as an emergency room doctor. Mark is also bi.

King Jotan Angelis
One of Marks father and fierce King who has hung onto the monarchy while his mates have been mourning.

Queen Corethea Angelis
One of Marks mothers, blonde with large white wings, and a talented healer.

Queen Tabbris Angelis
One of Marks mothers and also a talented healer.

PLANET RECCEDEA

A lush, foliage-covered, tropical planet with frozen poles on either end. It is the birthplace of the dinosaurs found in the circus. Many species of dinosaurs that once roamed the Earth continue to survive and thrive on this planet.

Vigolash

Viggy is a red and black tyrannosaurus rex. He was trained from a baby, and acts just like a giant, overgrown golden retriever.

Htaed

Htaed is a yellow and orange velociraptor, who was also trained from a baby, but is unruly and kind of crazy.

PLANET AAZ'AX

The leadership of this race was cruel and vicious and wanted to use the orb to conquer other lands. They possessed it momentarily and laid waste to a number of planets, but the Unas were able to take it back. By then, the Aaz'ax weren't doing well. A mysterious illness had taken most of their women, and women of other races wanted nothing to do with the men. Their species has been on the brink of extinction and were finally able to dispose of their tyrannical leadership. Remaining survivors scattered to planets far and wide. The Aaz'ax are distant ancestors of the Vilaxians. Although they do not require blood, they can consume it, but it acts much like alcohol and drugs to a human. They have the ability to glamor, and they have two natural forms, their warrior form which is humanoid, but their shoulders and backs are covered in ridges and their body looks like they are covered in thorns. With their green skin and blood-red hair, they resemble a rose. And their everyday form which is again humanoid but he is covered in spikes, long and short. Comparable to an Earth's lionfish. The long spikes have sheer membrane draped between them. They don't have hair, just a crest of spikes, but it's their color that is stunning. They look like an opal, all greens, reds, blues, yellows, and pinks. Originally people thought they were two separate races because of how different they look.

Brannock

Hiding on Earth. Escaped there with his unit over a hundred years ago when the Una's and Aaz'axian war finished. He moves every thirty years and changes identities. Uses a glamor to blend in. Can't hold his glamor when intoxicated.

PLANET ELEMENTAL

A race of beings capable of controlling the elements. Four different varieties Earth, Fire, Air and Water. HUmanoid in shape and features. They do have fated mates, but they are rare and only found within their own kinds so usually it will be a life partner pairing with no cosmic and divine intervention. However, it isn't forbidden to have sex outside of their own kind, it is frowned upon to choose a life partner of a different elemental and any children born from a non matched union will result in the child taking on only one element of it's parent. Those kind of pairings are often seen as outcasts in the community. In fact on the planet Elemental there is a whole city made up of odd parings as they often get shunned by their birth families.

Elementi need to breed with elementi. Children won't happen with another species.

Earth Elementi

The earth elementi have antler style horns, a tail with the end fanning out like a leaf. They have dark green wings that are also leaf shaped and double fanned and their skin tone is mottled shades of green. They are fine and almost fairy like in stature with long lithe limbs and a shorter stature.

Abilities include - They can manipulate, reshape, and control earth elements at will. Including all crystals, metals, and minerals. Make and command gollums which gives them access to an entire army of beings at their command. Create tunnels in the ground to transport themself by. The have the ability to create, control, and manipulate volcanoes, lava, and magma which is something they share with a fire elementi.

They have a second larger form that's like a bear, but green with antlers, wings and the tail. They are also herbivores.

Fire Elementi

Come in a range of solid colors, red/yellow/orange and amber. They have bat like wings that have a smokey shimmer to them. Horns on the head, kind of look like molten lava and their tail has flames on the end of it. The wings will flame up when you use them and their bodies can withstand any sort of flame or fire. They also have a second form, the wings, horns and tail stay the same but they get a lot bigger and more gray in color and have cracks in the skin that look like lava. They are meat eaters, they can eat vegetation, but prefer meat.

Abilities include create, control, and manipulate anything fire and heat related including plasma. As well as the volcano ability they share with the earth elementi. Generate and control a magical fire that will do their bidding. Control of fireworks and the ability to teleport through fire. Self detonation - phoenix like powers were they can blow themself up and then reform unharmed. Fire breathing.

PLANET CAREVASTA

Carevasta Bear - adult sized dad bod care bears with shaggy fur and now belly badges. Eyes are usually the color of the fur. All solid colors except for Ghosie who is multicolored. Fur has aphrodisiac qualities. Their race was cursed by a goddess when one of their leaders used his fur to seduce her. Before the curse it was a thing they could turn on and off. She was furious and cursed them so they couldn't be touched without seducing someone. She also cursed all of their women to change to men and they can no longer give birth to female bears. They have become a society who have to steal women to procreate. Any female child born of the union will be whatever the mother is, all male children are bears. They have been looking for a solution for years. They are a species divided. Half like their ways of stealing and coercing and half long for meaningful relationships. Carevasta bear gestation is three months.

Ghosie - bright multicolored, mink soft shaggy fur and eyes. Wants to find true love. Loves children because their fur doesn't affect them and it means he can get affection from them.

Osid (dec) - the bear responsible for Liliana being on Husdavia.

Lizis - blue carevasta bear. Responsible for Lila's capture. Had a deal with Glup to trade woman.

Straun

OTHER ALIEN RACES

Unas

A race of highly intelligent, peaceful, powerful beings who created the power orb that the Galaxy Circus protects. The now extinct race had powers that were fueled through sexual energy. They didn't have mates or partners, it was just a free-for-all orgy.

Their war with the Aaz'ax dwindled their numbers until there were only a handful left. Their energy was absorbed into the orb when they turned it over to the Adams brothers. They used the Adams' ancestors' blood to link it to them, and if it leaves their line, anyone remaining will be absorbed too.

The power orb was supposed to be a clean, free source of energy capable of powering planets across the galaxy. It can be used as a weapon of mass destruction, but cannot be destroyed because the galaxy would implode.

Utaz - Oshan's son. Pure Una and he would like Lila to meet him in the hope they will return the Una race to the Galaxy. Lila is reluctant.

Darklarkian (Planet Elos)

Elf-like race identifiable by their pointy ears and black skin, and green snake-like eyes.

Snarkle (Planet Cereabosto)

Humanoid bodies with two heads. Each head has a mouthful of sharp teeth.

Pistadon (Planet Laxo)

Bird like creature similar to a pterodactyl. Sharp beaks and beady eyes, they have no feathers, look like a freshly plucked chicken. The only feathers on their body surround their cloaca. Red and yellow spike-like feathers circle this opening protecting it from unauthorized penetration.

Seiomann (Planet So)

Magic race with subjugating powers. They can make it so a being can not access their powers. They also have the ability to freeze a person in stasis. They appear floating draped in a dark cloak with only discernible features are three red eyes.

Telazions (Planet Telaz)
They sold the tech for the iPhone to Steve Jobs.

Nengh
They perform as clowns in the circus. They have detachable limbs and are able to adjust their body's size and mass. They are humanoid in shape, but they are orange with feathery tufts instead of hair. They use a glamor provided by Xavier to appear human when on Earth.

Jelliads
A race of purple gelatinous amorphic creatures. They are sentient and communicate via telepathy. They feed from the atmosphere of their home planet but they can also feed on orgasmic energy. They can change their shape and they breed asexually.

Bacalacian
From the planet Bacalac they are humanoid in form in that they walk upright and have two legs but they have a red armor plated outer shell, bright red when on high alert, orange at rest. They have two pincers in place of arms that are razor sharp and dangerous. Their torso is triangular with two eyes on stalks sticking out of the top and a mouth opening with a single pair of teeth on top and bottom which grind food between them.

Dodarran

A demon counterpart to the Celestians.

Gilani: member of the circus. In the first act with Caspian, he is one of the jugglers. He's got red leathery looking skin, big horns,and his own set of large bat-like wings.

Filani

A race of being that can be likened to succubus and incubus. So beautiful they can seduce with their looks and can absorb someones life force during sex to feed.

Madova

This race has only females and they have two forms. Humanoid with hypnotizing gaze, snake like appendages for hair, fangs, nose slits, wings. A snake-like appendage that comes out of the vagina and penetrates the male to lay eggs. They have sex through an x like opening in their stomachs.

Animal form, shifts into a serpent like dragon with wings that spits venoms and bites the head off the the male they have sex with once the babies are ready to be born. Babies then consume the remaining body.

Tutva

Four armed humanoid race. The women have three breasts and two vaginas and the men have double cocks and only one nipple in the middle of their chest. Tall and built with trusts and horns. Kind of like orcs. The come in various shades of green gray and brown

Tully and **Sully** are sisters who run Orion's Belt

Vengii (Planet Sotda VX)

Tinka - No legs -mushroom style base long spindly arms with mauve skin. Round back skull like a human but the front half tapers down into a snout. Black beady eyes, no hair, ridges and bumps all over the back of their head. Snout ends in pouty lips. Seamstress and fashion designer for the Galaxy Circus.

Flobberstums (Planet Flor)

No human like features whatsoever. They are a large, flat and wide worm like creature, with brilliant colors and patterns covering the back of the bodies while the front is a smooth black. There are no discernible features. Flobberstums are neither male nor female but both, and they cock fight to see who will bare their young each year. Three prong trident penis that must pierce the opposing Flobberstum implanting their seed into the other and the loser is responsible for carrying their clutch to term.

Barcoa (Planet Barc)

Barcoa are are slightly primitive warrior race, that is big and beefy. They kind of look like rocks but the texture of their skin is more like leather. Not all that intelligent but good at following orders and almost indestructible. They are often used as security guards for high profile people. Humanoid in shape but they have a centralized mouth situated on their stomach and they eat moss. The thing that makes them good security is they have several decentralized eyes. One on their hand, one on either side of their head, and one on the back of their knee. It gives them three hundred and sixty degrees of vision. But their sexual organs are in their elbows. Both male and female, they have a vagina like slit on one arm and a penis which is retractable on the other.

Gurko

Short and stout gremlin like creatures that are very strong, with a mouth of sharp teeth. They are motivated by money and don't hold any loyalty to anyone. Would sell their own mother to make a quick buck.

Glup - Security guard for X68. Has a deal with the carevasta bears to let them know when women visit the station.

The Old Gods

The original inhabitants and creators of the galaxy. Once had names but they have been forgotten over the years. They are known as Life, Death, Water, Air, Fire, and Earth. Were responsible for the creation of all planets and life forms. They disappeared and the galactic council tried to erase all knowledge of their existence.

DICTIONARY

Phoeall (fo-all): Warlock for…
Vigolash: Obedient one in Aaz'axian
Sandar worm: native to the planet Westalin, they are large creatures that turn soil over in their paddocks between crops. They eat all organic matter left from past crops, leaving it free for farmers to plant the next crop.
Silax worm: Native to Rilu, it lives in the mines and is a pest. Their secretion kills the rilax berry plant. They are trapped, and their secretions are used to make achom.
Achom: A drink that is like a blend of coffee and chocolate with a chili vodka kick. Made from the anal secretions of the silax worm, found in the cave system of Rilu.
GIN: Galaxy Information Network.

Karta monster: A large, kaiju style creature the size of an elephant.

Cirillion: Little bundles of fluff with big eyes.

Lastovian hog:

Saturn's Rings: A restaurant on the Galaxy Circus mothership.

Edalaxion Space Station: A space station with dodgy bars and meeting spaces for the dregs of the galaxy.

Celesian Brothel: A popular brothel if you want to have sex with living beings as opposed to sex bots.

Jaxa bird: A bird native to Westalin, it looks like a cross between a peacock and a phoenix. Its tail is a fanned bloom of fire.

Kala mouse: A marsupial found on Westalin.

Coolmy shell: This is a crustacean found in Aquilian waters.

Farlucks: A creature from Westalin similar to an Earth fox with three tails and pink fur. They are an aquatic mammal.

Husad Mead: From Husadavia, an uninhabited planet in the Kavar system. The plants and animals on it are carnivorous and lethal and it takes a special kind of being to harvest the fruit from the Halla bush. It's quite popular and quite potent.

Mitavin: rodent found on space junk and in space stations. Skeletal beings with a tail like a beaver and body like a racoon.

Treason: board game like monopoly but you invade planets.

Toosook Flowers: shimmery pink and purple blooms shaped very much like a cross between hollyhocks and tulips. A special coral that grows deep within the ocean. They get their color from a species of fish that brush against them to keep clean. The shimmer is from their scales. They will also never die. If you put them in a vase at home and top the vase up with ocean water every few days, they will live continuously. Found only in the oceans of Fluxx.

Lemug: Round, smooth and blue about the size of a marble, they are very much like a pearl from Earth, in the they grow inside the shell of a sea creature. Found only in the oceans of Fluxx.

Catava grain: similar to Earth wheat used to brew beer on Fluxx.

Suva : A red fluffy moss substance that grows only on the cliffs next the Capsian's parents home. Used to make a recreational drug that gives a similar high to coke but is not addictive. Mira and Murphy sell it to drug manufacturers all over the galaxy.

Catsuva beer: A beer brewed from catava grain and suva moss. Has a high alcohol content and gives a burst of energy in the drinker.

Whathefucorcadiles- a cross between a crocodile, orca and a great white shark. Hungry aggressive predators.

Mallac bear - From westalin. Large stocky scaled beast with plates like an armadillo. Size of a hippopotamus with a mouthful of fangs that drip a paralyzing toxin.

Station X69 - Popular recreational and trading station.

Saluktat beans - A bean used to make a beverage similar to coffee from Westalin.

Earth Alien Aliiance (EAA) Located in Area 51. Keeps track of all aliens on Earth and assures they are dhearing to the visa laws.

Galactic Council. One member from all planets in the Galaxy ensuring smooth relations between all member planets.

Lollecado - Black banana shaped fruit found in the thermal caverns of Rilu. It is solid as a rock until cut in half. The inside flesh is seedy like a dragon fruit but blood red in color and steaming hot. Grows in lava pools, and is harvested by dragons or Riluense wearing special gloves. It's coveted by dragons because it makes their cum taste like the fruit.

Z68 - Space station for the dregs of the galaxy, drinking, fighting, and fucking.

CHAPTER ONE

Xavier

"Lila Adams." The loud, robotic voice comes across the speaker of the flight deck. "You are hereby charged with crimes against the Aquilian royal family. Surrender now, or we will be forced to board and take you by any means necessary."

My body practically vibrates with anger as I stare at the Aquilian attack birds through the control deck viewing screen. Their announcement causes a pause of shocked silence before Lila curses. The two cats, Silac, and Tirrian arrive, breathing heavily. Maxsim is naked, so I absently wave my hand to clothe him with his usual attire so that no one is distracted by his magnificent form.

"What's happening?" Silac asks, his eyes widening with surprise as he catches sight of the Aquilian army.

"Ah, it seems that the Aquilians have taken

exception to something I've done," Lila says flatly, and I feel her anxiety and annoyance as she crosses to Caspian and takes one of our children off his hands. She snuggles into a dripping Jack, so I wave my hand again, making towels appear for all of them. She wraps Jack in a towel, and Saxon takes Cally from Cas and does the same thing while he wraps a towel around himself and Cordy, drying everyone off. It's all I can do not to lash out and destroy the ships in front of me. It's yet another fucking obstacle in the way of my intimate getting her memories back. When am I going to get a fucking break?

My power crackles around my body, and everyone turns to look at me, worry and concern filling their faces at my agitation.

"What are we going to do?" Captain Broderick looks to Lila's grandpas for guidance. We could attack the blasted cans of tuna, as Lila likes to call them, but that doesn't bode well for Galaxy relations. We would probably get reprimanded by the Galactic Council and then my parents would have to take our side and, well, things would get messy.

William huffs out an impatient sigh. All three of the brothers are radiating annoyance and impatience. They, too, have goals that do not involve a side trip to Aquilia, but I guess there is nothing we can do to avoid this for now. "Hail the Aquilian ship please," he instructs the captain, who presses a few buttons.

"Okay, it's good to go." He nods at William.

"Aquilian ship, what crimes are you insinuating Lila has committed against the royal family?" he demands.

There's a moment while we wait for the ship to respond. "We are not at liberty to discuss this, but if she does not surrender, we will have no option but to take her by force."

"Can they do that?" she asks, biting her lip with worry, and I hurry over to her and wrap my arms around her, trying to feed her comfort and assurance, but without our intimate bond, the feelings are muted. Instead, I hope that my embrace does the same kind of thing.

She sags against me, and Jack wraps a tentacle around one of my arms, and I feel his little suckers give me kisses.

"The Aquilian battle birds are well-equipped to launch an assault on us," Saxon muses as he pulls one of Cally's tentacles off his face. "The circus ship, while equipped with weaponry, needs people to operate them, and we are short-staffed. We could appeal to my aunt for help, but it would take a few days for the Vilaxian fleet to get here, and I'm not sure if they will be patient. If we stall, they will think we are calling in reinforcements and take aggressive action."

"I think we should see what they want." Eric is glaring at the ships like he can pierce a hole in their hulls. "How dare they demand something from us? We have been nothing but generous in putting up with their arrogant son for as long as we have."

John runs a frustrated hand through his hair and paces back and forth. He's still a little pale, but all in all, he's doing so much better, the flamegem having done exactly what the Celestians promised us it would. Link says there is no trace of the virus left in John's system, but he continues to monitor him. "King Marlin is just as arrogant if not worse than Nikos. Where do you think he learned it? The only reason he sent his son and daughter to us was because he wanted them to learn more diplomacy skills to benefit him. He was hoping Nixie would make a lucrative marriage, and, well, Nikos is the crown prince. He hoped he would learn not to insult others and cause war. I'm not sure that worked out as planned."

"You think?" I say dryly. "You're not wrong about King Marlin. My parents abhor having to socialize with him. He's a man-whore despite being married and continually flirts with my mom to the point where I'm surprised my father hasn't blown him up on the spot. He also thinks his planet and species are so much better than everyone else's, despite having no power other than shifting abilities."

Tirrian snorts. "Yes, my father feels much the same way. Not to mention they choose to limit themselves to one environment and stick to the ocean. They would go further if they established more land-based cities, but they only have the one. They don't trade, they don't have any kind of commodities, heck, even tourism would be beneficial, but they are too arrogant to do that either. The whole race is the same, and I loathe having to interact with them."

"Well, that doesn't surprise me based on my interaction with Nikos, but Nixie isn't like that at all." Lila sounds surprised.

"She is most definitely the exception," Link says, smiling at her. Their relationship is much better now that they have bonded. All that uncertainty is gone, and Lila's mood swings seem to have evened out slightly as well, though from what I understand, that may not last. Who knows how many she's going to need in her harem to keep her stable?

"Okay, so let's do this. We will allow them to escort us to Aquilia," William suggests.

"That's a week in the wrong direction," I grumble. Everyone looks at me with sympathy, and I feel an itch between my shoulders.

"I'm sorry." Lila snuggles even closer, like she wants to join us together, and I feel waves of love and support and a small amount of shame.

"It's not your fault." I press a kiss to her now sparkling locks, and my hand drifts down to cup her ass. "Uh, Lila, why is there a hole in your pants?" I ask, poking a finger through the offending gap.

Maxsim chuckles, his hand in Echo's fur, who also chuffs with what sounds like amusement.

"Someone is having trouble handling the lightning whip. Luckily, she's immune to the actual charge," Tirrian says dryly, and I narrow my eyes at the dragon.

He is really pushing this aggression thing too far. Alright, we get it, he doesn't want to mate with Lila, but it's time he stopped being aggressive, and if he doesn't do it soon, I may be forced to make him. I'm the one who feels her hurt every time he speaks like that to her. Before, all I used to feel was annoyance or even humor from her every time he opened his mouth, but now that she knows she's his mate and he doesn't want it, all I feel is sadness, hurt, and resignation, and that pisses me off.

"Shit, I forgot about that," she says.

Now I can feel her embarrassment, and I quickly wave a hand, fixing the hole in her pants before patting her on the bottom again. I do like my intimate's ass.

She smiles up at me and winks. I guess she knows me well. "Fine, let's see what the king of canned tuna wants, and then we can be on our way again. I won't let them derail us longer than it takes to sort out whatever they have decided I have done to them. I can't imagine what it would be."

Over the top of Lila's head, I see Link wince. *Do you think this is about that bite on her breast?* I ask him telepathically, not wanting Lila to hear.

He nods his head slightly. *Yes, I can't imagine what else it would be. Lila doesn't even know she is half mated to Nikos. Shit, for all we know, they are fully mated. She might have bitten him during their swim as well, but if we ask her about it now, she's going to be suspicious.*

I don't like keeping things from her, I warn him.

Neither do I. I'm just not sure how she's going to react to the news. Her mood has been a lot better this week. I'm afraid if we tell her, it will make things worse. The self-loathing and guilt she felt after it happened took a toll on her.

I don't want her to be blindsided by it either, I tell him, and I can feel his resignation and know he's going to do the right thing. *We will just have to keep her distracted until we get to Aquilia, and then we will tell her before we go down to the surface.*

I pull out of his mind as I hear William respond to the Aquilians. "We will allow you to escort us to Aquilia, but you will not be taking Lila into custody, and we will meet with them in Aquila."

There is silence as we wait for the mer people to respond. "Do you think they are going to go for it, or do I need to prepare to create an international incident?" I feel my powers itching to get out and wreak havoc. It's been a long time since I needed to use them for defense.

"It could go either way. Their arrogance knows no bounds, but I'm hoping they are still trying for galactic harmony. By now, they must know that Lila is both Xavier's intimate and Saxon's blood rose—not to mention that she is also mated to Maxsim. That's three separate planets that would have our back if the Aquilians started anything with us."

"Don't rule out the Celestians either," Cas reminds Eric. "They will forever be in Lila's debt for returning Mark to them."

"And my father would throw the dragon support behind you too," Tirrian growls.

"That is all well and good, but if they get Lila and take her to their underwater cities, then there isn't much any of us can do to help her," Link argues.

"I could," Cas argues, "and my family would."

"Yes, we know, but you and your family of krakens are no match for a battalion of warrior mer people in their own environment. It's why I will insist on meeting in Aquila, the only city above ground, so that we can all be present." William crosses his arms and leans back in the chair he's sitting in. "I wouldn't put it past them to throw her into the dungeon, and we'd never see her again. Any perceived slight is dealt with harshly. If they hadn't appealed to the Galactic

Council, I never would have agreed to take them as an act."

"But they are popular, even on other planets apart from Earth. The love story they tell always sucks people in," John argues. "Adding Lila to the act was genius."

"I'm pretty sure Nixie came up with the idea. It's so much more fanciful than I would expect from the Aquilians as a whole. I'd like to know where she got the idea from," I muse. Nixie has a softer side to her than the others in their act. I know apart from her and her brother, the others are an established pod, and they are not going to be returning to the circus once it resumes. They are going to stay and give birth in their home waters. I wasn't sure if a new pod would be joining us or not.

"At least we will be able to demand a definitive yes or no about their act returning, but I'm guessing with this act of aggression, it will be a no," Lila says, her head still resting against my chest, and I feel her exhaustion. "I will miss Nixie, but then again, maybe we can offer her another position." She looks hopefully at William, who frowns.

"We will have to wait and see how this plays out," William tells her. "This is not exactly the act of an ally." He stabs a finger at the viewing window.

"No, it most certainly isn't," I growl, and Lila shivers in my arms, but I can tell she's turned on and not scared. "This is basically a declaration of war, and if war is what they want, then the warlocks will be happy to join your side. It's been a long time since we had a good fight."

Saxon smirks. "Yes, the Vilaxian army has been grumbling that they have become glorified security guards for our own planet. They will also eagerly join the fight against Aquilia. In fact, let them be stupid. I'm sure their blood is watery and gross, but I bet it flows fast when you rip their necks out."

Holy crap, our vampire general's eyes are flashing red, and I have a feeling the soldiers aren't the only bored ones. Lila shivers again, and I can tell she is turned on by seeing Saxon this way. Any normal person would be running in the opposite direction if they saw General Saxon looking like this, but not her.

"Now settle down." John, ever the peacemaker, holds up his hands. "Let's just wait and see how they respond before we start planning planetary annihilation." The tension in the room eases, and I relax slightly. All those amped emotions were making me twitchy.

"Yes, that's acceptable, but we will lock our tractor beams and cannons on you for the journey. If you try anything, we will fire," the voice says over the intercom, finally giving us an answer.

"Pfft." Bubby snorts and raises our own shields, protecting us from any fire. "Just in case they get itchy fingers," he says, and William nods his approval, but I'm not completely happy with that, so I add my own power to the shields, reinforcing them a hundred times. I'd like to see the Aquilians get through that.

My own wave of exhaustion washes over me. Without my harem to feed from anymore, and without Lila's intimate bond, I'm not feeding as regularly as I should to sustain my power levels.

"Xavier, are you alright?" Link comes over and peers at me in that all-seeing way of his. "You just turned a little pale. Would you like me to check over you?" He fiddles with the monitor built into his arm and holds his hand out, but I shake my head.

"No, my friend, I'm just a little down on energy. I'll be alright," I assure him, but now Lila has pulled away and is frowning at me.

"He's right, you do look a little pale." She raises her free hand to my cheek and rests it there. I lean into it. It feels nice, but I feel her temper rise. "Those blasted cans of tuna. How dare they get in our way? I'll be having very strong words with the king when we get there. This is ridiculous." We all chuckle. Her outrage is kind of adorable, just as she is. "What do you think it's even about? Do you think it's because I told Nikos to fuck off after what happened?" She feels confused and worried and annoyed, and I hate those negative emotions from her. They upset me.

"Actually, I have a theory," Link hedges, "but

how about we head back to our rooms, get the kids some food, and put them down for a nap before we discuss it?"

Silac has been silently watching the conversation. "That sounds like a good idea. Tirrian and I will remain here and assist with the flight deck in case we do need to use our defenses. I'm sure someone can show us how to operate them."

"That's a good idea actually. If we show you, Brannock, and Tirrian how to man the defense systems, we won't be completely blindsided if we need them. I hadn't considered that we would be attacked, but we usually have a full crew who knows what to do if we are." William nods his agreement, and I can feel the relief pouring off him.

"I would be more than happy to learn how to defend you. I can't thank you enough for giving me a home after being cast off of Earth—a home that allows me to be myself." The Aaz'axian who is not wearing his glamour and hasn't since it's just been us on the ship bows his head, and I narrow my eyes. This shiny spiky man is somewhat of a mystery to me. He has his emotions under lock and key, and they only occasionally leak through, but even then, I can't make heads nor tails of them. The only thing I can make sense of is that he means none of us any harm, and I guess that's all I can ask for at the moment, but I will be watching him closely just like I watch the snake and dragon.

"Alright, now that that's settled, tell the ship to lead the way, and let's get moving. This delay is maddening, so let's get it over with as soon as possible. We will return to our quarters and feed the kids. Let us know if you need anything," Lila agrees, sighing. "I swear I'm going to make sushi out of that damn merman when I see him."

CHAPTER TWO

Lila

My growing family makes its way back to our rooms. We feed the children and put them down for a nap, the three of them worn out after their big swim in the Aquilian pool with their daddy. None of them put up any argument, they just shift into their human forms, snuggle up next to each other, and are out within minutes.

"Holy crap, what did you do to them? I've never seen them go to bed so quickly before," I ask Caspian as I return to the living area where all six of my mates are waiting. Echo has returned to his humanoid form. I was freaked out when he shifted the first time after finding out he was pregnant. I read many shifter books that said they couldn't shift while pregnant, but they reassured me that it was fine.

Cas chuckles as I sit down on the sofa next to Xavier. "They had fun chasing Sweetpea around the pool. They were at it for ages. It seems to really love the children."

"Of course it does, they are amazing." I preen, not even slightly embarrassed about how proud I am of them. "Now why do I get the feeling you're not feeding properly?" I reach for my warlock's hand, and his skin is cool to the touch. I worry so much about Xavier. He's been dying to return home to have his parents return my memories so our intimate bond can be sealed. This is just another delay to something that has been put off for far too long. I'm surprised he's so calm. I thought he would lose his shit, but maybe he's too exhausted. Now that I look closely, I can see the bags under his eyes, his silver markings are faded, and he's much paler than normal. He even feels less powerful. When I first met him, he felt like a power station. He made my jaw ache with how powerful he felt, but now I don't know if I'm used to it, or if I'm immune because I'm his intimate, but he doesn't feel like that at all, and I'm worried it's because he gave up his harem for me, and without the bond, he's not feeding like he should.

A wave of guilt washes over me, and he huffs. "Don't feel guilty, Lila. I knew what I was signing up for. Things will be better once we seal our bond. I will be back to full strength."

His words basically confirm what I expected.

"You're starving? How long has this been going on for? Why aren't you feeding properly?"

"Be honest, X. We can't help you if you lie to us," Saxon scolds his sometimes lover, frowning with disappointment. If I guess correctly, he's feeling as guilty as I am.

Xavier winces, and his eyes shift from side to side like he's trying to think of an excuse. He isn't fooling anyone. "Just be truthful. We can't help you if you lie," I demand, and he huffs out a big sigh.

"I fed fully when we were on Station X69, with all those beings with all those vices. I felt full for the first time in a while, but when I let my harem go and promised to feed from just you, I thought our intimate bond would be established quicker. Once it's formed, I won't have any problems feeding from you exclusively. It's a part of what makes the bond so essential to a warlock, but without it, I run the risk of draining you until you're a husk like Mithus was."

"Damn it, Xavier, I told you to feed from the others." I wave my hand at the rest of my husbands. "I know Saxon will help you."

He wrinkles his nose, and a small blush rises to his cheeks.

Saxon chuckles. "Lila, he went from feeding from nine different people every day to just you and occasionally me."

"And by feeding, you mean fucking?" I ask

dryly, already knowing the answer. "How did you find time in your day to do anything else?" I ask sarcastically, hating the reminder that I'm not enough for him, not that I think that was Saxon's intention at all.

"Lila, *phoeall*, don't be like that. I only have eyes for you," Xavier lies, and I snort, not that I'm upset. He is a highly sexual creature and is used to having sex at his beck and call.

"And Saxon, and I'm sure everyone else in the room isn't on the no list either," I point out, knowing my warlock fiancé is somewhat of a man-whore.

He at least has the grace to blush a little harder.

"So what we need is an orgy then." I stand up and brush imaginary lint off my pants as a rush of excitement replaces the guilt. You have no idea how long I have been wanting to say those words. It's all I can do to contain my gleeful grin. "Right, who's in?" I look around the room and almost chuckle at the wide-eyed look Cas is giving me. Saxon and Link are less shocked—in fact, both of them look amused. They know this is what I've wanted for ages, but it's the first time I've had a chance to suggest it. I am all fucking in. My body starts to tingle with anticipation, and my mimic powers roll inside me. I feel that familiar itch urging me to change form. Maybe I should take my warlock form and feed too. Xavier hasn't taught me how to do that yet because he was waiting until our bond had been sealed so I can feed exclusively from him, but it really is something I should learn. If I need it for an extended amount of time, then I need to learn how to feed so I don't hurt myself while using my warlock powers.

"Well? Cas? Link? Want to come play in the bedroom with me and these two." I cross my fingers behind my back, but I think Link sees it because he chuckles.

"Sure, why not. As long as that's what you want, and Xavier doesn't mind."

"I mean, yeah, sure, it could be fun." I'm nearly about to bust out a happy dance, but I'm trying to play it cool.

"Of course I don't mind." Cas has recovered from his shock and looks almost as excited as I do.

When I look over at my warlock to see if I can gauge his feelings, his eyes are hooded and smoldering with desire. Okay, this is a go.

I turn my attention to my kitties. "What about you two?"

Before either of them can answer, Xavier uncrosses his legs and gracefully stands, his movements lithe and languid. "I know the pretty alpha kitty is probably feeling incredibly territorial with his pregnant omega over there, so I wasn't even going to ask either of them to feed me. Not at this stage."

Maxsim nods solemnly at Xavier, appreciation in his gaze. "You are right. I wouldn't want to share Echo with anyone but Lila at the moment." My glee dips slightly, but I also understand. The alpha whisperer side of me is agreeing strongly with Maxsim. It's so weird having all these different emotions tugging at me. It makes me feel slightly off balance. "But that's not to say things won't be different in the future." He shrugs casually, and my glee returns.

"I think I'll take a little nap in my nest. I'm feeling extremely tired. Growing babies is hard work," Echo jokes, rubbing his belly. I hurry over to my pretty kitty and wrap my arms around him, rubbing my cheek against his furry one.

"It sure is. I remember it well. Go rest, and I'll rub your feet when we've taken care of Xavier," I promise him, and he starts to purr, wrapping his arms around me.

"Or you could rub something else," he whispers into my ear, and I smirk. Ah, yes, pregnancy horni-ness. I remember that well too. I feel Maxsim at my back, his arms circling my waist, sandwiching me between the two cats.

"Settle now, Omega. I'm sure Lila will rub whatever you want her to once she's finished looking after the warlock."

"I sure will." My sexual appetite is just as big as Xavier's now that my mimic powers are fully active.

Although I haven't had the need to use them, they haven't fully settled, and according to Oshan, they won't until I have enough mates bonded to me. Who knows how many that will be? "Sleep well." I bid them farewell, and the two of them head to their shared room.

Much like their previous accommodations, it is designed like an Iceen den with temperature controls that lower it to the correct icy temperature. They still use their previous accommodations to run around in for exercise, since their room in our suite isn't big enough for that, and we kept the old Iceen den as is for when Minx and the other three return to the circus once it reconvenes. The only change they made was combining the multiple dens into one for the four of them. It also gives them a little more space to romp around in the snow.

I can barely contain myself as we head for our bedroom. It's all I can do not to use my Vilaxian speed to get there quicker. I hear Xavier chuckle behind me. He must be able to feel my excitement. I feel so bad that he's starving because we haven't been able to establish our bond yet. I will rectify that as soon as we are done with our sexual shenanigans. I'll have Saxon help me make a call to his parents. If we can't get to them, then I'll have them come to us.

We arrive in my newly designed bedroom. The room is huge, and its central focus point is the biggest bed I have ever seen. All of us could roll around on it, and there's still room for more. My mood dips slightly at the thought that there are two more men on the ship who could be joining us on the bed, but neither of them is interested. My mimic side is greedy, and although I have fairly good control over it, when it sees something it wants, it tries to force the change. I've spent most of my time avoiding both of them. Silac was helping today because everybody else was busy, and I have no idea why Tirrian was around. I just wish he would return to Fluxx, but Cas told me that he probably can't because his dragon won't let him. He told me he wouldn't be able to hold out against his creature forever, but that just makes me feel worse, because he obviously doesn't want it, and being a slave to another is really frustrating. I know this feeling intimately.

Hands snake around my body and cup my breasts quickly, drawing me out of my melancholy musings.

"Hey, none of those kinds of emotions when we're about to rock your world." Xav nibbles on my ear, making goosebumps rise across my flesh.

I'm wearing jeans and a hoodie, comfy but warm from working with the cats in the ice arena, but with a snap of his fingers, I'm naked. Saxon prowls to the bed, stripping off his shirt on the way, while Cas and Link make slower progress, both removing their clothes until they are only left in their underwear. Cas is in his human form, and as much as I love his tentacles, I'm not sure I want to share them with anyone else. I think it's my inner kraken, but I'm feeling incredibly possessive and want to save all that gloriousness for me. Maybe I'll eventually be willing to share that, but not yet.

"How are we going to do this?" I ask, enjoying the sight of my mostly naked mates in front of me, but unsure of how to get this show on the road.

"Tell us what you want, Lila," Saxon commands as he slides his pants off as Cas and Link join him on the bed.

I feel a pulse of lust rush through me, and I'm not entirely certain if it's from me or the delicious man behind me, whose cock is pressing against my naked ass. He must have removed his own clothes at the same time as mine.

"I want to see Link and Cas kiss." My voice is husky, and I can hear the desperation in it, but I don't care. I have been wanting this from the moment I learned I'd have multiple mates and that they were all bisexual.

Link smirks, crawls forward on his knees, and grabs Cas by his hair, turning his head before licking his lips. I moan and grind back against Xavier as they melt into one another, their clash of mouths almost violent but sexy as fuck. Both of them are turned on, the outlines of their cocks prominent behind their briefs.

"You like that a lot, don't you, *phoeall*?" Xavier's voice is guttural in my ear, and his hands tighten on my breasts. One of them slips down toward my already soaked pussy, and he runs a finger through the mess before bringing it up to my lips. "Suck," he demands, and I do as I continue to watch two of my guys make out.

As they pull apart, the sex fog lifts slightly, and I remember why we are here. I spin away from the warlock at my back and grab his hand, tugging him over to the bed. "Stop distracting me. This is about you. You need to feed, and you can do that while we sex you up. Now lie down."

Xavier chuckles and lies down on the bed like I instructed. "Far be it for me to argue with being sexed up."

I stand on the side and bite my lip, not sure how to conduct this orchestra. Saxon reaches out and drags me up onto the bed with them.

"Kiss your intimate, Lila," he commands me, and I slide over and kiss Xavier. Our tongues tangle together, much like Cas's and Link's had.

Saxon slides his hands around my waist, caressing my skin. I turn our heads slightly so we can both watch as Cas lies down next to Xavier, and his blue hand wraps around Xavier's thick purple cock. Link leans forward and spits on Xavier's cock, helping Cas with lubrication, before settling down next to Cas and leaning forward to give him an example of his mad blow job skills that I am intimate with.

I pull away from Xavier's kiss, completely distracted by the sexy sight in front of me. Cas has one hand wrapped around Xavier's cock and the other threaded through Link's shiny locks as Link bobs up and down on Cas's cock. The groan that leaves my mouth matches the one that falls from Cas's mouth as Xavier turns his head so he can kiss him.

Saxon slides in behind me and lifts my leg, notching himself to my dripping core before thrusting deep in one movement. I gasp and grab the sheets with my hands as Saxon's come up to cup my breasts. He thrusts in and out of my pussy as we both watch the sexy scene before us, but he doesn't let me stay distracted for long. He pulls out and maneuvers me so I'm on my hands and knees, my face over the top of Xavier's crotch.

"Suck your warlock's cock, baby," he growls, "while I wreck your pussy." He pushes my head down onto the thick purple length, pushing Cas's hand away before he starts powering into me.

With every stroke of his cock, he pushes me down onto my warlock's dick. My pussy ripples, the ridges and bumps on Saxon's cock hitting all the right places deep inside me. I swallow Xavier down, my throat constricting around his length as his sweet precum bursts in my mouth. He groans, and his fingers tangle in my hair as he holds me in place. I breathe through my nose as tears well in my eyes, but I have never felt more wanted. I love being used like I'm their fuck toy. I want to blame the kraken part of me, but secretly, I think it's all me. I've always loved to fuck, and the more depraved and desperate the sex, the harder I would come. That's why the tentacles, blood taking, and knotting have done nothing to turn me off or freak me out. My kinks seem to be limitless.

The tiny little tentacles at the base of Xavier's cock tickle my nose, and I feel the urge to sneeze, but another hard thrust from Saxon and his teeth sinking into my neck removes the urge as my orgasm explodes through me. Saxon's venom courses through my body, lighting my nerves on fire and creating a bigger ache that won't be satisfied with one orgasm. He drinks his fill and continues to thrust through my orgasm, but as soon as I start to come down, he pulls out, despite not having found release himself. I pull my mouth off Xavier's cock and look at him quizzically, but he wears an evil grin.

"Oh, you didn't think we'd be done that quickly, did you? I'll come, but it will be in his ass while you ride him to completion." He nods at Xavier, and I blink in surprise. I wouldn't have pegged Xavier as a bottom, but then I wouldn't have said Saxon was either.

I look up at my warlock, but I can tell by the hazy fog in his eyes that he is lost to the lust in the room. He was basically operating on empty, so I'm not surprised that he has been overwhelmed so quickly. I turn my head and find my cyborg wrapped up in my kraken's tentacles. I know that I was feeling possessive of them, but I mean sharing is caring and that is fucking hot. Cas has partially shifted and has Link suspended above him while he sucks on his cock and a tentacle slides leisurely in and out of his ass. It's a magnificent view, and I'm momentarily mesmerized by it. The look on Link's face is nothing short of ecstasy, and I know exactly how he feels, but I want to be involved, and I feel my own eyes flick back and forth as my kraken tries to push to the surface and force a shift. I will her down. She is not taking over, because this is my orgy, and she can back the fuck off.

Cas's gaze flits to mine, and he smirks. "Take care of them, and then come over here and join us," he suggests. "I'm going to edge our cyborg until you're ready to join us."

There's a hint of frustration in Link's gaze as he snatches one of Cas's unoccupied tentacles out of the air and starts to lick it with his tongue. Cas gets distracted and lowers Link slightly as he takes it into his mouth, sucking on it like it's a cock. It basically is, since he can come out of all eight appendages.

Saxon's hand tightens in my hair, bringing my attention back to him. He guides me up the bed and helps me straddle the fuck drunk warlock. He's actually not much use to us at the moment, and I can't help but giggle at his hazy grin and floppy arms.

"He can't sit up, let alone fuck me," I tell Saxon over my shoulder, and he nods.

"That's why you're going to ride him."

Ah, okay, I did this position with Echo and Maxsim. I start to lower myself down on to Xavier's cock, but Saxon spins me so I'm facing him, my back to my warlock. He lifts my legs and places my knees in the creases of his elbows. I'm balanced precariously on Xavier's cock, and I groan at the feeling of being stuffed as Xavier's hands come up to caress my breasts. "Gorgeous," he mutters incoherently. "You feel so good strangling my cock." Saxon leans in and kisses me as he breaches Xavier's ass, and we hear him grunt. It takes him a couple of thrusts, but he's finally seated balls deep.

"All right, baby, you just enjoy the ride," he tells me as he starts to retreat, sliding out gently before thrusting in hard. His movements have me sliding back and forth on Xavier's cock, the happy tentacles at the base of his dick stretching out to tease my clit with every pass. It doesn't take long until I'm worked back up, my orgasm just out of reach. Xavier groans, and in the mirror above us, I see that his head is thrashing back and forth as Saxon rides his ass hard.

I'm chanting both their names, praying to some unknown god with all the feelings assaulting my body. When I crack my eyes open again, Saxon is entirely too much in control. I want to see him lose his shit, so I lean forward as far as I can and sink my fangs into his wrist. I let my venom flow, giving him a bigger dose than normal.

A growl worthy of a lightning cat escapes his lips as he starts to use his vampire speed to fuck our warlock. This sends us all over the edge. Our orgasms detonate, and I can't stop the scream that leaves my mouth. I collapse back on Xavier's body, unable to hold myself up any longer as incredible bliss rolls through me. Saxon collapses on top of us both, pinning me between them as we all come down from our high.

"Oh no you don't, we aren't done yet." Cas sounds amused as a tentacle reaches in and wraps around Saxon's body, lifting him slightly before snatching me away from them. I feel Xavier's hot, wet cum dripping down the inside of my leg as my kraken brings me over to him and Link. When I turn my head to look back at the other two, Cas gently lowers Saxon back down. The two of them are still connected, and Xavier wraps his arms around Saxon as he snuggles into his abs. It's kind of adorable, but Cas and Link don't allow me any time to recover or watch the other two post orgasm.

Cas's tentacle manipulates me so that I'm on my hands and knees. Link is behind me, and Cas is in front. With a shimmer, Cas changes back to his human form, and I swipe my tongue up the length of his cock as I feel Link lean in and swipe his own tongue through the mess that is my pussy. I moan around Cas's dick, the filthy thought of him eating Xavier's cum out of my pussy making it clench in need once more.

"Fuck, what did you just do?" Cas groans as I swallow around his dick, but Link doesn't answer, he just swipes some of Xavier's cum up with his finger and spreads it over my tight ring. I feel him line himself up with both my soaked cunt and my asshole. I startle slightly and try to get a better look, but Cas holds my head in place.

"He's made himself a double dick," he mutters in my ear, "and he's going to fuck you in both hot holes while I come down your throat." My eyes roll back in my head as Link slowly eases forward, his nanobots making one dick thick and the other nice and slim for my ass. "Xavier's not going to need to feed for ages after this."

I'm a useless mess by now, and it's all I can do to hold myself up. Thankfully Link helps me out, his fingers digging into my hips as he powers in and out, his cock rippling and pulsing and vibrating like the best rabbit vibrator out there. Every one of his moves has me moving back and forth on Cas's dick. I try to suck, but I'm worn out now, so I just let him fuck my mouth. Link's cocks start to swell, and he reaches around and pinches my clit, and then another orgasm, this one stronger than all the others, tumbles through my body in never-ending waves. I feel Cas come down my throat, his grip on my head just adding to the sensation, and then nothing.

When I become conscious again, I find myself clean and tucked in my bed, my mates surrounding me in various states of sleep. The only one awake is Xavier, who looks like he's fucking wired. He's brilliant and pulsing with power, and he finally resembles the warlock I originally met. I smile, happy that we could help him with that. I take stock of my body, and despite a few pleasurable aches, I feel pretty good.

"Hi," I whisper quietly.

"Hi," he says just as quietly. "I didn't want to leave before you woke up."

"You look good," I tell him, and he leans in and kisses me.

"Thanks to all of you. You have no idea what it means to me that you're willing to share us," he tells me, and I shrug.

"Well, of course. I wouldn't want to deny myself the deliciousness of you all fucking."

He chuckles and pushes a stray strand of hair back from my face as Cas grumbles and rolls over, hugging Link to his body.

"I love you," he tells me.

"I know," I murmur.

CHAPTER THREE

Lila

After a very satisfying orgy, I can now officially tick it off my bucket list—not that I'm ever going to turn one down, that's for sure. Xavier is full to the brim and bursting with energy. He hurries back to the bridge so he can keep an eye on the Aquilian ships. Cas takes a nap, exhausted from swimming with the kids before our impromptu orgy, and Link decides to do some research on halla fruit harvesters and see how they can do their job without perishing on the planet. We need every possible bit of information we can get our hands on. He said he has an acquaintance, a doctor, who is in contact with one of the harvesting teams, because they procure a certain plant for him while they are on the planet that he uses in an herbal pain relief tea he brews for patients who are oversensitive to other medical means. He's going to see if he can facilitate a meeting for him so he can get firsthand knowledge.

While all of them do that, I grab my Vilaxian husband and pull him to his bedroom.

"Are you still hungry, my beautiful blood rose?" Saxon asks, putting his hands on his shirt to strip it off, and I'm momentarily distracted. Sure, I just had a number of mind-blowing orgasms, but I am a red-blooded female, and Saxon is gorgeously distracting.

"Ah, no. Well, I mean, I wouldn't say no to more sex, but first could you make a call and introduce me to Xavier's parents?"

He pulls his shirt back on and frowns, leaning against his desk. "Why?"

I sigh. "Because he has waited so long for me to get my memories back, and now we have another detour. I'm hoping that maybe his parents will meet us at Aquilia instead of us having to spend all that time traveling first there and then to Westalin. This way, we would also have a show of force behind us with the warlock royal family, which will make King Marlin think twice about how they treat me for some supposed slight, and Xavier and I can finally establish our intimate bond."

A smile slowly stretches across his lips, and his eyes sparkle with love. "You are amazing, did you know that?" he tells me, and I shrug.

"I don't know. With so many mates, I worry that

some of you will feel neglected and miss out, and my mimic powers are pushing me to add more. When is it going to stop?"

He shakes his head and walks over to me, pulling me into his arms. "No, baby, you are doing everything right. We are adults and can speak up if we ever feel neglected, but so far, you are doing a fine job balancing us and parenthood, so I'm sure you will have no problems no matter how many mates you add."

"From your mouth to God's ears," I mutter as I lean into him, absorbing all the strength he's giving me. "What I wouldn't give for a few days on a tropical beach with just my mates, the kids, a few cocktails with fruit and umbrellas in them, and the sun shining down on me while I get a tan."

"One day we will do that, even if Xavier has to conjure up something for me and the cats so we don't burn."

I feel a pang of guilt as I remember that some of my mates aren't so temperature compatible. "Ugh, sorry, I forgot. See? I'm so self-involved, I forgot that you guys can't do that." I pull away and start pacing back and forth. "I need a checklist to remind me of everything. How is that being a good mate?"

"Lila, stop it. Seriously, for the amount of time you've had to adjust to all of this, you are doing wonderfully. A lot of people would be in the corner, rocking and drooling," Saxon scolds.

"How do you know I'm not when you aren't looking?" I retort, and he chuckles.

"Because that's just not you. Sure, you mess things up, but you try to learn from your mistakes and keep moving forward. That's all you can do. Look at how well you dealt with knowing we're going to have more babies."

"Ha!" I exclaim. "Sure, on the outside I was the picture of poise, but inside, I was screaming," I tell him, and he shakes his head.

"You were not. You are just as thrilled as those two cats, but you've been programmed to want to be upset. Thankfully, you are letting go of most of your preconceived Earth ideals. Look, I get it, it's a lot, but just stop, take a moment, and breathe deeply every time you feel overwhelmed, or change and go for a swim. I know you like the bottom of the pool. We have one of our own now, and no one can bother you down there."

"Except three gorgeous yet exhausting kraken babies," I point out, and he shrugs sheepishly.

"Not if we do our jobs right. Now stop worrying. Let's deal with one thing at a time. We are solving Xavier's needs, and then we can talk about the can of tuna." He turns away from me to open up his communication screen, but not before I notice him grimace when he mentions the can of tuna. He isn't the only mate who has had this reaction. What the fuck aren't they telling me?

Before I can ask him, though, the screen activates, and we don't have to wait long until it's answered.

"Yes?" A warlock with pale blue skin and no visible silver marks answers the call. He doesn't look a thing like Xavier, so I'm going to assume this isn't his father.

"General Saxon of Vilax and Lila Adams for King Cronus and Queen Xylene." Gone is my warm, snuggly blood bunny, and in his place is a rip your heart out, rabid rabbit—or the imperial General of the Vilaxian army, nephew to the Vilaxian queen.

"I'm sorry, but the king and queen are unavailable without an appointment." This warlock is basically looking down his nose at Saxon, and I feel the urge to reach into the screen and rip his heart out. My teeth click into place, and I step forward so he can see me. I consider assuming my warlock form, but we're trying to keep the extent of my powers under wraps. Only the people on the ship know how many beings I've mimicked so far, and we kind of want to keep it that way.

"Tell them that their son's intimate would like a word with them regarding our bonding please." I don't hide the threat in my voice, but the warlock looks at me with undisguised disgust.

"You're the crown prince's intimate? Well, that is certainly underwhelming. Maybe he isn't as powerful as everyone assumed he was."

Saxon stiffens, and a low, rumbling growl can be heard in his chest, but I pat his shoulders and smile widely, my fangs on display.

"Oh, I can assure you that underestimating me would be a mistake." I allow the red to bleed into my eyes, but he still doesn't seem intimidated.

"They don't have time for some pretty twat who the prince thinks is his intimate. He will come to his senses soon and recall his harem when he can't be at full power just from feeding from you. I'm sure if you're lucky, he might keep you around in his harem. I've heard the Vilaxian bite is quite alluring. Maybe he'll lend you to me when he gets tired of you." He leers at me, and I just gape at him, not believing the crap that's coming out of his mouth. Who is this man?

Saxon chuckles darkly next to me, and the warlock flinches. He must have forgotten Saxon was here. "You claim they don't have time for Lila, but I'm sure they have time for me. Please tell them that I am waiting to speak to them."

He sighs like he is put out, but he must know exactly who Saxon is, because I see him look up from what must be a hand held communication device before he calls across the room, raising his voice.

"Your Majesty, General Saxon of Vilax is on a call. Do you wish to receive it?" Holy crap, they are in the same room. Maybe Xavier has this all wrong, and they aren't happy that I'm his intimate. Maybe it's all a mistake, and I'm not really his intimate. Surely they would have overheard that conversation. I gnaw on my lip with my fangs, feeling it pierce through. Saxon turns my head to face him, his nostrils flaring. He leans in and licks my bleeding lip. "Stop worrying, Lila. He's just a trumped-up asshole who has become too big for his boots. He will realize what a big mistake he made once Xavier's parents realize he was gate keeping you from them."

The warlock snorts and mutters, "Unlikely," but in the background, we hear, "Of course I will receive a call from Saxon. What are you doing screening my calls anyway? Give me my communicator," I hear an abrupt voice say, and the warlock sighs, sounding annoyed. Hmm, someone is confident in his position. I wonder if he would be so confident if Xavier was there.

"I put it on the main screen for you, sir," the warlock says and starts moving, but our screen changes images, and we get a view of a large office area. There are two desks, and sitting at each desk is a male and female warlock. The man is deep purple, almost eggplant in color, and the woman is the palest lilac I've ever seen, but both of them have many silver swirls and markings. I can see how Xavier came to be the color he is. The man looks so much like Xavier it's scary, but there's wisdom in his eyes that shows he's considerably older than my warlock fiancé. They both smile widely at the camera.

"Ah, Saxon, it's good to see you. How can we help you today?" the man booms joyfully but looks a little quizzically at me.

"I take it you haven't announced to the general population that Xavier has found his intimate and who it is," Saxon says a little dryly without any niceties.

The two exchange a confused glance. "No. We were waiting for them to return so we could have a large celebration," the woman says as the previous warlock joins them, standing between the two desks.

"Well, your lovely assistant there not only insulted Lila, but he also hit on her. I'm sure you can set him straight." He gestures to me, and the two older warlocks' eyes lock onto me. My eyes are still red, and my fangs are still down, so I shake off my anger and allow them to recede. Their gazes both soften, and Xylene smiles at me.

"Lila, honey, you look so much like your mother. You have no idea how happy we are that you have finally joined us. We were about to start our own search for you when you were found."

The previous warlock's mouth drops open in

shock. "That's Xavier's intimate?" He sounds disgusted, but he blanches as the warlock king and queen glare at him.

"You dare insult the crown prince's intimate?" Cronus looks furious, but it's Xylene's cold tone that makes me shudder. I don't envy him one little bit.

"But... I..." The warlock stutters a little, but Cronus holds up a hand, silencing him.

"Your family is treading on very thin ice at the moment, Eryan. Your sister has already been punished for her trespasses against the crown prince's intimate. Do not make us punish you as well."

Eryan pales at hearing about his sister. They must be talking about Elyan. His eyes narrow, and he glares at me as the king and queen turn back to face the screen, dismissing him behind them.

"Lila, we are looking forward to seeing you in a few days." Cronus steeples his hands in front of him but leans back in his chair.

"King Cronus, Queen Xylene, it's lovely to meet you," I say politely, but King Cronus frowns and shakes his head.

"No need for formality, we're family. You can call us Mom and Dad if you want." He beams at me, and Xylene rolls her eyes.

"Slow down, love. Ignore him, he's just so excited that you and our son can finally be together," she apologizes for her enthusiastic husband.

"And I can't wait either, but I'm afraid we are going to be delayed once more," I tell them, explaining that the Aquilians have placed me under arrest and that we are now heading toward the planet Aquilia instead of Westalin. They both get more and more annoyed as I speak, and Xylene gets up and starts pacing, making Eryan push backward and huddle against the wall. I can't say I'm sad to see that.

"I was wondering if maybe the two of you could meet us there. Xavier has waited too long already, and I don't want him to have to wait any longer." I side-eye Eryan, not wanting to announce that he's not feeding well in front of someone who is obviously so hostile.

Thankfully Saxon comes to my rescue, allowing me to remain silent regarding how vulnerable Xavier is at the moment. I wouldn't want anyone to get any ideas. "Lila would benefit from sealing the bond. It may help stabilize her own newfound powers."

The warlock sneers at hearing this, but I don't care. I would rather him think I'm useless than know the truth.

"Of course we will. King Marlin is a giant asshole. He always hits on my wife whenever we have official functions. I would love to show up and put a little bit of fear in him." Cronus smirks, and it's so much like Xavier's that I have to blink a couple of times.

Xylene grimaces. "Ugh, the man is an eel. He keeps the Aquilians isolated and doesn't allow visitors on the planet. It's why there is only one city on land. It's to keep his people ignorant so they don't rise up and overthrow him. The Aquilian royal family has had a history of doing that. It was why we were so surprised that he sent his son and daughter to the circus. Hopefully the next ruler will be better."

Saxon and I exchange a glance, and I shrug. "I wouldn't count on it. Nikos isn't really all that much better. He's horny and stupid." I feel an ache in my heart when I say this, but I'm still pissed at him for putting my babies in danger.

Saxon frowns disapprovingly at me, and I feel slightly guilty. "He's actually not that bad. He has potential, but I believe Nixie would be an excellent ruler. Unfortunately, Marlin is a sexist pig and won't consider naming a female as his heir."

"Never mind. Aquilian politics are the least of our worries, but they better have a good reason for detaining you. We will leave immediately. We should be there shortly after you," Cronus assures me.

We sign off, and I feel a rush of excitement, knowing that I'm going to get all my memories returned and Xavier and I will be able to bond.

"Thank you." I wrap my arms around Saxon, and he does the same. I just lean there, supported by his strength, grateful that he is so supportive of being mated to me and all that entails. "I am so lucky that I am mated to wonderful, kind, and understanding men. I don't know what I would do if you hated each other," I tell him, pulling back slightly so he can see all the emotions in my eyes.

"Hmm, I find it interesting that you are ending up with mates who were all previously friends or acquaintances."

I frown. "You don't think it's a coincidence?"

He shrugs. "So far, every one of your mates has been in the circus. I kind of feel like maybe something or someone has been manipulating us."

"You mean a greater power? Like a god?"

"Stranger things have happened," he replies, giving me a squeeze.

"Well, if I knew whom to thank, I would. Although it was a bumpy start with a few of you, I wouldn't change anything at all."

"Yes, just keep that in mind as we go along. Things happen for a reason," he says cryptically, but before I can ask him what he means, a childish wail is heard through the speakers of his room. Ah, one of the children woke up, and that means they are all awake now, because there is no way anyone can sleep through that noise.

"I'll get them," I call out as we leave Saxon's

room, not sure where or if any of my other mates are around. I try to spend as much time as possible with them while we have downtime. I missed them so much while we went to Rilu, and I know there will be another trip when we head to Husadavia where they will have to remain behind on the ship. We try to be hands-on parents, but we have so much going on that the idea of a nanny is becoming more and more appealing. So far, though, we've been resistant, but with two more babies on the way, it's not a bad idea to get one, especially once the circus is up and running again.

I may not be everyone's idea of a perfect mate or mother, but no one is ever going to accuse me of not trying.

CHAPTER FOUR

Lila

The five days it takes us to get to Aquilia are uneventful apart from the constantly looming presence of the Aquilian ships. I work on my whip skills a little more, but without the rest of the cats for the ice show, there isn't really any point in rehearsing. Saxon tries to distract me with flying lessons in Vilaxian form, but I still suck at it. Now that I have access to the Aquilian pool, I've been spending a lot of time in there in both my kraken and Aquilian forms. Thankfully they have no special powers, but I practice a lot of swimming with my tail and maneuvering. Their skills in the water are exceptional, and Caspian and I mock fight just in case I need to defend myself once we arrive on the planet. I doubt it, but I didn't want to be caught unaware again.

Eventually, I get bored and restless and decide to join the meetings discussing plans for rescuing my grandmother. Today's powwow involves everyone except the two cats and Cas, who are looking after the little ones, which is what they will be doing when we arrive at Husadavia as well. Apparently the three of them are not suited to go down to the planet. I'm almost certain they are going to try to tell me I'm not suited either, and I'm going to tell them they are mistaken. If my grandpas think they are going down to the surface, then they are sorely mistaken as well. Thankfully Xavier is on my side.

"We've explored everything we could find on the planet Husadavia, trying to figure out the best way to get into the death forest." Brannock has taken charge of this expedition, which surprises me. I didn't think we were at that level of trust with him yet, but obviously he has proven something to my grandpas and mates. Also, his experience during the war with the Una's is invaluable, according to my grandpas. "But there's just not enough information. Link has a friend who hooked us up with the leader of the halla harvesters. We have a meeting with him at Z68 in five days' time."

We're all sitting around the conference table, which is off the side of the flight deck. Saxon, Xavier, and Link, as well as Silac, Tirrian, Brannock, and my three grandpas are all here. Bubby is making sure the ship stays on course to Aquilia so we don't get shot out of the sky. "Z68?" I ask because everyone seems to know what he's talking about.

"It's another one of those space stations, like the one we attended before," Xavier tells me. "We should be able to find you a few more beings to mimic as well. Depending on what the imagined slight is to the Aquilians, we should be able to wrap up that issue and make it to the space station on time. It's not too far from here."

"It would be helpful if we could add the other two elementals, though the earth elemental is going to be an asset for this mission, and it certainly would be an advantage if we could get you to mimic another dragon. Their impenetrable hide would be useful on Husadavia." Link nods, and I see Tirrian's eyes narrow as his nose starts to smoke, but he's made it perfectly clear how he feels about me, so I ignore it.

"What's so special about the leader of the halla harvesters that he and his group can get onto this planet when nobody else seems to be able to?" I ask, worried we're getting scammed. "What's to say he won't just take us there and leave us to die?"

Everyone exchanges a glance. "We're not actually sure what species he is. It's all very hush-hush," Link tells me. "But even if we decide not to go ahead after the meeting, we're hoping that you'll be able to mimic him, and that should help us on the planet."

Tirrian snorts derisively. "That's reassuring."

Grandpa William scowls at the dragon. "Be careful, dragon. You are still breathing at this stage because I respect your father too much to kill his firstborn son. The fact that you may come in handy for this rescue mission is the only reason you are still on this ship, so shut your mouth unless you have something helpful to add."

"We are all very aware that you do not wish to mate with our granddaughter, and that is your decision, but you can keep all your derision and negative opinions to yourself unless you're offering a solution," Eric sneers at the dragon. He fought with the other two to send him home once he found out that he didn't want to seal the mating bond his dragon is insisting on, but John argued that it may make him even more volatile, and that we should just let him stay and leave him be. We can't force someone to do anything they don't want to, and I certainly don't want a mate who doesn't want me.

I'm sort of sad because I kind of felt like maybe we had a moment in the caves of Rilu, but I guess I was mistaken. Shaking myself out of my funk, I tune back into the conversation, but I see Xavier looking at me with sympathy in his eyes. Damn him and his warlock emotional radar.

"Okay, so we have a plan for navigating the planet. What about the other thing Zamala told us about? The something bears?"

There are audible groans around the table and muttered curse words, and I go on high alert.

"The carevasta bears are an all-male species. They are the pirates of space, capturing ships and pillaging both their cargo and their women. They need to use other women for the continuation of their species. They emit a pheromone that makes women crazy, allowing them to breed and impregnate them. The women are loved and cared for until they give birth to their offspring. Any males born will be carevasta bears, and the fathers retain custody of the child and return the mothers to their former lives. If the child is female and of whatever race the female is, they both get discarded," Silac explains, his nose wrinkling in disgust.

"They are foul-mouthed, arrogant creatures, but they have the ability to manipulate matter," Saxon grumbles, but I'm still confused.

"So why exactly do we need them?"

"Because Zamala said that Liliana is encased in something, and we need a carevasta bear to reach in and pull her out with his matter disruption abilities."

"It's what makes them such good pirates. Nobody is able to keep them in a jail cell or out of any vault or safe that they want to get into. As long as they can get close to a ship, they can board it."

"But if they are lacking in morals and complete assholes, then how are we going to convince them to help us?" I look around the group, my heart sinking with everyone's solemn faces.

"I'm not sure, to be honest," Xavier says, sounding worried, but he avoids my gaze, and again, Tirrian snorts.

"Are you really that stupid?" he asks. Everyone around the table glares at him, but I'm unfortunately still clueless.

"Shut up, dragon, or I will make you." Xavier starts to spark with power, and Tirrian just rolls his eyes, not caring that he's being threatened by one of the most powerful beings in the galaxy.

"Look, I'm not sure why you are tiptoeing around this. You need to let her make her own decisions," Tirrian argues, and Link just snorts and shakes his head.

"That's a bit rich coming from you. You've done everything you can to take her decision away from her." I can hear the venom in Link's words.

"Yes, because mine is being taken away from me as well." Tirrian straightens in his chair and thumps his hand down on the table, his wings fluttering behind him. Although my skin still itches to mimic both him and Silac, I am able to control it, so I haven't asked them to remain in their human forms. Silac has kept two legs instead of his half snake form, but the rest of him is partially shifted.

Silac just shakes his head in pity, his tongue flicking in and out in agitation, and I'm mesmerized by it. It's forked, and if my reading is correct, it's not the only thing on his body that's forked. "If you and your dragon are that disconnected, I would say you have bigger problems than who it's picked for a mate. Usually the human and the animal are in sync, so who is really the stupid one now? Maybe you should shift when we get to Aquilia and see if you and your animal can reconnect, because whatever is going on with you can't be sustained."

Tirrian's nose smokes, and there is a low grumble, but he bites his tongue and doesn't argue. He nods. "Maybe you are right. If you don't need me for the meeting with the Aquilians, I will take advantage of all that space to shift and see if my animal and I can come to an agreement."

He says this quietly, and everyone looks at me. Oh shit, they are all looking at me like he's asking me for permission. Is he? Because that can't be right.

I wave my hand. "Do what you want. Tirrian, I don't get a say in what makes you happy." There's a moment of tense silence, but then I remember how it got that way. "Anyway, what were you suggesting about the bears?"

Everyone glares at him again, and he ducks his head and mutters, "Never mind." Everyone relaxes, but I'm not happy with that answer.

"No, not never mind. If you have something to

say that might help us rescue my grandmother, then I want to know."

Everyone at the table starts to argue except Brannock. He's been quiet this whole time, but he is looking at Tirrian and kind of nodding to himself. "The dragon is right," he says, and everyone stops arguing. "And so is Lila. We are going to need every bit of luck to get your wife back alive. The reports of Husadavia do not do it enough justice. We used it as a base to hide from the Una's during the war. Our generals ordered us to establish a settlement in the mountains, somewhere we could hide from the rest of the galaxy if needed. We lost many Aaz'axians trying to build that base before they eventually gave up. Even with our superior fighting skills, powers, and weaponry, we were unable to stop our people from dying. The flora and fauna are completely adapted to be the only inhabitants, and that's how they want it. They have a symbiotic relationship, and they are aware of everything that happens on that planet. We must have every possible trick up our sleeve if we wish to survive."

My family still tries to argue until I grow impatient and look at the dragon. "Tell me," I command, knowing he will.

"You are the perfect bribe for a carevasta bear. You can give them what they need."

It all suddenly clicks in my brain, and I feel like an idiot. Of course it all comes back to sex.

"Right. If I mimic them, I become the only female carevasta bear in the world," I say flatly, and he nods.

"With the ability to birth both female and male carevasta bears. It's something they would probably kill for."

"Which is exactly why we don't want them to know," Xavier shouts at Tirrian, his eyes blazing with power. "Lila is not a broodmare. She's not there for every dying race to pin their hopes on."

"The carevasta bears aren't dying out anyway," Eric points out, and Tirrian rolls his eyes.

"No, but they resort to coercion and abandonment to get what they want, and everyone turns a blind eye."

"What do you want us to do? There is no jail cell in the galaxy that will hold them," Link argues, and Tirrian looks at my warlock.

"Are you sure? Xavier was easily able to create a spell to have the children's clothes change with them, what's to say he couldn't create something that would keep them contained. Instead of coercing women with their pheromones, they could be required to enter into some paid surrogacy program, because let's face it, what they are doing is essentially rape."

Wow, Tirrian really is passionate about consent, just as much as Xavier is, but I guess if he and his animal are not in sync, then his animal's insistence that I am its mate might feel a little like that to him too.

Xavier frowns and gnaws on his lip as he thinks about it. "We've never had reason to try. I was under the impression that they could interrupt any kind of matter, but maybe not magical fields."

"Look, that's beside the point for this mission. Yes, the carevasta bears would be very interested in Lila's abilities, which is why we can't give them a reason to find out. As far as the galaxy is aware, Lila is a low powered mimic whose database of forms is already full. The only way we can do this is by mesmerizing a bear and have her mimic them, wipe their memory, and send them on their way." William is back to business, blatantly ignoring all the tension in the room. He is focused on getting his wife back, and I don't blame him for wanting to use every ability he can, including mine. I would happily mimic any creature to help my grandpas— after all, they have given me everything.

"I don't like this." Xavier crosses his arms stubbornly, and I can see that both Link and Saxon feel the same way as well.

"You don't have to," Brannock says, "but it is the best plan we've had so far, unless you want to dangle her in front of a bear to get them to cooperate."

"That's not going to happen, and everyone needs to just take a moment to chill out." Silac shakes his head at my mates and Tirrian. "You're all talking about her like she's incapable of making a decision herself." He turns to me, sympathy in his eyes. "Lila, what do you want to do?"

Ugh, there is no way the attraction mark is going to fade off the naga if he keeps being so freaking thoughtful. I mean, I'm not mad at my mates, and I know they need to be involved in the decision too, but I think they lose their shit with their concern and forget that I am perfectly capable of being reasonable and seeing both sides of the story.

"While I understand my mates' unease" —I nod in their direction— "I will mimic the bear if it will help us rescue Grandma. Preferably, we'll wipe their minds, because I really don't need to be the hope of a complete society. Freaking Oshan is already pressuring me to meet his son, and from what I understand, the bears won't wait for me to 'think about it' like he is."

"No way, they'll hide you away, and you will be used over and over until you pop out enough females to kick-start a little breeding program. You and your daughters will essentially be a puppy farm for them." Link sounds disgusted, and I feel a little ill as images of me tied to a bed, popping out baby bears, flash through my mind.

"Yeah, no, that isn't happening, so mind wipe it

is. Now where are we going to find one of these bears?" I ask, and they all exchange a glance.

"I'm not sure, to be honest." John is staring out a window, mostly happy listening to the conversation up until now. "They have been banned from most of the space stations and planets because of their predilection to steal women. They've upset many nations, but there are still some places where they are welcome, and there is always their home planet." He turns back to face us. "But you run the risk of being caught there."

"Yes, we want to catch one on their own, not a whole ship of them, because we don't need anyone finding out the rumors about Lila are lies." Saxon gets up and comes over to where I'm sitting and starts rubbing my shoulders. I groan and relax into his hands. I'm not sure how he realized I was so tense, but his hands are doing a wonderful job of releasing it. Another groan leaves my lips, and Tirrian abruptly stands.

"I will make some inquiries on where to find one," he announces before leaving the conference room.

I blink at his hasty departure, and Link and Xavier exchange knowing glances.

"Maybe it would be better if you released the dragon back to his home planet. It seems cruel to have what his animal so desperately wants dangled in front of him," Brannock suggests, looking a little uncomfortable, and it suddenly occurs to me that his species is another one that is dying out. I must be the ultimate temptation for him, but so far, he has shown no interest except mild politeness.

"I tried," William tells Brannock. "We are not unsympathetic to his feelings. We don't want to force him to be Lila's mate either. We only want her to be happy, and he is making her miserable, but he refuses to leave."

"What about you?" I say quietly. "Is it uncomfortable for you to be around me?" I ask him, and everyone else looks confused, but he knows what I'm saying.

The sympathy in his eyes for Tirrian quickly shutters, and his face becomes blank despite his incredible coloring.

"No, Lila. I made peace with my lot in life many years ago. I enjoyed my time on Earth. I even married once. She died a few years ago, but I came to terms with the fact that the Aaz'axian race will die out soon."

"You can't have babies with other races?" I ask him, and a shadow crosses his face. This man is very good at controlling his emotions, but this obviously strikes something inside him.

"Our bodies are not compatible with other races," he says woodenly. I remember the sharp spikes all over his cock as he stroked it while he watched Xavier and I fuck. Yup, that would tear a female Earthling to shreds.

"So you never had sex with your wife?" Xavier asks bluntly, and I hiss at him.

"Xavier, what the fuck?"

"I could have sex with her, but never to my completion. It's only when I get close to my peak that the spikes activate. A female Aaz'axian secretes an enzyme that numbs the female's inner walls so that the spikes lock in and cause pleasure rather than pain, setting off the female's orgasm and allowing her to release an egg." Brannock's cheeks sparkle, and I realize he's blushing as he explains his species' reproduction to us.

"So you haven't orgasmed in years?" I ask, now unable to control my curiosity despite how much I'd hate to be questioned like this.

"Only by my own hand," he admits.

"And your wife never knew?" I feel incredibly sorry for this quiet man. I mean, orgasms are not everything, but they are pretty freaking awesome.

"No, of course not. I told her I had a low sperm count, and we would never be able to conceive a child naturally." His eyes cloud, and I can see this conversation is making him agitated.

"I'm sorry," I say, unable to stop myself from standing up and going over to give the guy a hug. He just seems to radiate sadness, and I can't help but want to make it better.

He flinches as I wrap my arms around him, not bothered by the spikes all over him. When he is not on high alert, they are quite flexible and not sharp. It's only once he goes into warrior mode that they become lethal.

I lean my head against his shirt-covered chest, feeling all the bumps and ridges underneath my cheek as his arms slowly come up and he returns the hug. I feel him shudder in my arms, and a tear streaks down my cheek before I can stop it.

"When we rescue Grandma, we'll sit down and work out a plan for you. If you want to return to Earth, we will make that happen. I know Aura also feels this way. Smith will be dealt with," I promise him fiercely, anger at the slimy little man flaring up inside me like it always does when I think about him.

Brannock's arms tighten, and he stiffens at my promise. "Yes, I need to go back to Earth," he tells me in a way that makes me feel like there is something there that he can't live without, which is how I feel about my mates and children, so I will do everything I can to help him.

CHAPTER FIVE

Lila

We finally arrive in Aquilian air space. They don't have a space station for us to dock at, so we settle into an orbit above the planet. The only ships allowed to land on the planet are their own, but for now, the ones shadowing us continue to remain in orbit as well.

"Bubby, is there another ship nearby?" I ask him from my seat on the flight deck. I needed a break from everyone to catch my breath and get my bearings before I have to deal with whatever trumped-up charges the Aquilians are trying to pin on me. Link was the one who suggested I come up here and hang out. Everyone else is distracted by the children or micromanaging our Husadavia plans.

I have no idea where Tirrian is, and Silac and Xavier have been locked in the conference room, having clandestine talks about something that I'm sure they will eventually share with me. When I asked Saxon while we were dressing the children this morning, he said something about getting Silac out of his arranged marriage. I didn't let myself hope it was because he wanted to be with me. Saxon said it involved some political maneuvering and sneaky shit, which Xavier excels at.

"No, Lila, love. Nothing that I can see on the long-range scanners either. Is there something specific you are looking for?"

I watch as the Aquilian ships hover off to our side, not willing to leave and land on their planet until they receive confirmation that I have reached the destination I am required to attend.

"Yes, the warlock king and queen will be joining us," I tell him, and a grin lights up his face and he chuckles.

"Those damn cans of tuna aren't going to know what hit them." Everyone has started referring to the Aquilians like I do. Poor Nixie is going to be pissed at me, but I will make it up to her somehow.

"No, but we may have to go ahead without them. Can you tell them to join us when they arrive?" I ask the captain of the ship who I've come to love like a favorite uncle.

"Sure thing, Lila. Make sure you don't take any crap from the pompous King Marlin," Bubby tells me as I take my leave and go in search of those who are going to join me on the surface. William and

Eric are both coming, but John is staying behind. He feels like he won't be any help if we encounter any trouble since he isn't back to full strength. Both cats and Link are also going to remain behind, as well as Saxon and Silac. The fact that the planet is ninety percent water is really going to work against us, but Cas and Xavier will both be accompanying me. Cas for obvious reasons, but Xavier insists his presence will unnerve the Aquilian king.

We were all supposed to meet in the teleporting room, and that is where I find everyone who is accompanying me, but there is a loud argument going on, and it doesn't stop as I enter. I try to make heads and tails of what they are arguing about, but I'm lost.

I lean against the wall and watch with interest. Maybe I should get a talking stick. I remember the sparkly, glittery version we had in elementary school, and whoever held it could talk and everyone else had to shut their pie hole. My family could benefit from one of those. I must put it on the shopping list.

"I'm just saying that having an Aaz'axian with us is enough to make King Marlin crap his pants." Cas gestures to Brannock, who is shaking his head.

"It's not a good idea. I'm sorry, but I will remain on the ship."

"I have to agree with Cas. The asshole is mostly all talk, and seeing you will throw him off, which will be to our advantage," Xavier agrees with my kraken, and Brannock starts to pace with agitation, his spines bristling with each step.

"I would gladly accompany you anywhere to keep Lila safe, but please don't ask this of me," he argues, and William frowns.

"Why not?"

"Hey, lay off the man." I step into the conversation, seeing as none of them are backing off. "I'm sure he has his reasons, and what business is it of yours?" I growl at the gathered men, who look slightly chagrined in the face of my annoyance.

I turn my back on my grandpas, mates, and Tirrian—I have no idea why he's here—and pull Brannock to the side, trying to use my warlock powers to reassure him that his decision is valid. I'm not in warlock form, though, which I kind of have to be to use them, so I guess it's pointless, but I feel him relax under my hand, so maybe just interrupting helped.

"It's okay," I assure him. "You have no skin in this game, and you owe us nothing. If you don't wish to come down to the surface, it's fine."

He just stares at me for a moment, and then he grimaces and looks down at the ground and mumbles something that I don't catch despite my enhanced hearing.

"I'm sorry, what?" I ask him, and he huffs before raising his head.

"It's not that I don't want to come. I can't swim, so really, if anything happened, you would be the one rescuing me."

I blink, startled by his embarrassed confession, before shaking my head. "Don't be embarrassed. Almost sixty percent of Earth's population can't swim. I completely understand. I wouldn't want to do battle in the sky. I can fly in my elemental forms, but in my Vilaxian one, I'm more likely to crash and burn. We all have our strengths, and that's okay, but if you'd like, once we get some downtime, I can teach you if you want. I'm pretty good at it, even in my normal Lila body," I offer, and he just stares at me for a moment, and I worry I've over-stepped.

His eyes brighten, and the smile that crosses his lips is one of pure joy, and holy smokes, the man is hot when he smiles. I feel tingles in places I shouldn't be feeling them for a man who isn't my mate, and I have to grit my teeth and shove my mimic ability deep, deep down so it doesn't rise up and tag this man as one of its mates.

It's too late, though, and I see the moment my attraction mark burns itself onto his body. Fuck my life. Brannock's sinful smile disappears, and his mouth drops open in shock. His hand comes up, and he reaches back, rubbing the spot on his shoulder.

Groaning with embarrassment, I turn away,

unable to look at him any longer. I'm also aware that my back is burn free. Of course the attraction is one-sided. I'm never going to be able to look at him again, let alone teach him how to swim. Maybe it's not a bad thing. Seeing his body almost naked and dripping with water wouldn't help things anyway.

As I go to move away from him, that familiar feeling starts to burn into my back, and Brannock grabs hold of my arms, spinning me back to face him. He leans in and whispers, "Don't think I haven't noticed how incredibly sexy you are, not to mention that you're kind and caring and generous, but there are things you don't know about me—things I can't share, reasons why you may change your mind about how you feel. I didn't want you to think that the attraction only went one way though. I'd have to be blind and dead not to desire you, and I am neither of those things." His voice is husky in my ear, and I can see that he isn't unaffected by what just happened, but as soon as he admits that, I see a shutter come down over his emotions, and he becomes that blank, almost robotic being that we have gotten used to.

He releases my arm and turns away, and I step back. I notice that everyone else gave us a moment of privacy and are discussing how they will deal with the king of the fish people.

"Right, Brannock won't be coming down to the

surface," I tell them, even though I'm certain they all listened into what just happened like the nosy busybodies they are. "Shall we just do this? Until we know what the charges are, we won't even know how we are going to respond."

I see Link and Xavier exchange a loaded glance, and I brace myself. I know that look, and they are about to drop a bomb on me.

"God, what now?" I ask, hearing the whine in my voice and not even caring that I sound like a petulant teenager.

"We think we know what this is about," Cas says, coming over to me and wrapping his arms and a tentacle or two around me, and I start to panic. He's obviously trying to soften the blow of whatever they are about to tell me. His tentacle caresses my leg, but I push it away.

"Don't try to distract me with your sexy as fuck tentacles, squid rings." I poke a finger into his chest, and he winces and shrugs at Xavier.

"I tried," he says and steps back as Xavier scowls at him.

"You weren't subtle. I said be subtle, but no, you had to go and grope her with your tentacles and try to distract her with your sexiness. I knew she wouldn't fall for it. This is serious."

With the way the two of them bicker like siblings, you never would have guessed they brought each other to screaming orgasms during our hot as fuck orgy a few days ago.

I cross my arms, trying not to get distracted by thoughts of tentacles and orgies. "Just spit it out. Obviously it's shitty news if you're trying to soften it in any way."

The two of them continue to bicker, and Eric rolls his eyes, wrinkling his nose. "When you had your 'swim' with Nikos, did he bite you?"

"Yes, he left a scar around my—" I break off, not wanting to share where he bit me with my grandpa.

Eric shudders and holds up his hand. "I don't need details, it's fine, and did you bite him back?"

I have to think back carefully. Mostly, I try to block it out because I feel guilty that I was so easily lured away from my precious babies. I also try to forget how incredible the whole experience was, how his cock felt in my slit, and how we spiraled through the ocean together, every beat of his tail sending my pleasure higher and higher, his cock moving inside me like it could bury itself in me forever. We connected on a level that we hadn't reached before, and that was ripped away once I came out of my sex-induced fog and realized his betrayal. He took me so far away from my babies that it made them vulnerable to the predator beast. I was completely relieved when I saw the sea dragon fighting off the whatthefuckasaurus, but angry at the merman.

"No, I did not bite him. I was pissed off and yelled at him and banished him. I told him I never wanted to see him again or something like that. Do you think he went crying to his dad? Is that what this is about? The poor little prince got yelled at by a woman."

Everyone in the room exchanges glances and knowing looks, and now I'm just getting pissed.

"What the fuck is going on?" I demand.

"What they are scared to tell you is that bite that scarred was Nikos claiming you as his mate," Tirrian tells me, leaning against the wall. There's no sarcasm or any of the aggression I've been getting from him since he admitted that his dragon picked me as his, just sadness and a hint of sympathy in his eyes, and my heart races as I recognize what he's telling me.

"He mated me?" I ask quietly as I try to play over everything that happened in my head.

"Yes." He nods as the tension ratchets up in the room. I guess everyone is waiting for my explosion.

"But Aquilians don't have fated mates," I argue, and he sighs.

"No, they don't. They choose whom they want to spend the rest of their lives with, unlike a lot of us, and he chose you."

"But I've been horrible to him," I whimper.

"How could he have chosen me to be his mate? Surely there are many other more suitable mer girls who wanted to be his mate?"

I look around the room, and no one seems to know how to answer the question.

"That's probably why." Tirrian breaks the tension again. "You treated him like he was normal, not the Aquilian crown prince. You didn't care if he was a prince or a circus performer, and you certainly didn't care what he could do for you or what your status would be if you managed to snare him in your net." Xavier stares at the dragon prince with an intense focus, but Tirrian ignores him.

Cas sighs and nods. "I have to agree with the dragon. You didn't take any of his crap, and he loved that more than anything else you could do. Despite how he acts, Nikos is not stupid. Most of that is an act to scare people away and get people to underestimate him. Yes, he is a bit of a himbo, so don't expect that to change, but he is smart, and he knows when someone is after him for what he can do for them or who he is. It's why he was with the circus in the first place."

"So what? I'm half mated to him?"

"Well, he has selected you now, but it will be a half mating, because if it's not fated, it will break after a period of time, and both of you can move on. He will be able to remate." I feel a sudden rush of anger and jealousy as Xavier says these words.

"But I would hazard a guess that the king is going to force you to accept him or ask for some kind of compensation. Rejecting Nikos will have far-flung consequences for him. Marlin may even remove his crown prince title and elevate one of his other children. He won't stand for the shame of his son being rejected, especially by someone he considers lower than him."

"So let me get this straight. Because Nikos chose me as his mate, he may lose his title and get banished from his home because his father is a bigoted asshole?" I'm fucking furious—mostly at Marlin, but a little at myself for not understanding the significance of what happened between me and my favorite can of tuna. I was angry, but over the last few weeks, I've come to recognize that I was just as responsible as Nikos, and I guess I'm slightly ashamed of how I treated him. He didn't deserve to suffer all my wrath because I felt guilty.

"Yes," Xavier admits, and I feel a whole new wave of anger wash over me.

"So all of this is because King Marlin is feeling slighted?"

"We believe so, yes." Grandpa William sighs and runs a hand through his hair in frustration. Luckily for them, they age slowly, because I bet since meeting me, their hair would have turned gray three times over.

"Well, let's go and tell the king of the cans of

tuna what we have to say about that. If he thinks he can blackmail me into accepting his son, he has another thing coming. As for compensation, I'll compensate him by removing his head if I have to." I step up onto the teleporting platform, knowing none of my words are making sense because I'm that furious. It is none of his business what Nikos and I decide to do, and he will not get away with threatening me and putting my family in danger.

CHAPTER SIX

Caspian

I smother the chuckle that bubbles up in my chest as I follow my mate up onto the platform and wait for the others to join us. She is hopping mad, as well as feeling a little bit guilty and confused. The words coming out of her mouth don't really make sense, but I'm not going to make her feel small. I just place my hand against her back in support as she mutters profanities and threats under her breath.

My life is freaking amazing. I have a beautiful, loving mate, three gorgeous children, and three other men whom I am allowed to enjoy in the bedroom. Even without that last thing, I would be beyond blessed. Sure, this is another setback in getting the Adams brothers' wife back and the circus up and running again, but I'm hoping Lila and Nikos can finally settle this thing between them. Lila's other mates and I aren't stupid. We know it's inevitable, but the fact that the Aquilian king is going to force this is somewhat of a surprise. I'm actually stunned that Nikos even said anything to his father. I know there is no love lost between them. He is the crown prince because of his first-born status, not because of his father's love. He has no love for his father, who is not faithful to Nikos's mother, his wife. He has a harem of women he keeps in the castle who have fathered his children. Quite frankly, it's disgusting. The galaxy isn't a bigoted place, but most cultures respect the sanctity of marriage vows, and if your race is a monogamous one, then you just don't do what Marlin has, but his arrogance knows no bounds.

"Why are you here again?" Lila snaps at the dragon who has followed us onto the platform, and he flinches slightly at the venom in her voice.

Xavier tells me that she's mostly resigned to how he feels about her, but there is a hint of hurt and sadness every time she looks at him. As for him, although Xavier doesn't like to pry into other people's emotions, he decided the dragon is fair game. He wanted to know exactly how Tirrian feels about Lila, and he confirmed that every word out of his mouth is a lie. Tirrian wants Lila like a dragon wants its hoard, but he is still stubbornly resisting the mate call. Who knows why, but if he doesn't modify his behavior soon, he's going to find himself floating out in space after we throw him out of the air lock. This will come to a head, but it has a reprieve while we deal with the Aquilians.

"I'm going to shift and be backup if you need me for any reason," Tirrian tells her, not flinching away from her glare. This dragon has big balls. Lila's glare is enough to make anyone shrink back with fear. "Also, you may want to glamour your hair so they don't suspect you now control the supply of the most precious gem the Rilunese possess." He turns his back to her, and her mouth drops open in shock as her body starts to spark. I tear my hand back as one of the sparks sends a jolt of pain down my arm.

"Holy shit, what's happening?" Eric asks as we all stare at Lila in awe. She hasn't shifted into her cat form, but it seems like she may be able to access her lightning while in her normal form.

"Lila, *phoeall*." Xavier holds his hands up, trying to calm her down, but it doesn't work.

"Don't you try to manage me, Xavier Colest. I'm allowed to have my feelings." She waves her hands around, and a bolt of lightning shoots out, luckily bouncing harmlessly against the ceiling, but it sparks where it hits the metal, and we all jump in shock.

"Lila, baby, we're not saying you can't be upset, but you need to take a breath and let it out," I say gently. "You're going to kill one of us if you aren't careful."

She stares at her hand in horror and yelps. "That's not supposed to happen," she says, looking around with a small amount of panic in her eyes.

"No, it's not, but it seems like maybe you are breaking all the rules," Tirrian mutters unhelpfully, and Lila's sparks increase.

"For fuck's sake, shut up, you idiot, or I'll let her use you for target practice," Xavier yells at the dragon.

Broderick is still watching us, waiting to send us down to the surface, so I take a risk that Lila actually won't hurt any of her mates, even subconsciously, and wrap myself around her.

She sparks a little more and shudders in my arms, but I bite my lip and take the small bites of pain. It's certainly not strong enough to kill me. Bit by bit, she calms, deflating in my arms and heaving out a large sigh. I press little kisses to her temple and coo words of comfort in the hopes it will help settle her.

"Thanks," she mutters, wrapping her arms around me. "I needed that. Ugh, after feeling slightly settled after Rilu, it suddenly felt like I was back on a roller coaster. My mimic self is going haywire." She pulls away reluctantly, and I let her go. I desperately want to keep her wrapped up and protected, but I know she needs to deal with this. "It feels angry and demanding. It kind of has this whole megalomaniac streak that says the Aquilians must pay for their treatment of me."

She sounds scared when she admits this, and I see her grandpas exchange worried glances. I don't blame them. Nothing Oshan shared with her mentioned anything like this.

"I now also know that I can access any power in this form. I just have to think about it." We watch on in sheer surprise and no small amount of terror as her hair slowly changes to what it used to look like prior to her connection with the larnuk.

"Did you just use warlock glamour?" Xavier asks, and she nods.

"Yes, it's like it's all just sitting at my fingertips. I'm not sure if I could access them from a different form like my half-kraken or lightning cat. It's something I'm going to have to play around with." The tension in the room has eased slightly now that she isn't sparking.

"Well, that's going to have to wait until we return to the ship," William says, looking at his wrist display. "Try not to fry the Aquilian king please. We don't want an international incident on our hands."

"Ugh, that's going to be hard." She turns to look at me. "Keep a tentacle wrapped around me at all times, and if I start to get out of control, give me a little squeeze?" she asks, and I feel my chest puff up that she's trusting me to do this for her.

"Of course, baby, but I wouldn't mind seeing

him fry, or maybe be a little singed, just saying." I wrap a tentacle around one of her ankles and rest my hand against her back again. I feel her relax under my touch, and she leans her head against my shoulder.

"Love you," she whispers, and I kiss her head again.

"Love you too," I tell her again, counting my blessings for everything I have.

Xavier heaves out a sigh of relief, and Eric gives Broderick the cue to send us.

Our bodies dissolve into particles, and within seconds, we reform down on the surface. The sun is high in the sky, and it's hot. The landing platform sits on a small area of land that's just out from the mainland. There is nothing but the platform, so if you arrived in bad weather, then you'd end up very wet.

The blue, sparkling ocean stretches out as far as the eye can see, and the familiar yet comforting smell of the sea wafts across my senses with a gentle puff of breeze. An ache to just dive in and swim hits me hard, and when I look down at Lila, I can practically see the longing in her own eyes.

"Maybe if we get this sorted out quickly, we could have a quick swim before we return to the ship," I suggest, and she looks up at me hopefully.

"That would be wonderful. I wonder if there are any great big sea beasts here?"

Before I can reply, the platform hums a warning, and I unwrap my tentacle from her ankle and we hurry off it. It activates again, and a phalanx of armed and scaled warriors appears before us. They are wearing chest plates with the sigil of the Aquilian king and carrying staffs and tridents that all point at us.

"Lila Adams, you will accompany us to the throne room." One of them steps forward, his whole demeanor screaming with aggression. I push Lila behind me and rise on my tentacles to make myself bigger, my colors flashing darker in warning. Both Xavier and Tirrian flank me on either side. Smoke pours from Tirrian's nose, and Xavier clouds himself in his mist for the first time in a while.

The rest of the troops bristle aggressively, and the tension ratchets up again.

"Easy." William holds up his hand and steps forward, putting himself between us and the group of warriors.

"We are here as requested. If you will show us the way, we will be happy to accompany you and get what I'm sure is a misunderstanding sorted."

One of the mermen snorts. "Misunderstanding, right."

"What the actual fuck?" Lila mutters behind us, sounding as confused as I'm starting to feel.

"She will answer to the king," the lead warrior

spits out. "You can't insult the Aquilian race and get away with it."

"What exactly did I do to insult the Aquilian race?" Lila pushes me out of the way and steps over my tentacles, her hands on her hips. "Because I was angry at the prince? Is that a crime all of a sudden?"

There's a rumbling within the ranks of the troops, but the lead warrior quickly silences them. "Quiet." He jabs his trident in Lila's direction. "You, start moving. The rest of you will remain here."

"Like hell we will," Eric says, raising his voice.

"You are not required at the tribunal," the warrior argues.

"But surely she's entitled to representation?" I can't help arguing, and William nods.

"According to Galactic Council laws, everyone is entitled to representation when facing a trial."

"The Aquilian court is not subject to galaxy law," the merman sneers.

"Oh, Marlin might think that, but I assure you they are." Xavier's voice booms out of his mist, the power behind it causing the lead warrior to flinch.

"Right then, shall we go?" Lila turns, not waiting for any more arguments, and starts marching toward the mainland. She startles slightly as she catches sight of the main building on the island. It's a castle-like creation, made from gleaming white sandstone, surrounded by palm trees and other tropical plants. Nobody else is allowed to have a dwelling above water except for the king, and anyone wanting to spend time on it must apply for permission. By order of the king, Aquilians don't get to spend much time in their human form, though I believe a lot of their houses below the ocean are water free.

The warriors hurry forward and surround us, but Lila doesn't stop. She keeps marching forward with Xavier, William, Eric, and me following. Tirrian remains behind. It's probably not a bad thing, because she is worked up enough as it is, and we don't need him to make it worse. I'm assuming he's going to shift and then soar on the small coastal breeze. Hopefully he can sort out his issues with his inner beast and come to some sort of agreement.

The walk to the palace gates doesn't take long, maybe ten minutes, but Lila is muttering about sand in her shoes and sweaty under boob by the time we get there, which doesn't bode well for the Aquilian royals. She was already annoyed, so this is just making things worse.

The warrior captain hurries ahead, shooting an annoyed glance at the pace Lila has set. We've all had to hurry to keep up with her. The thing is, she could have used her Vilaxian speed and been there within moments, but she didn't.

"I should have just teleported us all there," Xavier mutters to the side of me.

"Why didn't you?" I ask. My tentacles are feeling dry and sandy too.

"Dude, look at our wife. She is fucking mad. I thought maybe the walk would cool her down so we don't have an intergalactic incident," he tells me, nodding at Lila who is close on the heels of the lead warrior, the rest of them having to fall behind us in the narrower hallway.

"That was a bit of a failure, wasn't it?" Eric says dryly from behind us, and Xavier's hand pokes out of the mist and flips him off.

The doors to the palace are thrown open as we approach so we don't have to stop. Lila continues her march through the halls, not even stopping to take in the pearly wonder that is the inside of the castle. She just mutters about ostentatious hard to clean surfaces, and how it had to have been a man who picked such a vain thing.

"This is not going to go well." William sounds worried, and I can't help but agree with the man.

"You think?" Xavier's sarcasm is thick but unhelpful.

There is another set of large doors in front of us with two more mermen guarding them. They startle as the lead warrior approaches and jump to open them. They do, and we all file into a large, open throne room with dual pools of water running along either side, creating a barrier between the people spread out along the walls and the walkway to the front of the room. Up on a raised dais at the front of the room is a large, ornate throne made from dead coral. Sitting on it is a man, one I have never met in person but have heard many tales about.

"King Marlin, Lila Adams, as you demanded, is ready to stand trial for insulting the Aquilian royal family," the lead warrior announces, slightly out of breath.

Lila comes to a stop slightly in front of the dais. I can see her taking in the Aquilian king in front of us. He looks nothing like the rest of his fit warriors and citizens who line either side of the throne room. He is an immensely overweight man with jowls and rolls, covered only by a garishly ornate robe. Standing on either side of him are a number of women and children, one whom I recognize as his wife. She has her hand in Nixie's, who mouths, "I'm sorry," to Lila. Both of them look concerned.

"Whoa, man, you must look like a mantiti in your shifted form." Lila looks at the king with amazement. Xavier and Eric stifle snorts of amusement, but William groans. Crap, she just compared him to one of those Earth sea cow things she was telling me about once.

The king frowns and looks at his lead warrior. "What is this mantiti she speaks of?"

The warrior shrugs, and I sigh with relief that nobody knows what she is talking about.

"A great and powerful sea creature, no doubt," the king says out loud, and the rest of the Aquilian citizens murmur their agreement. As I gaze around the room, I can see the fear and worry on a lot of these people's faces. The king stares down at Lila like she's a piece of sea kelp marking the pristine sand of his beach. "Now in payment for insulting my son, I demand a half share in the Galaxy Circus and for you to be imprisoned for the rest of your life."

The crowd bursts into loud murmurs as Xavier starts to spark powerfully beside me, but Lila just laughs.

"Are you serious? I yelled at Nikos about something, and he comes running to you to cry about it?" Lila's head swivels between the king and Nixie. "I had every right to be mad at him. He put my babies in danger." She crosses her arms stubbornly.

"You ruined him for anyone else," the king sneers, looking down his nose at Lila. "He is useless to me now. I have had to raise Raen to be my heir." He gestures to a man just behind his chair who has the same kind of soulless look in his eyes that Marlin has. He has stringy, long black hair and glares at me before sticking out his tongue and waggling it. Eww, gross.

"What, because he decided to give me a mating

bite, but I didn't reciprocate?" Lila's disbelief is obvious.

King Marlin gets to his feet. "No, you worthless trollop, because he is with child, and nobody will want him now that he carries your bastard." With that announcement, two warriors wheel out a pod similar to what the children have for their kraken form, except this is adult-sized and contains a merman.

"Oh fuck," I whisper as Nikos floats around to display the very obvious bulge in his belly, telling us the king is not lying.

CHAPTER SEVEN

Lila

"Oh fuck," Cas whispers behind me as I stare in open-mouthed shock at the sight before me.

Gone are Nikos's very defined, sexy abs, and in their place is a very large, very familiar round belly —one I recognize from looking down at myself not all that long ago. Unlike the king behind him who is all fat, Nikos is most definitely pregnant. I blink a couple of times just to make sure, rubbing at my eyes and shaking my head, but sure enough, when my vision clears, he is still pregnant. My gaze rises up his floating body until it gets to his face. He looks at me with shame and embarrassment, and that wave of guilt that has been plaguing me rises up with a new force, as well as an overwhelming sense of jealousy. Why is my can of tuna pregnant, and how the fuck did he get that way? Which sea bitch am I going to have to kill for knocking up my mate?

A rumble starts deep in my chest, and it's only then that I notice his cheek and the very dark, defined bruise with knuckle imprints.

"Who did this?" I demand, pointing at Nikos. "Which woman is responsible for my mate being in this condition?" I ask him, looking around at all the Aquilian courtiers.

"Ah, Lila. Marlin said it's your bastard," Cas whispers behind me, and I freeze.

"Mine?" I ask quietly. "But how?"

"We don't have time for this, but I guess it's similar to Echo," Xavier says.

I think back to our swim and how my orgasm seemed to be so different from anything I'd ever experienced.

"Well shit," I mutter as William steps up next to me.

"King Marlin." He nods his head respectfully. "I wish I could say it was a pleasure to see you, but under the circumstances, I believe I won't. As far as your request for compensation, the Galaxy Circus is only to be passed down to a member of the Adams family, so you have no business asking for half of it."

"That is an Adams baby in my son's belly." He points at the bubble, where Nikos's golden hair floats around his face. I'm not sure if he can hear the proceedings or not. I'm not even sure how I feel about this. Even faced with the evidence of what we did, I still can't comprehend that I'm his baby mama. He looks miserable, and all I want to do is wrap my arms around him and hold him tight. I also want to kill whoever put that mark on his face. The need is fierce and all consuming, and when I find out who hit my pregnant can of tuna, they will die, and I will make them suffer.

"So you claim, but there are also five more babies up on the ship with equal rights, and it is them who have the right, not you. We will take Nikos with us, since you claim to have no use for him, and run tests to assure that what you say is true. If this is the case, he and his baby will be well loved." Eric steps up to show a combined force on my other side, and I feel Cas and Xavier crowd my back.

"I want compensation." The king struggles to his feet, huffing and puffing. "I am due some kind of compensation."

"You will get nothing, and you will tell me who put that mark on his face," I say through gritted teeth, trying to hold in the lightning power that begs to lash out and kill this worthless slug on the spot.

The king sneers at me and waves a hand. "Then you will rot at the bottom of the ocean in one of our prisons." We are suddenly surrounded by the warriors, and I hear a thud and turn to find my warlock in a crumpled pile on the ground, a warrior having hit him in the head with the blunt end of his trident. I go to raise my hands, but the lead warrior tuts, smirking at me as he shoves his trident deeper into Caspian's side.

"If you even twitch, we will kill them all," he threatens me. I look around, and both my grandpas have razor-sharp tridents pointed at them as well. I know that I could use my warlock powers and take care of these idiots, but I'm not experienced enough with them to be quick, and I don't want to risk them getting a little stab happy if I do that. I'm sure both my grandpas feel the same way about using their own powers, especially with Xavier on the ground.

"If you come quietly, I will allow the others to go back to the ship safely. If you do not, I will kill one every time you fight my guards," the king says, sounding as happy as a clam at the moment.

"Don't do it, Lila," Cas says, shaking his head furiously.

I look around, but for now, I see no options. My heartbeat is steady, and I have a plan forming in my mind. With my earth elemental powers, I should be able to get out of any prison they put me in, and I have options once I'm out, so now I just have to make sure that everyone else is okay.

"Let them go," I demand, and he shakes his head.

"You really have no room to negotiate, but I am wise and kind," he announces to the room. As I look around at his gathered people, I see the skepticism in their eyes. Marlin's gaze narrows on my Cas, and he grins evilly. "I will allow them to return to their ship, but I want a galactic ton of suva delivered to me, and I want sole distribution in this quadrant of space, and I want that to continue every month."

"No, that's unreasonable," I argue with him.

"Agreed if you let Lila go as well," Cas says quickly, but the king snorts.

"No, that bitch is mine. She will spend the rest of her life in my cells." My grandpas and Cas start to argue, and I hiss at them.

"Be quiet. I have a plan." Thankfully they do as I ask, though I can practically feel Caspian glaring at me. "Fine, as long as you allow my family to take Nikos with them."

Marlin sneers at me but waves a hand. "They can take him. I have no use for him."

I turn to face my family. "Go, I will be okay. I have all my forms. They won't be able to keep me contained for long. Just have Bubby watch the transport platform, since I haven't mastered teleporting yet, and don't let Xavier lose his shit when he wakes up."

I can see that it's killing Cas and my grandpas, but they readily agree. William and Eric gather Xavier's slumped form between them as Cas goes over and retrieves Nikos's pod. He still hasn't really looked at me, and I feel terrible. Not a wink or a smirk or a flutter of fins to be seen. He's listless and unresponsive as Cas wheels it down the hall, followed by my grandparents with an unconscious Xavier and half the mermen warriors.

"I don't need to tell you that you won't be welcome back here," Marlin calls, and William and Eric stop, glaring at him.

"The Galactic Council will hear about this. I hope your people won't be mad at you when you are completely cut off from everything else when I demand sanctions against Aquilia."

King Marlin laughs evilly as murmurs travel through his people. "My people have no need of anything else the galaxy can provide."

I'm still surrounded by some of his warriors, and I hear one of them mutter, "I wouldn't be so sure of that." When I look up, a few of them have worried frowns. All is not right with this planet. King Marlin is more tyrannical than anyone could have known. I look closer at his surrounding citizens, and they look pale and gaunt and very unhappy. This planet is ripe for an uprising.

The doors close behind my family, the loud clang sounding awfully final, but my heart rate is steady and my brain whirls as I try to make plans despite the anger building inside me.

Marlin looks back at me and demands, "Change forms."

I feign a frown and shake my head like I don't know what he is talking about. "What?"

"I know you have an Aquilian form. My son wouldn't be pregnant unless he fucked you in it. If you had done it in two-legged form, you would be the one who was pregnant."

Oh crap. I haven't completely studied up on my Aquilian knowledge yet. Had I known I was mated to Nikos, I would have. I didn't even know that their males gave birth like Earth's seahorses.

"If you don't, I will kill my daughter," he threatens, and I watch in horror as his other son, the one who is now crown prince, grabs Nixie and holds a knife to her throat. Fuck, I was so worried about getting Nikos to safety that I forgot about my friend. I allow my Aquilian form to wash over me and collapse to the ground when my legs disappear, my tail flapping, and King Marlin smiles triumphantly. "So you are a mimic. I had my doubts, but now I am going to be able to make a galactic fortune by hiring you out to whatever race wants to make babies with you."

"Like hell I will do anything for you, and my family won't let you either. The minute Xavier wakes up, you will have the warlock and Vilaxian armies on your doorstep."

King Marlin's laughter echoes around the ostentatious room. "And how will they get to us deep under the ocean? Sure, your kraken mate may be able to, but there is no one else who can come to your rescue."

I snort. "And how the fuck are you going to hire me out if no one can get to me?" I ask him, and he rolls his eyes like I'm an idiot.

"They can transport directly to my palace under the ocean if they have the right code, which changes daily."

"And you don't think a warlock can't." I smirk too, but my amusement disappears when he just tuts.

"Ah, Lila, I am not an idiot. My palace has been warded against warlocks. Even the warlock king and queen couldn't get into it."

Damn it. Iceen was the same. I was hoping maybe he was too stupid or arrogant to consider it.

"I wouldn't be too sure of that," a voice I've recently become familiar with says from behind me.

Marlin's smug look disappears, and he glares. "Cronus, I don't believe I invited you to attend me. Seize them and take her below," he orders his warriors, waving his hand at us. The room breaks into chaos. All the citizens start yelling and shouting before throwing themselves into the pools mid-change and disappearing into the deep. I guess they aren't just pools, but access to the ocean.

More warriors appear from who knows where and surround Cronus and Xylene. They don't look too concerned. In fact, there's a glint of excitement in their eyes that I recognize, but before either of them can react, the head warrior grabs me by my tail and tugs me into one of the pools. My body slides across the smooth surface, and I splash down into the water. All the frantic sounds from above disappear in a loud splash. Mer bodies torpedo deeply all around me, bubbles exploding from the rush of water. It's disorienting and confusing, and I can't get my bearings as I remember to breathe through my gills and not my mouth. The warrior has a tight grip on my tail as I try to thrash myself free, but he tows me deeper. I glance around, trying to get my bearings, and there are five or six more guards escorting me, including Nikos's brother Raen, who has been promoted to crown prince.

The warrior who has my tail releases me, and two more grab my arms so I can't get away.

Raen jabs me in the side with his trident, his black and silver scales glimmering in the pale light of the deep. I flinch because he pokes fucking hard and actually makes me bleed.

Fuck you, asshole, I say to him, hoping he can hear it, and from the grin on his face, he can.

No, bitch, I will be fucking you. Dad didn't say you had to be well looked after. I want my turn at that golden pussy before he starts hiring it out. His voice is greasy, and a shiver runs down my spine.

I'm almost certain I have to be interested in him to have sex in this form, so I'm probably pretty safe.

He opens his mouth and starts to sing, and my body becomes languid and relaxed as my mind starts to float. Fuck, I forgot about the seductive sounds of the Aquilian people. I try to struggle, but it's like I'm not even in control of my body anymore. He runs his trident across my scale-covered breasts, coaxing me to let the scales drop away. I'm unable to stop myself from complying, and his eyes narrow as my naked breasts are exposed to him. He swims toward me while I'm still being held by two of the other warriors, who seem happy to gawk at my breasts too.

We should secure her in the prison, I hear the original warrior captain tell Raen. *The warlocks may figure out a way to get down here.*

Raen chuckles wickedly. *How? Neither of them can breathe under water. I want what I was promised. My brother doesn't get to have all the fun.*

He hands his trident to one of the other mermen swimming close by and reaches out to pinch my breasts. I can't help but gasp in pain. He pinches them so hard, despite feeling languid and pliant, I am not turned on in the least.

Ow, asshole. If that's how you treat a female, it's no wonder you have to rely on rape. The pain has chased away the trance he attempted to put me in.

He backhands me, and I'm so shocked that it actually hurts, I'm speechless. How did he do that? Surely the water should have slowed him down, but no, he connected just like he would have on the surface.

You're a mouthy bitch. I can't wait to shove my cock in it and choke you with it.

I look down, and sure enough, his cock is wriggling beneath his scales. I struggle again. There is no way I'm going to let that anywhere near my mouth, but the two mermen just tighten their grip.

I hear a loud roaring sound, and everyone stills.

What was that? the merman on my right asks, looking around.

Nothing, you're imagining things, Raen sneers and reaches out to tweak my nipples again, but before he can, the head warrior's eyes widen.

Holy fuck, what is that? he asks and starts to swim backwards away from me, and so do the others who aren't actively involved in my attempted rape.

Screw this, one of them says and turns to flee.

I try to see what they are looking at, but I can't turn my head around far enough. Raen isn't distracted though. His cock has forced itself out of his slit, and he's stroking it with one hand as he runs his other over the front of my tail where my sexual slit is, but that sucker is closed tight with a no entry sign on it as far as my body is concerned. He tries to poke a finger into it, and I flip my tail up to block him. Whoa, my tail moves like normal too. He yanks it back, and I bare my teeth at him—the shark ones, not the normal human ones. If he wants to put his cock near my mouth, I'm going to fucking bite it off.

He glares and yanks his trident back from the Aquilian he'd given it to and stabs me with it again. This time, it punches deeper, and I scream as he yanks it back out, my blood pouring into the water around us. He watches it, sticking out his tongue and tasting it as it flows past him. Another loud roar sounds, and the rest of the mermen surrounding us back off and swim away, leaving just the four of us. I feel tears trickle from my eyes and merge with the salty sea around us as I try to staunch the blood flowing from the wound in my side. I attempt to stop my tail from beating back and forth, because with every movement, blood pulses out of my body, but it's tricky.

He starts to jab his stick at me again when something huge barrels past us, knocking him away from me. The flash of a green body triggers a memory, and I struggle to get a better look.

The two mermen holding me have loosened their grip in shock. *What the fuck was that? I don't recognize it.* The one on my left releases me completely and starts to swim away.

Come back, you fucking coward, Raen calls, but the huge beast barrels toward us, and the man on my right also loses his courage and swims away, leaving just the two of us. Raen goes to reach for me, but he's too late. I watch with glee as the big green water dragon snatches him up into his mouth and crunches down just like he had with the whatthe-fuckasaurus. Raen's blood tints the water around us, but the dragon finishes him off quickly.

I hope for your sake they really do taste like canned tuna, I say to my heroic rescuer and reach out to stroke his whiskers. I hear a purring sound vibrate in my ears, but the pain in my side is too much, and I've lost too much blood. I start to feel a little dizzy. I sway and grab hold of those long whiskers to keep myself from sinking to the bottom of the ocean.

Please help me, I manage to mutter before everything goes black.

CHAPTER EIGHT

Tirrian

My dragon scoops her up into his mouth and starts swimming for the surface. It's all I can do to stop him from giving her a bite and making her ours. *No, not without her permission*, I tell him, and he grumbles but listens. All three of us are on the same page. Despite everyone thinking I was going to shift and fly, I've been swimming since they disappeared from sight. It's been long enough for me to finally get over myself.

I've finally caved to my feelings and admitted that I want her as much as they do. I just hate that they made the decision for me, but if I'm truthful with myself, I've been interested from the start, even when I thought I had to be on Dylan's side. But he has proven to be everything they said he was and more. I have no idea what happened to him. He is nothing like the dragon I grew up with. Both he and his dragon have become bitter and twisted.

I've watched her carefully over the last few months, and she is nothing like he said she was. She's kind and caring and does her best to make sure everyone she loves knows it and feels it. I know I have a lot to make up for. I've been an asshole, I can't deny it, but hopefully she will accept our mating bite. I know she could mimic one of my dragons, but I don't think it would give her both forms, and they are insisting she has a form for each of them.

It's unusual for a dragon to have two forms, and my Chinese dragon is the only one I know of. He is lonely and would love another one to swim with, but first, the warlock needs his time. He's been waiting long enough, and we need to rescue her grandmother. My dragons are going to have to be a little more patient. When I explained this to them, they accepted it reluctantly as long as I wasn't actively trying to sabotage them anymore, and I agreed. I will be helpful and kind and her friend— or I will try. It really does go against my core makeup. I hate having to bow to anyone. I am the prince of dragons, after all, but for my mate, I will do anything.

We swim upward toward the pools in the palace. From the way mer people were swimming away from it, I would say something significant is going on, but hopefully the warlock will be able to heal Lila. I have no idea who I ate, but that's going to have to be explained as well. How dare they hurt our mate? Damaging the dragon prince's mate is a death sentence, and ignorance is no defense.

My head pokes out of the pool, and I look around, trying to take in the throne room, but there's smoke in the air and a keening sound coming from somewhere. I can't make out anything through the smoke, so I climb out, my large, serpentine body trailing behind me. I hold Lila carefully in my maw, my whiskers touching the ground. There are more screams as my body fully emerges, and as I pad through the smoke, I find two warlocks at the center of all the chaos, and not the one I had been expecting. In fact, neither Xavier or Cas are to be seen, nor Eric or William. The man looks like an older version of Xavier. These are his parents. I've met them on a few occasions with my father. They seem to have the same love of chaos Xavier does. How they managed to set fire to a palace made of limestone and coral, I have no idea, but they have achieved it.

"Oh, darling, would you look at that?" The male turns to face me, interested surprise on his face. "That's a different form of dragon than normal."

He's right. Dragons are mostly like my other form, but occasionally, there is a throwback to dragons of long ago, and we are able to take dual forms, making us lethal in both the sky and sea.

"I remember the dragon king's line had a ferocious female queen who was quite fond of this form," Xylene says offhandedly as she keeps her attention on the crying, stuttering people they have corralled in one corner of the room. She's talking about my great-grandmother, which is where I get the genes from.

I lay Lila down at their feet and back away before changing shape. "Lila's hurt. Can you fix her? Or can you take her back to the ship?" I stand naked in my half form, unashamed. Xylene smirks, getting a good look, while Cronus scowls before waving a hand and covering me with jeans and a shirt.

"Of course I can fix her," he tells me before squatting down next to her and running his hands over her injured side. I watch as the open wounds knit themselves back together, and then he covers her with a sheet that he conjures out of thin air. "She lost a lot of blood. She will probably need to feed. I could…" He trails off as I glare at him, and smoke pours out of my nose in agitation.

"No! I will help her," I argue, and he just grins and backs away, Xylene scolding him.

"Stop teasing the dragon. Regrowing skin is not a fun job if he decides to cook you."

She grabs him by his robe and pulls him toward her while still keeping an eye on the Aquilian crowd. I take his place by her side, kneeling down and using one of my claws to open a vein on my wrist. Retracting the claw, I gently open her lips and dribble blood into her mouth. It trickles down the side, but it doesn't take long for her to start swallowing. Suddenly, her hands grab my wrist and bring it close to her mouth, where she latches onto the wound, sealing her lips around it and drinking deeply. Each tugging pull of blood sends a shot of pleasure straight to my cock, and it rapidly hardens beneath my jeans.

Mate now, my dragons mutter inside my head, but I ignore them. Now is not the time or place.

Tastes so fucking good, also reverberates inside my mind. This voice is softer and familiar. Lila's talking inside my head like Aquilians do when they are beneath the water. She's probably not even conscious of it, and I won't point it out to her no matter how smug I feel that she likes how I taste.

Her eyelids flutter open, and she blinks a couple of times, looking at me before they widen in surprise, and she drops my arm like it's a hot rock. Using her finger, she catches the dribble of blood that escaped her mouth. I don't even think she realizes she's licking it, her surprise at seeing me in my human form too great, but I can't help the wave of desire that floods through me at the sight.

"Fuck, Tirrian, where did you come from? I'm sorry, did I attack you?" She looks around and struggles to get up, holding the sheet up to preserve her modesty. Her body shimmers like it does when she changes forms, and the tail disappears, replaced with long, shapely naked legs. I almost reach out and run my hand along them but stop myself before I can make a fool of myself. "What happened to that dragon? Did you see it? I can't be imagining things, can I?"

"Lila, thank fuck." A female voice has us both turning to the group of people huddled in the corner away from the warlocks. It's Nixie, Nikos's sister. She has her arms wrapped around a woman, and there are more women and children behind her. One of them is bawling loudly and annoyingly. Nixie and the woman with her glare at the stupid woman.

Lila wraps the sheet around herself and struggles to get up. I reach out, putting my hand under her elbow, and help her to her feet. She blinks with surprise but then gives me a shy smile. "Thank you," she says before looking around the smoking room. "What the hell happened here?"

"That idiot aimed a laser weapon at us, but he's so inept, he missed and set his own palace alight," Cronus scoffs, gesturing at a lump of flesh sitting at the base of the throne. I can barely make out what used to be Marlin, but there is a scrap of the gaudy robe he was wearing. Lila wrinkles her nose.

"Everyone panicked, and we've been trying to put out the fire ever since. Every time I think it's out, it flares up again. I've never seen anything like it." Xylene sounds put out, and I have to smother a smile. The two of them are so much like their son, it's uncanny. I only hope that my own father and I are not so similar.

"So the king is dead?" Lila asks, gagging slightly at the sight of the lump of flesh.

"Of course he is. You don't take a shot at the king and queen of warlocks and expect to survive." Cronus sounds affronted. I chuckle, and Lila rolls her eyes.

"And the dragon ate Raen, so I guess he's out. What happened to that dragon? It was the same one that saved my babies on Skarr and the one I saw on Fluxx." She looks around the room, and Xylene frowns.

"You mean Tirrian?" She points at me, and I wince slightly. Lila hadn't put two and two together yet.

"You're the Chinese dragon?" Lila's mouth drops open in surprise, and she almost loses hold of her makeshift sheet dress.

I push my hair back from my face and shrug. "Yeah, I have two dragon forms, meaning I'm good in the air and under the sea."

She throws her arms around me, forgetting about her sheet which drifts to the floor. I hear Cronus snort with amusement, but I'm distracted by the little naked woman pressed against me.

"Thank you so much. My babies would be dead without you." She rests her head against my chest, and I bring my arms up to return the hug, but there is so much naked flesh I don't know where to put my hands so it doesn't upset anyone.

"You're very welcome." I go with patting her awkwardly on the back, even though my dick is now hard again. "I wasn't going to let anything near them. I was swimming nearby when I heard the Aquilian's song. I arrived just in time to see you taken in by it. I thought it was the least I could do, considering my dragons have declared you as my mate. To be honest, they wouldn't let me leave until we knew that you had returned safely. They could feel the vibration of those predators in the water."

She pulls back and just stares at me. It takes all my willpower to avert my gaze from her luscious breasts. Lila has most definitely lost her Earth modesty.

"Thank you." She leans in and presses a small kiss to my lips. I don't pull away, and I lean into the small gesture from my mate. She gasps and pulls back again, her eyes even wider than before, and I can't help but smirk at her. She shakes her head, confusion in her gaze, before pulling away.

I let her go, and suddenly, she's fully clothed. We both turn and look at the two warlocks. Xylene points at her husband.

"We need everyone fully focused on the situation and not your tits, Lila," he grumbles.

"Thank you. So what happens now? Do they need Nikos to return? Or is there someone else who can rule?"

All four of us turn to face the remaining group of Aquilians. Nixie and her mother, who is still the queen I guess, step forward.

"My mother will rule, as is her right. There is nothing that says it has to be a male on the throne. Now that Nikos is with child, he won't want to leave his mate," Nixie declares loudly, and there's a rumbling of dissension from behind them, but Xylene just raises an eyebrow, and it quickly shuts off.

"The warlocks support and acknowledge the rule of Queen Nerissa. Please let us know if we can aid in any way."

"And I name Nixie as my heir." Nerissa, her mother, steels her spine, and instead of being the meek, cowering woman I have met before, she is now all steel and strength. "And anyone who is not happy about that can go swim in the Molastay Trench."

She walks over to the throne, stepping over the lump that is her former husband, and takes a seat on it. "If you could kindly release my guards?" she asks the warlocks and looks upward. Following her gaze, Lila and I look up, and there, high on the ceiling of the massive throne room, are two dozen uniformed guards just floating amongst the now thinning smoke. There is a massive hole in one wall, which I'm assuming the king's laser tore through, and it will need to be repaired.

"Fine." Cronus waves a hand, and they come hurtling toward the ground, their shouts of horror echoing through the large room.

"Tst," Xylene hisses at her husband and stops their plummeting descent so that they land gently.

"You're no fun." He sticks his tongue out at her, and she rolls her eyes.

"You've had enough fun. You killed the king. I think that's enough mayhem for one day."

The guards scramble to their feet, and they look dazed and confused, but Nerissa doesn't allow that for very long. "Swear your fealty to me," she commands loudly, and that has them jumping to attention. All of them get down on one knee, their fists to their breast plates, and bow their heads.

"All hail Queen Nerissa," one of them calls out, and the others follow suit.

"Hail Queen Nerissa. Long live the queen." The rest of the people come out from the corner they were huddled in and also take a knee, though one or two of the older women look disgruntled. Nerissa turns her attention to them, looking scornfully at the majority as Nixie steps to her side, showing her support for her mother.

"Since my husband is no longer breathing, he has no need for your... services." Ah, I can tell by her tone that these are his remaining harem members. There are a couple of small children who bear a slight resemblance to the former king. "Those of you who have children will be provided for, though none of them will have claim to the throne from now on. As for the rest of you, you reap what you sow. You knew he was a married man and in no position to make any of you promises. I have put up with you for long enough. You may leave the castle with any belongings that you brought with you. Anything my husband" — she spits this word like it tastes bad in her mouth— "gave you is property of the crown and belongs to me. Guards, escort these women below so they may retrieve their belongings." Most of the women readily agree, but one of them glares at her.

"What about my son? Where is he? He was named Marlin's successor." She has the same long black hair as her son and a hawk-like nose.

"He was eaten." Lila points at me, and the woman turns her glare on me.

"He damaged the crown prince of the dragon's mate. It is a death sentence, and I carried it out," I tell her flatly.

"I demand compensation." She doesn't look upset at the news her son is dead, just annoyed.

"Compensation denied," Nerissa says dryly.

"And if you're not careful, you'll find yourself in the dungeon for your son's crimes. You're lucky the dragon prince is happy with the outcome." She turns her attention to a couple of gentlemen who I hadn't noticed cowering behind the women. They are real heroes! "Also, I will be assessing all positions granted by my husband over the last few years. Please have ministers and advisors assemble early tomorrow morning in the palace below. Nixie will be my only named advisor until I've had a chance to assess loyalties. Make no mistake, things will change in Aquilia. My husband kept us cut off from the galaxy for too long, and that will no longer be the case. Please remove this from my sight. Throw it into the Molastay Trench for the sea monsters to devour." Four guards get to their feet and quickly do as commanded. A trail of blood leads to the pool as they drag the king's mangled corpse before they all leap into the water. Hopefully those sea monsters stay in the trench and don't go in search of what's causing the blood.

I look around the room, and while she has been talking, a few more people have appeared from wherever they were hiding. They look like staff members, but I can already see that having a new queen is giving them a reason to smile.

She finally turns her attention back to us. "King Cronus and Queen Xylene, I owe you a great debt of gratitude. My former husband was actively working to repress our people so they didn't rise against him. How can we ever repay you?"

"Never make a pass at my wife, and we'll call it even," Cronus says, and the queen smiles and nods her head regally.

"Of course not." She turns her attention to me. "Prince Tirrian, it is a pleasure to see you again. I hope you will convey my well wishes to your father, and know that you are welcome on Aquilia whenever you wish to swim in your dragon form. Our waters are your waters."

"Thank you, Queen Nerissa, and may I say it is lovely to see you on that throne. I'm sure my father will be in touch with you to discuss trade or a treaty. Your ex was never open to anything."

She snorts derisively. "Why does that not surprise me?" She finally turns her attention to my mate. Her eyes narrow slightly, and she takes a moment to really study Lila before asking, "Now, what are your intentions toward my son?"

CHAPTER NINE

Lila

"Well, I really think that's between your son and me." I bristle a little at the woman's tone. "Considering I knew nothing of any of this until we arrived on the planet, and then I was dragged below and tenderized a little until Tirrian helped me out, I would say I'm entitled to a moment to catch my bearings."

She continues to look at me like I'm the dirt under her bare feet. I mean, I guess I can't blame the woman. Nikos is her son, after all, and she seems to care more about him than his father did, though I didn't see her stepping in when that asshole was alive.

"Mother, give Lila a break. Her and Nikos's relationship has been... trying," Nixie says diplomatically, giving her mother's hand a squeeze. "I'm sure we don't know the whole story." There's sympathy in her eyes when she turns her attention to me. "All he would say is that you rejected him and wouldn't give us any details."

I stomp my foot. "That damn can of tuna. I didn't even know that him biting me meant he'd chosen me as his mate. Like you said, our 'relationship' has never been particularly normal. I only swam with him because he lured me with his song. I was guarding my damn babies from predators, and we swam too far away from where I laid them. If it wasn't for Tirrian, they would have been eaten." I wave my hand at the dragon who has been surprisingly noncombative. Shit, he even fed me in his human form. You could have knocked me over with a feather when I woke up and found my mouth latched onto him, sucking like he was my favorite Slurpee, but I don't have time to examine the dragon's newfound attitude at the moment. I need to focus on the stupid can of tuna and his surprising news, and then hopefully go back to the ship and make my warlock happy.

"He mated you without asking?" Cronus starts to crackle with power. "That is forbidden."

Nerissa straightens her back, bristling at his tone. "He would not be with child unless she was receptive of it."

"Bullshit," I tell her. "I didn't do anything. His penis jacked my eggs. I just had three babies, I was not looking to add to my family just yet. What is it with males who can just steal eggs willy-nilly? This is bullshit."

I'm angry now. It's the second time in just a few weeks that this has happened. I know Echo didn't mean to, and I'm assuming Nikos probably didn't either. I don't think it is something they can control —or that's how Echo made it seem—much like a man can't help impregnating a woman if he comes inside her, but surely they must have some kind of galactic protection to prevent this.

"If you consented to having sex with a male who is capable of this then you consented to possibly having babies with them. Ignorance is no excuse," Nerissa retorts, and I want to use my lightning cat powers and strike her down, but damn it, the woman's kind of right.

"But surely you have birth control. I'm not the first person Nikos has had sex with, and he hasn't ended up pregnant before," I argue, not even believing the words that came out of my mouth, but Nixie is biting her lip and screwing up her nose.

"Actually, you are. Mermen are very careful not to have sex in their Aquilian form unless they are ready to have children with their partners. Most sex is had in two-legged form. Swimming with someone is reserved for mates."

Oh shit. Again, something else I hadn't known. That's it, my ignorance is getting me into trouble. I will be reading everything I can about all the males who I may be having sex with. I need to protect myself better, and I can't expect to put it on them. First up, warlocks! Because who knows what will happen once I get my memories back and can feel the intimate bond. Xavier did mention that there was some mystical process involved, so I think we're okay, but it doesn't hurt to read up. I most definitely need some kind of galactic birth control, so Link will be my first port of call once I return to the ship. Hopefully he will be able to help me.

"Well, how was I supposed to know that?" I throw my hands up in the air, done with all this bullshit. "Look, for now, he will stay with us. He and I will discuss what is to happen because it is none of your damn business. How about you worry about getting your planet in line?"

I'm not willing to kowtow to this woman. She just completely benefited from the death of her husband, and only time will tell if she will do a better job than he did. For all I know, she's as horrible as he was, or maybe she just wants revenge for how badly she was treated.

The queen gears up to argue, but I see Nixie reach over and grab her shoulder, squeezing it tightly and shutting her up. "That sounds reasonable, Lila. My mother and I will look forward to hearing what resolution you come to."

"I take it you're not coming back to the circus?" I ask her, feeling a little sad both for myself and for

Majenta.

Her eyes glisten with unshed tears, and she shakes her head. "For now, my place is here with my mother. That may change eventually, but I will help her transition Aquilia into a healthier nation."

"You will always be welcome. So will there be any Aquilians interested in performing in the circus, or should my grandpas replace the act?" I don't tell them that I am in charge of finding the replacement act, and it seems like it may be the right choice. Mentioning my grandparents causes a different reaction in the queen.

She shakes her head violently. "No, we will contribute a group for the act. Please allow us a week or two to ask for volunteers. Send my best regards to the Adams brothers. Having an Aquilian act in such a prestigious show has always been a point of pride for us." Huh, well she wasn't earning any brownie points by being such a cunt to me. I wonder if she doesn't even see me as the next generation circus owner.

"I can give you two weeks, but if I hear nothing by then, I will be looking for another act. My grandpas have put me in charge of hiring since I will be the next ringmaster of the Galaxy Circus and responsible for all that, but I can't give you more time than that. I was checking out applications, and there was an amazing warlock illusionist who applied. He would make a good substitute. There was also someone who has an animal act that could work. They were these adorable little sea creatures that had little sheepy faces, who jumped through hoops and played games." I break off as horror infuses her face. I'm assuming she goes to say something nasty, because Nixie steps between her and me, blocking me from her view.

"Leave it with me, Lila." I can see her pleading with her eyes, so I back down, but I am sick of people underestimating me, and I won't be treated like trash.

"Can we go yet? I'm bored," Cronus asks, yawning, and Xylene smacks his arm.

"Hush now."

"But the killing and maiming is over. I thought it would be more exciting." He pouts, whining like a toddler.

"Yeah, let's go." I don't wait for Nerissa to allow us to leave, turning and hurrying back the way we originally came. I can hear the other three trailing behind me. Tirrian is a quiet, solid presence at my back while I mutter about arrogant Aquilians, and I can hear Cronus and Xylene bickering softly.

"I'm not sure she is going to be any better than her husband," I say mostly to myself, but I feel Tirrian step up and walk by my side.

"No, you might be right."

"If we have to kill her to get your friend on the

throne, we can do that," I hear Cronus call out, and I stop on the spot, whirling to face him. He startles backward slightly as I start to spark.

"We will not be killing indiscriminately." I poke him with a finger in the chest. "Okay?"

He grins, and it's so much like Xavier's, I almost melt. "But if they insult you, can we?" he asks.

"Hmm, I'm not sure if insults are worth death."

"The galaxy is not like Earth. Insults require action. Some people use stronger actions than others," Xylene explains, and when I look at Tirrian for confirmation, he nods.

"Yes, that's why I killed that idiot hurting you."

I throw my arms up in the air and turn around, stalking toward the platform, muttering about trigger happy, teeth snappy aliens.

"Lila, I can just transport us back to the ship," Cronus calls, and I keep walking, ignoring him.

"You know when I'm mad at you and just need some space?" I hear Xylene ask him.

"Is this one of those times?" he asks, and she replies with an affirmative. "Okay, I'll be quiet. Hey, Tirrian was the Aquilian tasty?"

Oh my god. The man can't just shut up.

"Actually, he tasted a little fishy," Tirrian replies, and I hear Cronus chuckle.

"Of course he did.

"Lila, Lila." I sigh with frustration but turn around to find my friend hurrying after us. Thankfully Xylene has some tact, and when Tirrian and Cronus stop to listen, she grabs both of them and drags them away.

"You know I'm still going to hear them over here," Cronus tells his wife. She waves a hand, and a bubble surrounds them. The man stomps his foot childishly. I think I'm really going to like my mother-in-law, but I'm still on the fence about my father-in-law.

"Thank you for stopping. Can you forgive me?" she asks, and I really look at her. She's lost weight, and her eyes have dark circles around them and look a little hollow, like all the life has gone from her.

"Why didn't you at least send a message warning me about what your father was going to do?" I'm still hurt that we were blindsided.

"The minute I arrived back after Nikos called to tell me what happened between you and him and about his condition, my father put us on lockdown. There was no communication allowed except on planet. I tried, but I was punished."

I make the split-second decision to forgive my friend. None of this is her fault, so how can I be mad at her? I wrap my arms around her and give her a hug. She sort of sags against me like it's taken all her strength to stay upright. I feel her shudder and hear her start to sob.

I just give her the comfort we both need for a

moment. I would love to be able to have a good cry too, but that's not going to happen anytime soon.

When she finally pulls away and wipes at her face, she grabs my hands and gives them a squeeze. "Don't be too mad at Nikos. Despite all his bluster and ridiculousness, he is a big softy and is madly in love with you. Although you rejected him, he was so proud to be carrying your baby. We hid it from Father as long as we could, but once a merman starts to show, there is no denying what it is."

I think back to him floating in the tank, his large belly on display with shiny yellow and blue scales scattered over it.

"I didn't reject him so much as I had no idea about any of it. I was so mad at him because he put my babies in danger."

"When mermen sing to their chosen partners, they go into a trance where nothing else matters to them until they finish the mating swim. He was horrified that he had endangered your children and was despondent because he thought you would never forgive him, let alone accept him and his child," she explains with hope in her voice.

I shrug. "I've mostly already forgiven him, but he and I need to have a long talk. I'm certainly not going to jump in and give him a mating bite."

Nixie's eyes become shadowed. "The longer you don't accept it, the sicker he will get."

"Will that hurt the baby?" I ask, and she shakes her head.

"He is almost due to give birth, so it shouldn't."

"Seriously? It's only been a month!"

Nixie smiles a little. "It's one of the best things about being an Aquilian."

"Do the women have babies as well?" I ask her.

"Yes, women can as well. It depends on the man. Someone like my father thought it was beneath him to carry his children. Most men consider it an honor to have their pod's babies."

"Your father had a pod? Were those the other women your mother dismissed?"

Nixie shakes her head. "No, they were his mistresses. He only became king by marrying my mother. She was the rightful ruler of Aquilia, and partners usually share the duty. He couldn't take those women into his pod because she would have had to agree, and she didn't."

"Ah, okay, I think I understand, and now you are the crown princess. Where does that leave you and Majenta?" I ask, and Nixie sighs heavily.

"Nowhere. I will have to find a male partner whom I can have children with, and they will have to be Aquilian. We may be able to have a pod, but there must be a male in it to allow for succession." I feel a pang of sorrow for her. "I didn't want this. I was thrilled that Nikos was crown prince and then when Father skipped over me for Raen, despite hating him with a passion, but I will do this because it's what's required of me. I was never going to be able to choose my partner, so I made the most of it. It's also why I chose Majenta. She didn't want anything serious either. Don't worry, she won't be too upset. She has many lovers." She's trying to reassure me, but I can see she's lying—maybe not about the Majenta thing, but she doesn't want to be Queen of Aquilia. She loves the circus and traveling, but who am I to tell her she's wrong? She's an adult who can make her own choices.

"Just know that you will always be welcome at the circus in any capacity," I tell her, leaning forward and giving her a kiss on the cheek. "And if you need anything from me, just let me know."

"Thank you, and be kind to my brother. He does love you, and I'm sure if you allowed yourself to, you would love him. You've come so far since you were that scared human and embraced all your challenges with grace and dignity. This is just one more challenge to embrace. Send me photos of my niece or nephew when they are born."

She backs away, and without another word, turns and heads toward the palace. I will miss my new friend. I hadn't had all that much time to spend with her, but hopefully we can rectify that in the future. After all, she is practically my sister-in-law. It's only one, sharp bite away from being a reality.

I turn and walk toward the platform. I hope Nikos doesn't mind a bit of pain. If we mate, I'm going to make my bite count just for a little payback. I haven't tested my shark teeth in Aquilian form yet.

CHAPTER TEN

Lila

The transport deck is empty when we arrive. Bubby can remotely trigger it from the flight deck. I press my communicator and use the open broadcast channel. "Hey, where is everyone? I'm back and have Tirrian, Cronus, and Xylene with me."

"Lila, thank fuck." Cas's voice is breathless when he responds not moments later. "We're in the med bay. Come down and bring Xavier's parents please."

My heart starts to race. Fuck, Xavier must be more hurt than I thought he was. What did they do to him to render him unconscious?

"Come on." I start to leave, but Xylene grabs me.

"Think of the med bay, Lila," she instructs me, so I bring up Link's domain in my mind, and within a flash, we are there—Tirrian included.

The room is in an uproar. My grandpas are all arguing in the corner about something, but what grabs my attention is Xavier's still figure on the exam table with Saxon standing next to him, holding his hand. Cas is also there, and Link is running his diagnostic hand scan.

"Oh good, you're here," Link says, looking up from my unconscious fiancé. "It's been a shit show. You two had just left when these four returned with an unconscious Xavier and a pregnant Nikos." He waves his hand, and farther in the room is Nikos's water pod. He floats listlessly, the water suspending him in the pod. He doesn't meet my gaze, just stares off into nothing. "Cas was shouting about you being detained and he had to return, because he was the only one who could get to you, but William stopped him. We wanted to give Xavier's parents a chance first."

I go over to my kraken and wrap my arms around him, pressing a kiss to his lips. He shudders in my hold and releases a huge sigh of relief. "Thank God you're okay. What happened?"

"Do you remember that dragon I was telling you about back on Fluxx? The water one that you told me wasn't real?" He nods, and I turn and point to Tirrian. "Turns out I wasn't imagining things." I think about what the dragon had done to the mating dome and snort with amusement. I wonder if Tirrian is horrified at his animal's behavior. "He also saved our babies on Skarr and me just now on Aquilia. We owe him everything."

Cas pulls away from me, marches over to the dragon, and pulls the shocked man into a huge hug, wrapping one of his agitated tentacles around the poor man as well. "Thank you. You will always be welcome in our family," Cas tells Tirrian, and the poor dragon's eyes widen comically as Cas's tentacles caress his leg. Cas's kraken is as bad as mine and gets away with a lot more while in half form. It's why I avoid mine most of the time. She ends up groping everyone around us.

"It was nothing," Tirrian mumbles gruffly, patting Cas on the back. Holy crap, he really is trying to make an effort. "I would protect your family like it was my own." He pulls away and leans against the wall in his favorite spot. Cas rejoins us around the table.

"What is wrong with our son?" Xylene takes the other hand that Saxon isn't holding. Neither her nor Cronus raise an eyebrow at the fact that Saxon is indeed holding their son's hand. I guess it's normal for warlocks given their harem proclivities if they don't have an intimate.

Link shakes his head. "Nothing that I can find apart from the goose egg on his head where the Aquilian knocked him unconscious. There's a small amount of swelling, but nothing that should be keeping him unconscious. I was just going to suggest that Lila change to her Celestian form and heal him."

"Lila, what happened? We were just in the process of working out which nations we could call on for assistance, but it seems you've already gotten us one of the most lethal." William and my grandpas approach, smiling at Cronus and Xylene. The five of them exchange hugs and greetings.

"I dealt with that fat slug. He took a shot at me. No one lives to tell the tale. Nerissa is taking his place for now, so hopefully there will be some positive changes," Cronus tells my grandpas when they all finish.

"Couldn't have happened to a nicer man." Eric smirks. "But what about the crown prince?"

Cronus points at Tirrian. "You have the prince of dragons to thank for disposing of that one."

Eric turns a questioning look on the dragon who shrugs. "He hurt Lila, so I ate him," he tells everyone succinctly without an ounce of remorse in his tone.

Eric narrows his eyes. "Maybe you will be an asset to this team." He still hasn't forgiven Tirrian for all the hurt he caused me, but it seems he may be thawing, not to mention Tirrian seems to be changing too, but that's for later. Now, I need to fix my warlock so he and I can get on with the intimate bonding.

I allow my Celestian form to wash over me, and

I lose my clothes again. I stomp my foot, annoyed that I didn't ask Xavier if he could create a spell for me like he did for the kids. There is only so much nudity that should be happening in front of people who are not my mates, and that is zero. It's Xylene who waves her hands and clothes me this time.

"Thank you," I say, ruffling my wings and stretching them wide. It's weird. I don't know where they go when I'm not in this form, but they always feel like they need a long, hard stretch when they first emerge. I haven't actually attempted flying with them yet either. I was so embarrassed at my lack of flying ability as a Vilaxian, I haven't wanted to try with these wings, even though I have mad skills as an elemental, but my whole body is different. I'm slight and dainty and delicate. This form is no different than my normal form except for the giant ass wings, but they are pretty, and now they are the same color as my hair, a rainbow of opalescent colors, which I allowed to change back to normal the minute we returned to the ship.

I allow my Celestian powers to take over. Xavier and Saxon took great pleasure in sword fighting— the metal kind, not the fun kind—and cutting each other, giving me wounds to practice my healing on. Seriously, they were like two school boys, giggling and taunting each other as they parried back and forth. Who would have thought that the galaxy had their own version of yo mama jokes?

I close my eyes and scan Xavier, and find that Link is right. There is a lump on Xavier's head, and I heal it, but it's not what's keeping him asleep. I snort, and a smile creeps across my lips as I shake my head at the ridiculousness of my fiancé. I can feel his own amusement. He's not unconscious but playing possum. He wants true love's kiss to wake him up, so I lean in and brush my lips across his, muttering, "Do you need all the guys to lay wet ones on you as well, or is this something you reserved for the Earth girl whose fairy tales you are mocking?"

His eyes pop open, and he hauls me up onto the exam table, my body on his as my wings flutter behind me at the sudden, unexpected movement. "No, I just needed my princess to wake me from my enchanted sleep." He grins and nuzzles his nose against mine before grimacing. "I can't believe those eels got the drop on me."

"Me neither," his dad mutters, and Xavier's head turns, his eyes wide.

"Dad?" he asks. Well, maybe he really was unconscious if he hadn't realized that his dad and mom are here. "What are you doing here?" He struggles to sit up with me still clasped to his chest. Saxon just tuts and lifts me off him and puts me back down on the ground before helping Xavier sit up. Xavier, the ungrateful ass, just slaps at Saxon's hands.

"I don't need help," he mutters but also pales slightly. Shit, did I miss something when I healed him? I let my powers scan him again, but I realize he's actually down on the tank again and needs to feed. Before I can allow myself to feel guilty, he slides off the bed. "What are you guys doing here?" They hurry over and hug him.

"Well, Lila called us and told us you'd been waylaid by that idiot King Marlin and invited us to join the party. Most fun I've had in ages. Now, that's a real welcome to the family present. Best daughter-in-law ever." Cronus slaps his son on the back. "But then I wouldn't expect anything less from Alina and Marcus's daughter. Absolutely a chip off the old block."

A pang of sorrow hits me in the chest. I'm never going to know my parents like these people do. Xylene smiles at me with sympathy, no doubt feeling my emotions with her warlock powers. Despite all my own abilities, I haven't been able to keep my emotions under lock and key, but I guess there are worse bad habits to have.

"How about we get on with unblocking your memories so you can at least have those ones back?" she suggests kindly.

"Definitely," I agree, but Link jumps in.

"Actually, can you just put that on hold for another twenty minutes or so?" Xavier growls at the cyborg who has the grace to look chagrined. "I'm sorry, but Lila and I just need to check on Nikos before you disappear for however long it takes for a warlock intimate bonding."

Xavier's growl instantly cuts off, and his eyes fill with worry as they slide over to the listless merman. "Of course. How about we all go and have a drink at one of the bars?"

"There's no staff," I point out, and Eric chuckles.

"You don't need staff when you're the owner, Lila. Our passcodes unlock everything." He waggles his fingers at me. I no longer have the lanyard they first issued me. The ship is coded to my biometrics, specifically my fingerprint. "And I happen to be a deft hand at mixing cocktails." Eric offers his arm to Xylene. "Shall we?"

"Actually, I could go for a drink. Killing off that fat slug worked up a thirst." Cronus nods enthusiastically. "Hail us when you're ready to get this show on the road, Lila. Until then, we will be catching up with our old friends and grilling your other partners." He grins wickedly, and I see Cas gulp with nerves, but Xavier just slaps him on the back.

"Don't worry, my dad is all talk. He's really a big softy," he tells my kraken, leading the group out of the med lab. "And we can always use the children to deflect. They will have him wrapped around his fingers within seconds."

"No, it's Xylene they have to be careful of,"

John mutters. "Are you okay, Lila? Do you want one of us to stay?" He gestures between himself and William, but I shake my head.

"No, I have Link, you go ahead. We probably shouldn't stress him out any more than he is, considering the state he's in," I say quietly, unsure if Nikos can hear us or not.

"We won't be far away if you need us," William says, and they both take their leave. I love the fact that they just trust me to get the job done. It is a big boost to my confidence that they have faith in me.

"Okay, Doc, what do we need to do?" I ask him, and he moves over to a screen and presses a few buttons before an image of a pregnant Aquilian appears on one of the screens.

"As far as I can tell when I compare the date that you and Nikos had your swim with the average gestation of an Aquilian, I would say Nikos is due to give birth in the next week or two. Ideally, I'd like to scan him, but they can't shift out of mer form when pregnant, unlike lightning cats or Fluxx shifters."

"So you need to strip and get in there with him?" I ask, and he looks from me to the pod where Nikos still floats with his eyes closed, looking pale and drawn.

"Yeah, I would say so, but it would probably help if you were in there too. Judging by the looks of him, I would say not only is he malnourished, but he seems to be suffering from antenatal depression, probably stemming from the one-sided mate mark."

"Antenatal depression?" I ask, not having heard the term before.

"Yes, it's similar to postnatal depression, but it occurs during pregnancy. A one-sided mating is difficult on the mate. The hormone that would be present if you had bitten him and sealed the mating is missing. From what I can read, Aquilians do not have fated mates, and his mate bite will fade on you, but until it does, he will always long for you to return the bite. If you decide not to go ahead, I would suggest that we send him and his child back to Aquilia and arrange some kind of visitation schedule with Nixie facilitating the swap over, because it would be cruel to prolong Nikos's yearning by having to see you constantly even if you do share a child." He doesn't say this with any judgment, just straight facts, which I appreciate. "He also looks pale. I don't think he's seen enough sun like he should have during his pregnancy. Pregnant Aquilians like to sun themselves while pregnant on special platforms provided specifically for this. It allows them to bond with other expecting parents, and there is something in the sun of Aquilia that aids fetal growth. Nikos is too pale to have been doing this, which may have affected your child's development."

Simultaneous emotions hit me—fury at the former King of Aquilia and guilt for my role in all of this. If only I had kept my temper in check, but I treated him abysmally. It looks like he had about as much choice as I did when we swam that day. Now I only have myself to blame if something is indeed wrong with our child.

"Is there anything I can do?" I ask him, a lump developing in my throat that's hard to talk around. He can obviously tell, because he moves away from the console and wraps an arm around me, drawing me into his chest.

"What do you want, Lila?" I start to answer, but he places a finger over my mouth, stopping me. "Just take a moment and think. I don't want to hear what you think you should do or what you think others, including me and your other mates, might want. What do you want? It's okay if you don't want to make Nikos one of your mates. We will work everything out."

"Is divorce common in the galaxy?" I ask while I think about what he just said. He's quiet for a moment.

"Not for races with fated mates. Most of the time, probably eighty-five percent of the time, fate, or whoever controls those mate bonds, gets it right. Occasionally it doesn't, and there is a way out of most fated matings that doesn't involve the death of one of the partners. There is a magical race of beings at the end of the galaxy—I think we've told you about them before—called the Seiomann. They have subjugation powers, and they can break a fated mating for a price."

"And for the other races who get to choose? Like you?" I ask quietly, because although I have complained about all these fated mate bonds, they are reassuring in that I probably won't be hurt by the men who have them with me, but neither Link nor Nikos do. I worry they will grow tired of having a relationship with me, especially when whom I add to this group is out of my control and with no end in sight.

"Probably a forty percent chance they will break up or something will happen, but hey…" He lifts my chin so I can look at his gorgeous silver eyes. "That won't be you and me."

"I don't want it to be me and Nikos either," I tell him, feeling tears well in my eyes. "I feel like this has all happened the wrong way. How am I ever going to get him to see that I want to explore the growing relationship between us? That I want him and our child to stay and see what we can become? I can't make promises I can't necessarily keep. You know what we were like together."

He chuckles. "Yes, you two are volatile, but I think you will find that given the chance, he will be a different man now that you have opened your eyes to what could be between the two of you."

My eyes drift over to the pod. He's floating with his eyes closed, his golden hair floating around him like seaweed on the currant. Even his beautiful gold and blue scales are dulled.

"Can he hear us?" I ask Link, and he shakes his head.

"No, the speaker is switched off. I didn't want to make him any more uncomfortable or sadder."

I go over to the pod and hold my hand up to the glass wall. Nikos must feel my presence, because his eyes crack open. He peers at me for a moment, his pretty eyes cloudy and unfocused, but then they widen minutely, and he slowly reaches up, placing his webbed hand against mine. I press my forehead against the glass too, and he flicks his tail just slightly and does the same thing, his large belly also pressing against the glass. Holy crap, that's my baby in there. I feel a rush of joy, overwhelming pride, and no small amount of desire. I think I know exactly how Caspian felt every time he looked at my pregnant belly.

CHAPTER ELEVEN

Earlier on Aquillia
Nikos

"Lila is here."

It's the first coherent thought I've had in weeks since I realized I was pregnant. Shamed by what I did to her when my mating urge took over and horrified that I put her and her babies in danger, I didn't put up much of a fight when my father confined me to my rooms in the palace below. She had every right to banish me from her sight and not return my mating bite. I am not worthy of her love or attention.

Panic washes over me when the guards wheel my pod out into the land palace and put me on display. I just knew my father was going to use me and our baby to get her to comply with his wishes, but I didn't think it would work. I thought I burned all of what might have been between us down to a fiery heap. What is she doing here? She can't be

143

here. My father will use her and our baby as a pawn, but I am so starved for affection, not to mention proper nutrition, that I don't have the energy to do anything but float listlessly and watch. My father has ruled over us for so long, none of us risk fighting back. Nobody wants to be thrown in the dungeon or worse, the Molastay Trench.

I thought for sure she would outright reject any manipulations from my father. I didn't think she cared enough to rescue me, but I was wrong. I watch silently and listen with growing awe and gratitude. Not only does she bargain for my and our child's freedom from my father, but she also swaps herself so we can go free. How can she be so kind and generous and brave after what I did to her? I can't allow even just the smallest bit of hope to creep in, though, because things might not be exactly how I've dreamed them to be. Now I just have to hope that my father's plan is foiled.

There is no way my father will be able to keep her contained with all her extra mimic abilities, but he doesn't know of the full range. He will allow his arrogance and confidence to cloud his judgment. Although I wish she didn't swap herself for me, I am grateful our child will be safe once more, and I don't doubt she will be able to get herself out of any place my father may keep her.

I feel our child growing in my belly. It is everything I thought it would be and more. I spend most of my time thinking about what he or she will look like. Father wouldn't let me go to the surface and sun with the other expectant parents. He thought I would use it as a chance to escape. I did consider it, but where would I go? I am not welcome anywhere else, and I thought my child's mother hated me because I put her other children in danger. I haven't been eating well, since he's deliberately been starving me in the hopes it will control me. I worry that it has done some damage to our baby. I haven't been allowed to see a doctor either. He's tried to keep my pregnancy hush-hush, not wanting to be shamed that I don't have a matching mating bite or mate in tow, but of course nothing like that can be kept quiet. He stripped me of my crown prince title, which is rightfully mine through birth, and gave it to my younger half-brother Raen.

I hate him and his mother. They make mine so very unhappy. Nixie and I were barely born when he moved his pregnant mistress into the palace, and then less than a year later, he moved another one in until my mother had five of them living with us. Thankfully, there were no more children until about ten years later. Now we have a few half brothers and sisters who constantly remind my mother of his infidelity.

I lose interest as Caspian approaches the pod and starts wheeling it in the direction of the transport pad. I feel my heartbeat pick up slightly at the thought of leaving Lila behind, but it slowly settles as I realize Lila is capable of looking after herself. My father has well and truly underestimated her, and I feel a small smile creep across my lips at the thought of what might happen. Even I don't know the full extent of her abilities. Seeing that Xavier is unconscious between the two Adams brothers is not going to go favorably for my father, and I almost raise the energy to chuckle, but even that is too hard.

I drift in and out of sleep, struggling to keep myself alert and awake. I'm not sure how much time has passed when I open my eyes and find Lila on the other side of the glass. Her beautiful green eyes are filled with sadness as she looks at me. She puts her hand up on the glass, and I stretch out my own, mirroring her as she leans her forehead in. I give a small flick of my tail, the only movement I can really manage, but it's enough for me to rest my own forehead against hers, just the glass between us. My belly presses against it too. There's a small flutter of movement, the first I have felt in days. It's as if our baby can sense its mother's presence.

Dr. Link's voice comes through the speakers in

the side of the pod. "Nikos, I'm going to pump a supplement into the water. Just keep breathing in and out. It might feel a little funny, but I'm worried about your and the baby's health, and this is a good start." I turn my gaze so he comes into my line of sight. He presses a few buttons, and I hear a whirring sound before something pours into the pod where he has it hooked up to his machines.

The solution disperses through the water, and I keep breathing normally. I feel exactly when it hits my system. There's a big jolt, and for the first time in weeks, my body doesn't ache.

"I'd like to come in there and do a scan if you don't mind. I want to assess the baby's health. Lila is going to assist me." They both climb the ladder on the side of the pod while I allow the medication to circulate, drawing it into my body through my gills as well as absorbing through my scales and skin. Bit by bit, it feels like I'm waking up from a long sleep. I'm still not back to tip top shape, but it's an improvement.

I watch with a glimmer of interest as Link removes his Galaxy Circus uniform, leaving him in just his briefs. His shiny silvery skin shimmers in the bright light of the exam room as he pushes off the side and plunges into the water. He splashes beneath the surface, sending up bubbles, but quickly rises to the top, and then he holds onto the side of the pod. He looks at Lila who also strips off her clothes, tossing them onto the floor. My interest in life suddenly returns when I see the silver scar of my mating bite around her nipple. Pride swells deep inside at the fact that this gorgeous, amazing woman wears my bite. I couldn't be prouder to be carrying her child, even if she never returns the mating bite.

Lila's body shimmers like it did the first time she mimicked me, and when the mist clears, she's in her Aquilian form. I have never seen a more beautiful mermaid before. Her hair retains the opalescent colors that it now is, and her tail also shows the same coloring instead of the color it was when we swam together originally. She sparkles and shines as she drops into the water too. I watch as she and Link have a conversation before she dives down toward me. She approaches me slowly, holding her hand out cautiously.

Nikos, can you hear me? Her sweet voice echoes through my mind as our fingers touch, and my soul seems to sigh with relief. She's here. Everything will be alright.

Yes, my beautiful pearl. I can hear you, I reply, and I see her release her own sigh of relief.

Grabbing my hand in her tight grip, she gives it a squeeze. *Link wants to look at you and our baby and make sure everything is okay, but to do that, he needs you to go to him. He can't breathe underwater like we can*, she explains, but my head is practically singing songs of triumph as I focus on the words "our baby." She acknowledged our baby, she's not going to reject us.

She frowns, the worry lines between her eyebrows making a cute wrinkle that I want to reach out and smooth away, but that is still too hard. *Yes, Lila, take me to your cyborg so he can check on our baby. They haven't been very active, and I am worried I have failed at keeping them healthy and safe.* I wrap the hand that is not holding hers around my distended belly like I can protect the baby like that. If only.

She must hear the shame and worry in my tone, because her frown turns to a scowl. *None of that is your fault. It is all your father's, and he paid for that.*

What? He did? I look at her with surprise, and the scowl softens as she looks down at my belly, taking her free hand and placing it over mine.

Yes, no one treats my mate and baby like that, she tells me, looking into my eyes, and my heart sings. She's claiming me. My heart and head pound with the knowledge, and happiness fills my soul. *If Cronus hadn't killed him, I would have.*

The warlock king? I'm confused but also so incredibly relieved that my father is dead. *Who is on the throne now? Raen?* I ask her, and she tugs me slightly, flipping her tail and swimming us up toward the cyborg who is waiting patiently for us.

Yes, it's a long story, but no, not Raen. Tirrian ate him. I'll tell you everything once you're back to full health. That's all you need to worry about for now.

But my kingdom. I can't leave the throne vulnerable like that. I will need to return and take my birthright. We breach the surface of the water, and she shakes her head before speaking out loud.

"No, you won't. Your mother is sitting on the throne and has every intention of making Aquilia great again. She has named Nixie as her heir."

I grimace at that. My sister is going to kill me, but my mother is probably the best choice. It was her throne to start with, and she was groomed to rule, much like I had been before I left to join the circus.

"Nikos, how are you feeling?" Dr. Link asks as Lila and I approach him.

"Tired, hungry, sad, and mad," I tell him, embarrassed as the words tumble out of my mouth.

"Of course you are. You're pregnant. I remember it well," Lila coos and rubs a hand over my aching back. Her willing touch is enough to make the hurt go away. "I felt all of those and more, and what your dad did to you would have made everything worse. Link's going to scan you, and then I will heal you and we'll get you into the Aquilian pool where you can spend some time under the lights on that platform in there."

"Will you be with me?" I ask her, hopeful she will join me.

She shakes her head, and my heart sinks. "Not to start with." She must see my disappointment because she continues in a hurry. "But only because the warlock king and queen are here to return my memories so Xavier and I can seal our intimate bond. He has waited long enough, and I wasn't waiting any longer while your father played his games."

My disappointment abates. "Of course, that would be cruel to make him wait longer than he already has," I agree, and her eyebrows jump in surprise.

I guess she was expecting me to be unreasonable and ridiculous. It's the act I have always put on in the past. I use it as a way of weeding out sycophants and people who don't care about status. Anyone who was happy to be treated like that was instantly dismissed. I was a real asshole, but it was fun playing the idiot. Maybe I can have a little fun with my mate.

"I will need some time to recover my stamina before we can swim the dance of love again," I tell her, winking suggestively, and a wide grin breaks out on her face.

"Now there's the Nikos I know and love. You really had me worried when you hadn't even made a comment about my naked breasts," she tells me, but I am focused on the word "love." She loves me.

"When I am back to full health, I will show you exactly just how much I appreciate your naked breasts," I reassure her and feel my cock stir beneath my scales for the first time since we did our mating swim. I was worried it was broken, but now I know it's a one woman cock.

"Well, let's just see exactly what's wrong with you, and then we can decide on a plan of action to get you back to full health," Link suggests. "Lila, if you bring him over here and support him by letting him rest against you while I scan him, that would probably work best."

The doc has to hang onto the side with one hand while he holds out his diagnostic one to sweep over my body.

Lila assists me in helping me lie with my head on her shoulder and body flat for Link to get the best angle on the baby. He frowns and mutters under his breath, but Lila and I are patient while he finishes his examination. He curses quietly when he gets to my belly, and both my and Lila's hearts start to race almost simultaneously. Lila rubs a hand along my spine, stroking back and forth reassuringly, and I want to melt into her, but I keep my body where it needs to be.

He finally pulls his hand away, frowning. "Well, you are malnourished mostly because the baby has been stealing all of your nutrients to sustain its life. If you hadn't been so healthy, I'm not sure either of you would have made it. While Lila can heal your aches and pains, she can't actually fix that. Only a few good meals will be able to counteract the neglect, but it doesn't look like it's done any damage to your baby. It's just a little smaller than I hoped considering where you are in your pregnancy."

"Smaller?" Lila sounds surprised. "But look at his belly." She reaches around and runs a gentle hand over it, and I feel my cock twitch again.

"Yeah, there's a reason for that. It also explains why Nikos is so unwell," Link says slowly, and he looks at Lila like she may freak out from what he's about to tell her.

"And that is?" she asks as I realize what he's about to share with her.

"Nikos is carrying twins. Do you want to know what you are having?" he asks, and I hear Lila gasp behind me. I struggle to sit up, and she lets me, but she doesn't let go of my body, which is a relief because hearing we're having twins probably is a bit of a shock for her. She probably doesn't even realize Nixie and I are a set ourselves.

"Seriously? What is with you guys and multiples?" she grumbles. "How can we go from no children to seven in a matter of months?"

"Seven?" I ask, trying to do the math. Lila sighs and spins me around so I can face her, her tail beating fiercely to keep us both afloat.

"Yes, I mated with Maxsim and Echo. My whisperer abilities allow me to be both alpha and omega, so I am compatible with both of them. Like you, Echo penis-napped an egg or two while he was lodged deep inside. He is pregnant with two. Add in Cas's three and yours, and that brings our child total to seven. We are definitely going to need a nanny." She turns to Link and pouts. "But I really don't want to share their love with a stranger."

He smiles sympathetically at her as I allow the information she just shared to run through my mind. I don't feel anything but joy. My babies are going to grow up with a big, wonderful, loving family, unlike my childhood which was uncomfortable at best.

"No, don't tell me, I want it to be a surprise. Will they be born in mer form if Nikos gives birth in the water?" She looks between me and Link, but he allows me to answer.

"Yes. We give birth in the water. I can give birth in the Aquilian pool."

"You can, but we also have a pool in our quarters now, so that's an option too. Now that the others have shifted, they don't need the water pods to sleep in, so they are available for your babies."

I just stare at her, my mouth and eyes wide with surprise. She looks confused.

"What's wrong?" she asks, and Link chuckles.

"I think Nikos is surprised that you are inviting him to live in your quarters." Link starts to climb out of the pod, using the ladder on the side.

"Oh, well, he's my mate, so I want him to live with me, but if you don't feel comfortable with that, it's fine," she says, biting her lip with her blunt teeth.

"I would be honored to live with you, but it would probably be best if the children and I stayed in the Aquilian pool until they shift for the first time," I reply, thrilled and disappointed at the same time.

"When will that be?" she asks, and I have to think about my baby knowledge.

"When they are about six weeks old."

"And how old will they be when they shift?" she asks worriedly, and I frown.

"Six weeks old. Why?"

"Because the kraken babies are already presenting as the age of Earth toddlers," Link explains from the other side of the pod, a towel in hand as he rubs his silver hair before drying off the rest of his body. "Lila was a little surprised."

"Oh, I understand. Our babies will be something similar," I tell her, and Link looks fascinated.

"I wonder if it's a survival thing. There are many more dangers for shifter and Aquilian children, so evolution has helped out by maturing them quicker."

"Sounds reasonable to assume," Lila says before she turns back to look at me. "I have to go, but Link is going to wheel your pod to your living quarters and make sure you are properly fed and stay with you to monitor your progress while I complete my bond with Xavier," she explains, and I nod, not wanting to ask about our bond, but I must not do a good job of hiding my yearning.

"We need a little more time, but I want this, I promise. I'll swim with you before I have to leave to rescue my grandma. I promise I'll tell you everything when I do, okay?" she says.

"Of course, my little sea squirt. I look forward to seeing you again. Maybe you can enjoy the sun in your beautiful form with me. You will look gorgeous in that bright light," I tell her, taking in her new shiny colors.

She smiles. "I'd like that, and I can change into my Celestian form and see if I can do anything to heal you as well." She flicks her tail and swims closer, wrapping her arms around me, and I shudder from feeling her tail flick against mine. "I would like to swim with you again too, if that's possible," she whispers in my ear, her hands caressing my back. "I find the sight of you pregnant with my child quite erotic, and I would like to feel your cock in my slit again."

Holy coral crusts! Lila is flirting with me. My life is complete. I return her hug, my large belly making it a little tricky, but my cock writhes beneath my tail, trying to push out. I will it to behave. "I'd like that," I tell her honestly, and she pulls back, but not before brushing a kiss across my lips.

"I'll see you soon," she promises before

releasing me, and her body shimmers, changing into human form before she climbs out of the pod. I sink down to the bottom, the smile on my face as big as it has ever been as I watch Link wrap a towel around our beautiful mate. Now I just need to get my strength back so that when we do swim, I can keep up with her.

CHAPTER TWELVE

Lila

I leave Nikos in Link's capable hands. He assured me he would work hard to ensure Nikos is eating well and will stay in his and Nixie's house until I return from my intimate bonding. I don't know what I would do without Link. He is the glue that's holding me together. Without him, I think my mind would have shattered into tiny little pieces from everything that's happened since I found out I inherited a circus.

I quickly make my way through the ship. I've well and truly taken up the twenty minutes we promised Xavier, but he's going to have to wait a little longer. I want to check on my babies and my cats. I'm not sure how long intimate bonding takes, so I want to assure myself that they are okay before I disappear again. When I get to my room, though, I find something I hadn't expected.

The door to our suite slides back, and I hurry

in, hoping that they aren't in the middle of a nap, and slide to a stop. In the large living area, which has been widened and decorated with more furniture, I find an amazing sight. Curled up in his snake form with his back against a couch is Silac. He has a child in each arm, snuggled against him, and my third child is curled up in his tail. All four of them are fast asleep. I wonder why he's watching my children and what happened to the cats.

I try to tiptoe past them so I can go in search of my missing cats, but the sound of scales sliding against one another has me stopping. My eyes meet his orange ones, and he smiles before closing them again. He's perfectly relaxed and content with my children, so I leave them be and head in search of my cats. They will either be in Echo's nest in the library or in their den. Are they taking advantage of the kids being asleep and taking a nap, or will they be getting some exercise? I think I'll try the den first. There's a nest in there as well, because having sex in the other one is no longer an option since the kids are with us. Their little footsteps are mostly silent on the floors, so we decided it would be safer for us to only use it for napping—not to mention they like napping in there with their pussycats as well.

I push my hand against the door sensor, and it opens up with a gust of freezing cold air. Crap, I can't go in there as Earth Lila. I strip off my clothes and leave them in a pile on the floor outside the door where they won't end up damp and covered in snow, and I allow my cat form to wash over me. I yawn and stretch, flicking my tail around and shaking out my mane before I step into the freezing cold room. The door slides closed behind me as wind and snow batters my body. Holy crap, it's a blizzard in here. I hold my hand up to shield my eyes from the onslaught and try to look through the sideways falling snow, but it's useless. I think about trying to shift into full cat form, but I haven't actually done that yet. There's been too much going on, and I haven't felt the need. I kind of wish I had now. I lean into the snow and make my way to the entrance of their den. They are definitely not out playing in this weather, or even if they are, I'll wait for them in the warmth. I'm sure they'll realize they aren't alone soon enough since their senses are heightened.

When I walk down the short tunnel to their nest area, my nose twitches as a familiar scent hits it. When I stop in the entrance, I don't know whether to be pissed that they left my babies to fuck or be excited. Meh, who am I kidding. My babies are being well looked after, and seeing Maxsim fuck our omega is pretty damn irresistible. Maxsim has Echo pressed up against the wall, his hands pinned against it, as he leisurely fucks his ass and bites his neck, growling dirty words to him. Echo's whimpers and groans have me squirming and desperate to touch myself.

"Such a good omega, taking your alpha's cock. You feel so good. Your ass grips me like a fist." A whimper escapes my lips, and Maxsim freezes before he turns his head and looks at me. "Get over here and help me take care of our omega," he growls, his eyes flashing with so much heat that I almost melt on the spot. He pulls Echo away from the wall and shifts so his own back is to the wall with Echo splayed out before me. His cock weeps with precum, and I sink to my knees in front of it and lap at it with my tongue.

Echo groans and throws his head back, resting on Maxsim's shoulder as he continues to lazily fuck him. With every thrust, I allow Echo to fuck my mouth, and as Maxsim withdraws, I apply suction so that Echo's cock is dragged out of my mouth. He tangles his hands in my still wet hair. There's a slight pull of pain that makes my own pussy weep with need, so I reach down and play with my clit.

A big paw reaches down and slaps my hand away from it, and I can't stop the whine from escaping my mouth. Maxsim growls again.

"Make our omega come, and then it's your turn," he tells me, so I renew my enthusiasm for Echo's blow job. I use one hand to fondle his balls while the other wraps around the base of his cock and slides up and down with the movement of my mouth. It doesn't take long for him to beg and plead. I feel his cock swell just as Maxsim bites his neck, and then he floods my mouth with his icy cold, slightly sweet cum. I swallow it down before easing back.

"But aren't you going to knot him?" I ask, unsure if he can do what he told me. He eases out of our mate's ass and nuzzles his neck as Echo smirks at me, then marches away to the bathroom, leaving Echo to help me to my feet.

"No, now that I'm pregnant, he won't knot me again until I go into heat. It's your turn." Maxsim returns with a cloth, wiping his cock before tossing it to the side. I appreciate that they can think to be hygienic, because I probably wouldn't have.

The two of them guide me over to the nest and help me down before they take turns kissing the hell out of me. Their large fangs are retracted so they don't tear up my mouth, but their tongues are rough. Maxsim pulls away and moves down my body as Echo stays with me. Echo licks and nips down my neck before turning his attention to my breast. His rough tongue feels amazing against my sensitive nipples as Maxsim's tongue pays attention to my clit. It only takes a couple of swipes before I'm squirming in need.

He pulls away, and I feel him line himself up. He pushes my knees wide so I'm as open as I can be as Echo slides farther south. As Maxsim starts to thrust, Echo laps at my clit.

"Oh my god," I exclaim as the two of them work me up into a quick peak, my pussy pulsing with every lick and stroke of their tongue and cock, but it's just not enough to push me over the edge. "Please, I need more," I beg, and Echo starts to purr, his lips working just like a vibrator against my clit as I feel Maxsim's knot start to swell. It locks in behind my pubic bone, finally giving me what I need, and I soar as he roars in triumph, his seed painting the inside of my cunt. A strangled yowl escapes my mouth as my whole body arches with the pleasure coursing through me. He can't thrust, but every small movement sends another pulse of pleasure through me. Echo moves away from my clit and back up my body, pressing little kisses to everything he can touch before snuggling into my side and stroking my hair, purring with contentment as we are joined together.

I'm breathing heavily, and my body is coated with a sheen of sweat despite the cool temperatures, when Maxsim's knot finally releases. He rolls to the side, and the two of them cuddle into me. It takes me a moment to get my breath back, but I run my fingers through their fur, and they purr with contentment. "Not that I'm complaining, but why is Silac with the kids?" I mutter when my heartbeat finally returns to normal.

"They begged to play with the snake man, so I asked him if he would mind," Maxsim tells me, nuzzling his face against my neck, his tongue flicking out and lapping at my salty skin.

"He was wonderful with them," Echo murmurs. "And when they fell asleep, he suggested we take a nap as well."

"And Echo's pregnancy hormones are causing him to be needy, so we took advantage of it."

"Yeah, I remember that. What is it with pregnancy hormones? You're already pregnant, so why do they make you want to fuck even more?" I kind of just talk out loud, but I feel Maxsim shrug in response.

My eyes start to drift closed, but instead of succumbing to sleep like I want, I struggle out from between my two cats. I lean in and give both of them a kiss before standing up. "This was fun, but Xavier is still waiting. I'm going to have a quick shower and let his parents return my memories. I was hoping to have a cuddle with the kids because I don't know how long I'll be away," I explain, and Maxsim just waves a hand at me.

"They will be fine. We've got this, and Cas, Saxon, and Link are also around."

"Oh, and Nikos is back too." I bite my lip, looking between them. "And, well, I guess there's no easy way to say this, but apparently we are half mated."

Echo sits up slightly, resting his head against his hand. "We thought you might be with that bite around your pretty nipple."

"And he also penis jacked some of my eggs, and he's having twins, so yay, more babies." I hurry through the rest of the news and brace for impact.

Maxsim's eyes widen comically, but Echo just smiles serenely and holds his hand over his own stomach, which isn't really showing yet.

"That will be wonderful. Our babies will all be close in age."

"Yeah, but will they stay that way? Do yours grow quickly as well?" I ask, and Maxsim nods.

"Yes, but not as fast as the shifters. Theirs stems from when all shifters used to war, and it was evolution's way of helping maintain the population. Our race has never been like that, though they have been known to have clan fights, but nothing on a large scale, so while our children age faster than humans, they are not as fast as shifters."

"Yeah, I think we may have to start looking for nannies sooner rather than later, but that's future Lila's problem. I'll see you both later. We need a sit-down family meal as soon as we surface from our intimate bonding. I don't know what it entails, so I have no idea how long we will be," I tell them, and they smirk, dirty pussies.

"If I know Xavier, he will make the most of it," Echo says, but Maxsim shakes his head.

"It takes two days to get to station Z68 to meet the halla harvester, so he's going to have to be done by then."

"Yeah. Are you going to join us on our mission?" I ask Maxsim, because there is no way either of us are going to let Echo go, even if he wanted to.

"No, Brannock informed us the planet is tropical. Xavier did offer to spell me, but Brannock insisted the less people who went, the better. I will stay back with Cas and Link and guard the children and your grandpas."

I chuckle. "Don't tell my grandpas you are guarding them, or they will put you on the roof and leave you there, but that makes me feel relieved. Echo, maybe you could go and visit Nikos? You can talk pregnancy with him. Link thinks he has antenatal depression, and seeing another pregnant person might help. He wasn't allowed to socialize with anyone on Aquilia. It might be a bit hot for you though."

Echo sits up, instant concern on his face. "I will ask your warlock to spell me so I can go and see the can of tuna. I think it will be good for both of us."

I lean in and kiss them quickly again, delighted at how well our relationship is just going. It's like we've been together for years now that we've sorted everything out.

"Love you," I tell them, standing up and

hurrying away, but not before I register the shock on their faces. I haven't said it to them before, but it's true. I'm still too chicken to stay and see if they say it back to me. I don't want to be disappointed if they aren't there yet.

I head to my room and hurry into my closet. I practically live in my uniform these days or conjured jeans and shirts, but I want to find something for my intimate bonding. It's kind of like a wedding, I guess, and all of my other matings have been frantic and unprepared. I just want to make this one feel a little special.

I search through the clothes I brought from Earth for something a little dressier than usual, but I stop when I find an outfit I'm not familiar with. I haven't seen this one before. It's a gorgeous, diaphanous lavender gown with streaks of silver thread woven through it. On it is a note.

I was hoping maybe you could wear this for our bonding ceremony. It is tradition for the warlock to give their intimate a pre-bonding gift. 🤍 *Xavier*

I melt and feel a tear prickle my eye. He must have put this here before we were waylaid by the Aquilians. Smiling like a loon, I hurry into our communal bathroom and use the large shower, washing the smell of sex and salt off me. It's been a hectic day. I also wash my opalescent locks. They were starting to look a little straggly.

I hop out and dry off, moisturizing my whole body before going back into my closet for my beautiful new dress. I shimmy into it and look at myself in the mirror. Holy hell! It's mostly sheer, and I can see the shadow of my nipples through the fabric of the top part. There are gorgeous long sleeves that split from shoulder to elbow, showing off my arms, but then they drape to the floor from my elbow. The neckline is a dramatic V that plunges just below my breasts. The waistline flows into a long skirt, but it has two splits up either side of the front, showing leg every time I move. I giggle with girlie glee before hurrying back into the bathroom to use the hair machine to dry my hair. I don't bother with makeup. Since my mimic powers kicked in, my skin has been blemish free and luminous. The only thing I do is add a bit of lip gloss. Happy with the way I look, I leave the bathroom. I don't bother with shoes because they aren't going to stay on long, and I noticed that Xavier doesn't wear them a lot of the time, so I think it might be a warlock thing.

Taking a deep breath, I go in search of my fiancé and his parents, eager to get this show on the road.

CHAPTER THIRTEEN

Lila

I find everyone else in one of the bars on the communal part of the ship. It's weird walking through it with no one else around just to arrive at the bar, finding it full of people laughing and trying to talk over one another.

All noise grinds to a halt when I enter the room. "Hi." I wave awkwardly, feeling self-conscious now that everyone's attention is on me.

"Lila, you look beautiful," Xylene says when nobody else does. She glares at my mates. "It looks like you've rendered everyone speechless."

Cas, Saxon, and Xavier all jump to their feet and hurry over to me. Tirrian stays put, but smoke starts to drift out of his nostrils, and when our eyes meet, I see approval in his gaze before I tear mine away. Tirrian is a problem for another day. I don't have the mental capacity to cope with his mood swings. Who knows if he really has changed his mind or if he is just giving in to his animals? Only time will tell. He is going to have to grovel a little before I decide whether I want to forgive him or not.

"*Phoeall*, I knew that dress was perfect for you. You look breathtaking." Xavier has lost his usual cocky smirk, and I can tell I've shaken him. Saxon and Cas both tell me how gorgeous I look before pressing kisses to my cheeks and returning to their seats, but Xavier and I are locked in a trance.

"Well then, let's get this show on the road, shall we?" Cronus's voice booms out, making us both jump. Xavier chuckles sheepishly and runs a nervous hand through his hair before grabbing my hand.

"Where are we going to do this?" I ask, not really wanting to return to our shared quarters, what with Silac and our babies in there. I'm almost certain things are going to get loud and freaky.

"I thought we could go to my room in my old quarters." I wrinkle my nose at the thought of smelling everything he did with his harem in there, but he shakes his head, obviously reading my mind.

"I never fucked my harem in my own room. Saxon was the only one who was ever invited there, and I've cleaned the rest of the quarters of any trace of my former harem."

"As you should," Xylene agrees. "A warlock with an intimate has no need of a harem. Only those of us who don't find them or have yet to find them continue to use them."

"Okay then," I say, and within moments, I feel us dissolve into particles before reforming in a room I've never seen before. I look around. The low lighting makes it a little difficult to see everything in my human form, but Xavier's familiar, exotic spicy scent is present, albeit faded. He snaps his fingers, and the ceiling lights up like it's been lit by thousands of lightning bugs. It's breathtaking, and I can't stop the smile that crosses my lips.

Before I can say anything, though, both Cronus and Xylene arrive, their bodies appearing from nowhere.

Cronus frowns. "That was mean. You know we've never been to this room before."

Xavier chuckles. "You're just annoyed you had to work a little, Dad."

"How did you get here if you haven't seen it before?" I ask, curious about how teleporting works. We haven't really worked on that skill in my warlock form. There are just so many new and different skills I have to learn, and I really haven't had time to master all the forms I've acquired.

"Xavier is our child, dear. We could find him anywhere because we have a blood link. You will be able to do the same thing with your children," Xylene explains.

"And you can do that with your mate bonds too.

Xavier will teach you how to do that when you've sealed your intimate bond," Cronus adds as the two of them move closer. Cronus moves Xavier to the side so that both he and Xylene have me between them—Xylene at my front, and Cronus at my back.

"Okay, Lila, we're going to return your memories. Don't be upset at your mom and dad for asking us to remove them. They were worried you were in danger, and rightfully so."

"Why didn't you take me with you?" I ask the question that has been plaguing me. "If you had to return to Earth to take away my memories, then why couldn't you just take me to my grandparents?"

Xylene and Cronus exchange a glance over my shoulder. "Alina and Marcus asked us not to. We would have loved to have taken you home and raised you with Xavier, but they told us it couldn't happen," Cronus explains, but I'm sure they can see my confusion because Xylene sighs.

"Your grandmother, Liliana, has seer powers as one of her Skarrian gifts, and she was the one who told them to hide your powers and leave you on Earth. You would be found when the time was right. If you had been with the circus this whole time, you would have been killed by the faction after the orb."

"Did they know they were going to die?" I ask them, stunned about what they just shared.

Xylene sighs. "They never said, but we have

talked about it over the years, and I think they may have. Alina was extra teary when we parted that day."

"We hated lying to your grandparents. Xylene and I dropped you off at the foster home and changed your name. We hated doing it, and she cried nonstop for a week after. But Marcus and Alina made us take an oath, so there was nothing we could do but pray for your safe return." Cronus is the most serious I've seen him since we met. "You have to remember that we knew you were Xavier's intimate, and we already considered you our daughter. It was heartbreaking to have to do what we did, and both of us hold no small amount of resentment against your parents despite us missing them like crazy."

I feel tears well in my eyes for the pain my parents put their best friends through. I can't imagine asking something like that of Susie. I'm going out on a limb and guessing they were desperate. Xavier's hand slides between me and his father, and he rubs my back, obviously feeling my inner turmoil.

I brush away the tears and take a steadying breath. "Well, let's not wait any longer."

Xylene smiles at me and brushes a strand of hair back from my face, her eyes shining with pride. "This may hurt a little, but once the pain stops, all of your memories from before should be returned. We will leave you to complete your bond."

"Could you please check on my babies while we're here? There's an awful amount of testosterone around and not as much estrogen. I'd love it if they could get cuddles from their grandma," I ask Xavier's mom, who beams at me.

"I would love it. Don't you worry about a thing. I'll make sure everyone is looked after until your return," she assures me.

Return? Are we going somewhere? Before I can ask any more questions about this mysterious bonding ritual, they place their hands on my temples, and a blinding pain shoots through my brain. I gasp and feel my knees give way, but they hold me in place. Blackness surrounds me as bright flashes pulse inside my mind. Fleeting images of eyes and smiles and laughter that I recognize make me feel dizzy and disoriented. My stomach lurches, and a wave of nausea rolls over my body.

"Almost there," Xylene croons. "You're doing so well." The pain increases, and I bite my lip to stop myself from screaming, but a groan of pain still escapes. I ball my fists and feel my nails bite into my skin from how tight I'm clenching. The scent of blood permeates the air, and I realize my cat claws have popped out despite me being in my human form.

"Well, that's interesting," Cronus mutters, and

Xavier responds, but I'm too lost in the pain to pay any attention.

Just when I think I can't take anymore and I'm going to sink into sweet oblivion, it all ceases, and a wave of soothing energy caresses my throbbing mind, easing the pain and bringing me back to awareness. My eyes pop open, and I look at the woman who I now remember fondly from my child-hood. Xylene always gave the best cuddles apart from my mama. I smile at her.

"Zeze, I remember you giving me cuddles and telling me I was the prettiest girl in the universe. You still smell the way I remember. Like cinnamon sugar," I tell her, and she grabs me and hugs me hard.

"I always wanted a little girl, but unfortunately we weren't able to have any more after Xavier. You more than made up for it. You were such a delightful little girl. We snuck onto Earth to visit you all the time."

I tuck that little bit of information away. I knew there had to be another way to visit Earth after Susie told me all about her Jelliad experience, which is something I'm still dying to try. Xylene lets me go, and I whirl to face Cronus.

"And you were always sneaking me candy from your home planet. I can't remember what you called them, but they were so tasty, like chewy ice cream. Cold and sweet."

"Ah, yes. You really did love those. Your mother would scold me, but Xavier insisted we always had some with us when we came, even before he knew you were his intimate. He had such a soft spot for you. We really wanted you to grow up together in the hopes that maybe you would be together. We were ecstatic when we found out you were his intimate so early on, and equally devastated when we had to hide you from each other."

He hauls me into a hug that I remember, and I feel tears flow down my face as my memories turn to my parents. I have a few very vivid memories of spending time with them, but lots of flashes of broken memories. They are the memories of a small child, but what stands out in all of them, both the broken and vivid, is that my parents loved me very much, and as a child, I already had levitation powers, but there was no sign of my mimic or whisperer powers. I do vividly remember hearing my parents talk about all the possibilities and thinking I would like conjuring powers. How much fun would it be to make something materialize in front of me? But the most overwhelming breathtaking memory of all is hearing them tell me how much they love me and knowing I felt the same way about them. My parents were amazing. New grief, grief I don't remember experiencing previously, hits me hard, and I start to sob in Cronus's arms. He stiffens briefly, but then he just pats me on the back and croons to me gently.

"Ah, pretty Lila. They loved you so much. They would be so proud of the woman you are now."

Another whispered conversation comes to mind, and I remember my parents talking about being followed and arguing about whether they should leave Earth. My mom wanted to, but my dad told her everything was supposed to happen that way, and that his mother foretold it. If we were to run away from our fate, then I would die. I remember her tears and him holding her much the same way that Cronus is holding me now.

"They knew they were going to die," I say, pulling away and looking between the two warlocks.

Xylene nods solemnly. "Yes, and we were not to interfere. They insisted your life was more important than theirs and that they would do anything to keep you safe. But come now, dry your eyes. I know everything is overwhelming, and we can talk more about your parents at a later time. This is supposed to be a joyous occasion."

Guilt hits me, and I whirl around to find Xavier. This is our warlock wedding, and I'm bawling like a bullfrog, but when my eyes meet his, and Xylene places my hand in his, all the guilt, sadness, and negative emotions drift away as I'm hit by a sense of wonder and knowing. This man is mine to love and cherish and share my life with. I'm seeing him with new eyes. Although I knew I wanted to be with him, this is something deeper, soul deep if I'm being honest. It's no silly surface level attraction, but right down to my very core, and it feels incredible.

"Hi," I say, feeling shy all of a sudden. His lips turn up in that familiar smirk, and the slight hesitation just floats away like dust on a breeze.

"We'll be heading out. I want to go and snuggle with my grandbabies now," Xylene says, but neither Xavier nor I acknowledge her, and she huffs.

"Stop it, X. I remember our bonding night well, and I wouldn't have wanted any attention on us either," Cronus soothes his mate before I feel them teleport out of the room, but none of that matters to me. All that I'm concerned about is the man in front of me.

"Are you ready to be my wife?" he asks, his eyes sparkling, and I nod.

"I've been ready for a very long time, I just didn't know it," I tell him.

"Let's go then," he says, and I frown as he drops one of my hands and holds his out in front of him.

"Go?" Maybe I didn't hear him right. I thought we'd just fuck and say some magic words and it would be done.

I couldn't have been more wrong.

Xavier weaves an intricate pattern in the air, purple and silver sparks lighting up the space in front of us before it's like the atmosphere splits in two and a large hole opens up, widening with every breath I take.

"What the hell?" I mutter. On the other side of the hole, something shimmers in the distance, but I can't make it out clearly.

"This is the most sacred secret of the warlocks. Our original home planet is on another plane of existence. We can access it for our intimate bonding ceremonies. It is what gives us the power to only be sustained by one another apart from a harem of people."

I gape at him, trying to understand what he is saying. "So not only are you an alien to me, but you're also an alien to everyone else?" I ask, and he chuckles.

"Yes and no. I was born in this realm, as were my parents, but originally, our species is from another plane of existence. We are a curious species, and exploration was our number one pursuit. Come on, I don't think I can wait any longer. I will answer any questions you have later. Right now, I just want to be your husband." He steps forward, my other hand still clasped in his, and leads us through the split in the space-time continuum, while various time travel rules play over and over in my head. Man, I hope we don't fuck up the multiverse.

CHAPTER FOURTEEN

Lila

The world that we step into is breathtaking. We seem to be on a small island with a gorgeous grove containing big, beautiful weeping willow type trees, except they are in shades of purple. The grass below our feet is silver, and there is a giant, canopied bed in the middle of the clearing with vines twirling around the posts. We're surrounded by snow-covered mountains, but the air within the little grotto is balmy. The sky itself is a spectacular shade of pale pink that is unlike anything I've ever seen before, and the fluffy clouds are pitch black.

"This is Warlock, our home world. Don't worry about the clouds, that's normal, and it's not going to rain. They turn blue if rain is coming," Xavier says, still holding my hand in his as I take in the beauty that surrounds us.

"The air is different," I say as I breathe. My

whole body feels lighter, and I feel rejuvenated with every breath.

"Yes, the air is a different makeup than on Earth, and it has something in it that makes you feel revitalized. Every intimate bond is formed in this little grove. Something here changes our makeup so we can sustain one another without having to feed sexually from others."

I wrinkle my nose as I look at the bed, and he chuckles. "The bed isn't always there. A new one appears for each couple." Well, that's a relief. I wouldn't like to think about all the previous bodily fluids on it, but then I realize something.

"So no more orgies?" I ask, whirling to face Xavier, unable to tamp down my disappointment.

He snorts out a blast of laughter before pulling me to him and hugging me tightly. "They won't be necessary to keep me fed, but who am I to deny you all that wonderful fun?" he whispers in my ear, and I sag against him.

"Thank goodness," I mutter, and he shakes with laughter.

The air starts to prickle against my skin, leaving little biting stings on my exposed arms and face, and I pull away from Xavier. "Ouch." I try slapping at whatever it is, but it doesn't look like some random bug.

Xavier grabs my hands and stops me. "It's okay,

just let it happen," he tells me as my body starts to rise into the air.

"What the fuck?" I scramble, trying to grab onto something, anything, but Xavier just pushes me away.

"It's because you're not a warlock. The land is trying to take your measure," he explains as I settle down and allow myself to be poked and prodded by some mysterious force. If I have learned anything by now, it's that fighting any of the weird shit is only going to make things worse.

As I drift, I feel something pushing at my mimic abilities, trying to force my shift. I fight it for all it's worth, but it overpowers me, and my body shimmers. Holy crap, what is it forcing me to change into? I heave out a sigh of relief as the mist clears, and I see my warlock form. After a few more stinging bites, I'm lowered to the ground, and the invisible presence fades away.

"Oh, good, you were accepted." Xavier can't hide his worried look quickly enough.

"Accepted?" I screech. "What would have happened if I had been rejected?"

Xavier shrugs. "It differs from person to person. Most just get kicked out of the realm and returned to wherever they started, while some are obliterated."

I start to hyperventilate. "Obliterated?"

"For not being pure of heart or worthy of being

a warlock," he says nonchalantly like it's no big deal. Well, I beg to fucking differ.

"Not being worthy? Did you ever think that maybe my mimic abilities would have made me unworthy, or maybe the fact that I already have five and a half mates?" I yell at him, and he shakes his head.

"No, *phoeall*, calm down." He holds his hands up to placate me, and I slap them away. Damn man, I'm entitled to my annoyance. "Warlocks value strength and power, and your mates and your mimic abilities give you that. You are more than worthy. I never had any doubts." His eyes are wide and admiring as he looks me up and down. "Just look at you," he marvels.

His words calm the raging beast inside me, and when I follow his gaze, I see the silver marks on my skin are glowing and swirling chaotically. When my gaze returns to him, he drags his shirt off. It's like a hypnotic dance, and I can't help but suspect it's all part of the bonding process.

Sure enough, he snaps his fingers, and the rest of his clothes disappear, and the marks start to lift off his skin. They dance around in front of us as he steps closer to me. "Did I tell you how beautiful you look in the dress I picked?" he asks, his voice husky as he looks his fill.

"I mean, you might have, but a girl likes to be complimented," I tease him, still watching the marks float around our heads, my annoyance disappearing with the distraction of the magic.

"Well, you do, but now I want to see something even more beautiful." He pushes the material off my shoulders, and the dress falls down my body, leaving me completely naked. His eyes become hooded, and his mouth drops open as he takes in my naked form.

"Fucking gorgeous," he mutters, but then the swirling silver marks start to jump off my skin and join his in the air, where they swirl together. I watch in awe as they leap and twirl amongst each other, but Xavier walks us over to the bed before helping me down. The swirling marks follow us, always floating just above and out of reach as he climbs up on the bed next to me and lies down, stroking one finger between my breasts, over my stomach, and to my pubic mound and back again. "I need to talk to you about this process," he says calmly, but that instantly puts me on alert.

I struggle to get up on my forearms so I can look at him. "You mean there's more than almost getting obliterated by some mysterious force?"

"Yes, my sweet, warlock princess. All those marks up there" —he nods to where our joined marks are whirling above us— "determine how powerful we are. The two of us combined have more strength than either my mother or father, but we need to prove we are worthy of carrying those marks."

That doesn't sound too hard, but I'm sure there is more to it. "And how do we do that?" I ask him.

"We need to orgasm for each pair of marks to return to our bodies. It's a way of proving we can feed and sustain each other without needing a harem. Only the strongest of warlocks can pass the test and prove they deserve their intimate bond. If we fail, then we will return unbonded, and I will need to continue to feed from others."

My eyes widen as I think about the number of marks he had on his body. There has to be at least twenty of them. There is no way my body can orgasm that many times without me passing out. "I'm not sure I can do that," I stammer. "And I know your recovery period is good, but it can't be that good."

He chuckles and narrows his eyes. "Are you doubting my sexual prowess, *phoeall*?" he asks, and I shrug. "I'm pretty sure if I can keep a large harem satisfied, I can manage to keep one little Earth girl well fucked," he growls, and I let my kraken flash into my eyes.

"Not just an Earth girl anymore," I argue, feeling a little stabby at the mention of him servicing his harem.

"There is another component to the ritual that requires us to deposit three bodily fluids from each of us into the sacred cup of the motherland, mix them together, and drink them."

"Three bodily fluids?" I'm trying to work out what the hell he's talking about.

"Blood, cum, and tears. They need to be taken during our love making."

A shimmering orb appears just above us, and as the shimmer fades, it leaves behind an ornate cup not dissimilar to the one the Vilaxians have for their non-Vilaxian blood roses. This one is purple and iridescent with the same silver markings that were on our bodies. It hovers above us, and Xavier reaches up and plucks it out of the air.

I'm suddenly wondering if everything in the universe is connected—if there are a bunch of higher beings bored as fuck who like manipulating and controlling the people they consider beneath them. Gods, I guess, but I don't have time to think on that too long because vines twirl out from the posts and capture my hands. They wrap around my body, crisscrossing between my breasts, around my waist, and then down to my thighs, spreading my legs open and lifting me into the air.

"Agh." I reach out to Xavier for help, but he just watches with heat and lust in his eyes, the goblet clasped in his hand. I'm not sure if he's controlling the vines or if it's some other mystical force, but he approves no matter what. The vines have thorns, and I feel them pierce my body all over as they dig into my skin. I gasp, gritting my teeth as the pain soaks into my being, and I feel small droplets of blood start to pool in places.

"That's one fluid taken care of." Xavier leans in and allows a particularly deep wound to dribble freely into the cup. I growl at him and feel my Vilaxian fangs drop into place despite being in my warlock form. He startles, his eyebrows jumping in surprise. "Well, that is unexpected. I think you, my darling intimate, are more powerful than anyone was expecting. I really do pity the Syndicate when they eventually decide to make a move on the orb."

"Wait until it's your turn for blood. I will drink my fill, and only then will I allow it to drip into the cup," I tell him, violence in my tone. I'm simultaneously annoyed and turned on as fuck, being trapped and suspended with pain running through me. I'm almost certain I could get out, but I want to see what Xavier is going to do to me, and I don't want to fuck up the ritual.

"With each orgasm, our marks will return to us, but I will have yours, and you will have mine." I'm now suspended above the bed, spread open like a sacrifice to a cruel god. My warlock climbs to his feet, stroking his cock as he steps between my legs, which are conveniently at head height for him. He leans in and swipes his tongue through my folds, and I can't stop the moan from leaving my mouth. "Let's get this first one out of the way, shall we?" he mumbles against my core before diving in like I'm his last meal.

It's not long before I'm screaming like a banshee as he uses his fingers and tongue to wring my first orgasm out of me. I feel my eyes drip with tears, and the chalice, by some magic of its own, manages to swoop in and catch them for the so-called magical process. I mean, I think it sounds like a gross concoction, but I guess I've already drunk Xavier's blood and cum before. He's the one who has to stomach drinking my blood.

The chalice floats away once it's satisfied with my tears, and the vines holding me start to move, manipulating me so I am now hovering in front of Xavier's cock, perfectly in position for him to fuck my mouth. He's wearing that sexy, wicked grin that makes me melt every time. His hands stroke my hair before he takes hold of it in a grip that has a pinch of pain. My core clenches with need as he uses my mouth. He thrusts in and out with no care for my breathing or well-being. All I can do is moan around his fat length, turned on that he is using my body in such a way. I feel my pussy drip with need, dying for him to pound his cock into it, but she's going to have to wait. My mouth is being punished first. One of his hands leaves my hair, and then he leans forward, holding his cock deep in my throat as he pinches my nipples before giving each a long suck. I feel the suckers deep inside my throat flutter over his cock, and he groans and pants.

"I'm going to come," he says roughly, and the cup suddenly appears next to my head. I moan in disappointment as he pulls out. Using his hand, he floods the cup with his release. I love swallowing Xavier's Twizzler-flavored cum. I could suck his cock every day and not be sad.

As soon as he finishes, the cup floats away to wait for the next time it can claim our bodily essence. Three fluids down, three to go.

The vines start moving again, manipulating me into position. This time I am face down, ass up, and ready for Xavier to slide into me from behind. "Does that count as two?" I ask him, unsure if we have to come twenty times each or in total.

I feel his finger slide over my back. "Two marks have returned to your body, so I'm guessing they indeed count as two."

"Well, twenty orgasms between us isn't such a chore then."

"Let's see if we get two marks or only one if we orgasm mutually," he says as I feel him line himself up and ease slowly inside.

I groan and hang my head forward, completely restrained and unable to do anything. He rolls his hips, teasing me and building me up, but not giving me exactly what I need to push me over the edge. "Please," I beg, and he chuckles wickedly.

"I love having you at my mercy. It makes me feel dark and possessive. Thoughts of keeping you bound and ready for me anytime I or any of your mates feel like taking you flood my mind. Our pretty little fuck toy."

My pussy clenches, and he starts to thrust a little harder. "Oh, so you like that idea, don't you? Blindfolded and bound as we use any hole we want for our pleasure. Taking turns fucking our cum into your pussy. Breeding you and keeping you pregnant and horny."

I'm so turned on by everything at the moment that all of the dirty things he whispers in his gorgeous voice sound perfect to me. I'm sure once the fog of lust leaves, I will draw the line at being permanently pregnant, but that's another future Lila problem. At this rate, future Lila is going to fucking hate present Lila.

"Please, make me come," I beg, sounding desperate and needy, and I am. I want to feel my cunt clench around his cock with this orgasm. I want to grip him so tightly he struggles to move.

He takes mercy on me and speeds up, his clever fingers sliding around to play with my clit at the same time. It doesn't take long before we come together, our voices mixed as we shout our mutual pleasure.

"Lila, fuck, your pussy is so fucking tight, and the suckers feel unbelievable." Xavier is muttering incoherently now as I chant his name. "Two more power marks returned. Can you feel yourself getting stronger?"

Now that he mentions it, my body does feel stronger, like I could break out of the vines no problem, but I don't try. I like the pain, and I like the restraints, all of it ticking every kink box I have.

"Four down, only a few more to go," he says as he pulls out of me, and the vines change my position again, this time rolling me so I'm facing up.

The air in front of me shimmers, and when it clears, there is a range of sex toys floating in front of Xavier. He reaches up and grabs a butt plug out of the air.

"Perfect, I can't wait to feel your ass grip my cock," he says as he runs it through my pussy, lubing it up before gently pushing it into my ass. I bear down, helping him, but it still pinches as it slides past my tight ring of muscle.

"But how about we try to get your contribution of cum for the cup? I can't wait to see you squirt." He plucks another of the toys out of the air, and I feel it suction onto my clit as he inserts a thick dildo into my pussy. "I'm going to have fun wrecking your pussy." The machine turns on, and my vision blurs as I'm assaulted by sensation. All I can do is hang on for the ride.

CHAPTER FIFTEEN

Lila

When we return to the ship, I am the one who opens the split in the space-time continuum or whatever it is that gets us from one plane to another. I'm brimming with power after our joining, and I hope that it will settle, because at the moment, I'm feeling a little like I could become the galaxy overlord with how much power thrums through me. Xavier's marks buzz and twirl around my body, not content to settle into one spot, but thankfully the minute I step through the gap and back into Xavier's old room on the ship, that power instantly dulls, and my whole body sags. Xavier reaches out and catches me.

"Holy crap," I mutter, feeling drained, and he nods as we drop down onto his bed together, exhausted.

"Yeah, it's a lot to take the change in power." He sounds as weary as I feel.

"You've felt it before?" I ask him, confused. "I thought it was an intimate bonding thing?"

"No, the royal family of Westalin can access the power of the motherland whenever they need a power boost. My parents taught me how to do it when I was younger, which means if either of us need a power boost, we can open a gate and the power will channel through to us."

"Well, that's good to know, but right now, I think I need a nap. I'm exhausted all of a sudden." I flop back on his bed, and he follows me down. I curl around him, and he uses his magic to pull the covers up over us. "I wonder what day it is or how long we've been gone. We must be getting close to the space station."

"It's actually about an hour after we left. Time runs differently on the other plane, so what felt like multiple hours wasn't. We definitely have time for a nap before we get to station Z68."

"Thank fuck," I mumble. "I don't think I could mimic an ant, let alone a whole host of new creatures at the moment."

Now that I can feel Xavier's emotions, his smugness at fucking me stupid reverberates through my body, and I roll my eyes. He wasn't the only one dishing out orgasms, but I'm too tired to play the orgasm count game. I'm going to let him have the win, though I vividly remember him calling me a goddess and the best fuck he has ever had. I think that was sometime around when I allowed a few tentacles to come out to play. It's strange that I can still retain the bottom half of my body, but a couple of tentacles can also appear and fuck his ass and mouth while I ride him like a cowgirl. That's when I was able to gather his tears for the cup.

"I can feel how smug you are," he mutters, and I giggle.

"I guess my sexual prowess is as impressive as the mighty warlock prince's." Okay, I'm not letting him have the win. I'm not that magnanimous. "What was it you called me? Goddess of sex and love?"

There's a twinge of embarrassment, and he puts an arm over his eyes. "Don't make me spell your mouth shut, Lila," he threatens, and I giggle again. Even if he does, I can project my thoughts into the rest of my mates' brains. I'm sure Saxon would love to see our warlock begging and pleading like he did a few times.

Lethargy drags me under, and I fall asleep wrapped in the arms of my newest husband, content and satisfied with only a small thought to what I'm going to do about Nikos and Tirrian, but those are future Lila's problems.

"Mama." A little voice and a small hand patting me on the cheek has me cracking open an eye, seeing Cordy peering down at me with a small amount of worry in her eyes. Panic rushes through me. Shit, are we still naked? When I look down at my body, I find that Xavier clothed us sometime during our nap. "Wake up, Mama, I miss you."

A wide smile crosses my lips as I drag Cordy down to snuggle with me. Her giggles are music to my ears, and it's not long before I feel Jack and Cally bounce up and down on the bed.

"Daddy X!" Jack shouts with excitement, and when I turn to look, I watch our son launch himself at his still sleeping father, landing with his knees right in Xavier's happy place. Xavier's eyes pop open, and he groans, curling in on himself and wrapping his arms around Jack.

"Holy sh… shocking wake-up call," Xavier corrects himself as he nuzzles Jack's neck before pulling Cally closer for her own snuggle. We lie back down with the three toddlers between us. Thankfully they haven't turned into small children while we've been gone. I'm not sure I could have handled that.

"Hello, my beautiful babies. What have you been doing while Daddy and I have been away?" I ask them, and all three start to talk at once. They tell us about playing with Silac and then meeting Poppi and ZeZe, which I'm assuming are Xavier's parents.

"They wanted to give us candy, Mama, but Daddy Sax yelled at them," Cally tells me, her bottom lip jutting out in a pout. I chuckle and exchange a glance with Xavier, who looks horrified at the prospect.

God, I hope Saxon didn't tell my father what candy does to the children. He'll go out of his way to give it to them just for the chaos, he says inside my head.

I'll kill him, I mutter, and his eyes widen. *Okay, maybe just maim him a bit.*

"I didn't yell, I just explained calmly that candy wasn't good for a young shifter's metabolism," Saxon says dryly, and when we both sit up, we find him, Link, and Cas all leaning against the wall, watching us.

"I see the bonding went well," Cas says, smiling. "You two are brimming with power. It kind of makes my jaw ache." He clutches his jaw with his hand and gives it a squeeze.

"Can you tell me a little bit about the process now please?" Link looks between us, desperation in his gaze. I know he nagged Xavier to explain the process to him, his thirst for knowledge eager for information he couldn't find anywhere, but Xavier is an ass and wouldn't tell him about it, claiming it's a sacred ritual that only the warlocks are allowed to know about.

I'll tell you about it later, I promise him inside his mind as Xavier shakes his head.

"Nope. No can do, man. It's a trade secret." Link fakes disappointment for Xavier's sake, while I hear his internal glee at my promise.

"Your parents felt your return a couple of hours ago, and we've been busy organizing a huge meal with everyone to celebrate your bonding. Come on, get changed into something a little fancier, and we can get this party started," Saxon tells us, coming over to grab Cordy from me as Link and Cas do the same for the other two. He leans in and gives me a kiss on the cheek. "Was the warlock good to you?" he whispers in my ear so our babies don't hear.

I project some of my memories into his mind, especially the one of me making him beg and cry. Saxon's eyes flash red before he shakes his head and steps away.

Fuck, he mutters inside my mind. *I want to play that game too.*

"One day," I promise out loud and throw the blankets off me. I need a shower. We cleaned up magically when we returned, but I still feel like I'm covered in blood, tears, and cum—so much cum. At one stage, he painted my body with it, and I feel the lingering stickiness, even if it's all in my mind. "Give us half an hour to clean up, and we will be there."

"We're getting pretty dresses, Mama. Zeze said we could," Cally announces before sticking her thumb into her mouth and snuggling into Link's side.

"I get a warlock robe," Jack declares, puffing his

chest out, proud as punch. "Poppi says Daddy X wore it when he was young."

I look at Xavier and see him smiling, his eyes shining with unshed tears, and his emotions pulse with love. I know this man loves me, I can feel it, but he would burn the galaxy for our children. All of them would. Thankfully before we returned, Xavier taught me how to block out everyone's emotions, but my control isn't great yet, and stuff still flits through, but I don't have the urge to devour the feelings. He explained that's how it felt before we cemented the bond. He said he was ravenous all the time, desperate to feed on anything he could, but they are taught that consent is critical from a young age, so they are disciplined at keeping those urges controlled, especially warlocks as powerful as Xavier. It's why he needed so many in his harem. Most only have one or two and it's a reciprocal relationship.

"Come on then, let's go and let Poppi and ZeZe dress you, and we'll meet Mama and Daddy X at the table with all our other guests." Cas bounces Jack on his hip, and he giggles before changing form and scooting out of the room, his little tentacles moving across the floor rapidly. "Hey," Caspian shouts, hurrying after him. "What have I said about running in hallways?" Link and Saxon follow him out of the bedroom, and I look around the room.

"I guess we can repurpose this room now that

you're living with me." I bite my lip, worried that he's going to want to keep it, but he's quick to jump out of bed, his sweatpants hanging low on his sharp hips and distracting me from my worries.

"No, *phoeall*. Do what you want with them. I'm sure there will be some new performers who may want a new space."

"Ugh. That's if everyone comes back to the show. What if our performers are mad about all this time we're taking to settle our affairs?" I've been worrying about it for a while, but Xavier scoffs like I just said the funniest thing in the world.

"One, this circus makes them superstars, so that's not something most of them will give up easily, and two, they are being paid to take a break. I assure you, not many of them are complaining."

He takes my hand and leads me into his bathroom. He turns on the big, overhead waterfall shower before snapping his fingers and divesting us of our clothes. He tugs me under the water and proceeds to gently wash me.

"I am happy to help you with the administration side of the circus. It's my job as your husband to make sure you are getting everything you need. It's not like I have a huge role with the show anyway. I'm just hanging out in case something goes wrong, and I have to spin some untruths or remove memories or control unruly dinosaurs."

"Why are you with the circus?" I ask, knowing

that he's probably way too important to be playing circus security, and he spins me around, smirking.

"Well, I always wondered why my parents insisted I needed to be here, but in light of everything we've recently learned, I'm going to guess that they wanted me here for when you finally reappeared."

I think about that for a moment. "Yeah, you are probably right. I can't believe we've known each other since we were children." Warmth flows through me as I have brief, fleeting flashes of our childhood interactions. "You were so kind to me, and I loved you fiercely," I tell him, thinking about young Lila's crush on her best friend. "My mom used to tell me that I was lucky to have someone who would love me as fiercely as my daddy loved her." I can't help but feel sad at that particular memory. They were dancing, and I wanted to dance too, and they scooped me up, sandwiching me between them as they continued dancing. Mama told me that one day, Xavier would be big enough to dance with me like Daddy danced with her. I don't tell him this though.

"*Phoeall*, I have loved you from the moment I knew you were my intimate, but now it's different from the love I felt back then. There is a reason most warlocks don't discover their intimate bond until they are in their late teens, but what I felt for you then was the need to protect you and keep you safe."

"And now?" I ask, knowing full well how he feels. I just want to hear him say it out loud.

"Oh, I still feel the need to protect and cherish you, but I also want to do dirty, filthy things to all your holes."

Laughter bubbles out of my mouth, and I shake with amusement. There's my dirty as fuck warlock. "I can't say I'm disappointed, because I want to do nasty things to you too."

We hurry through our shower, both happy to keep our hands to ourselves after our epic marathon fuck-fest on the warlock home world.

Once we dry off, Xavier snaps his fingers, and I'm draped in the dress he picked for me for our bonding. "Where did this come from? I thought it was left on the home world?"

He shrugs. "It was, but I pulled it to us. Seems my powers have grown," he says modestly before clothing himself in his traditional warlock wide-legged pants and tunic that I love so much. His marks shine against the black fabric he's chosen. Those marks were mine, but now they are his. I feel a wave of possession and satisfaction from seeing my marks all over him. It's like he's been stamped with "Property of Lila," and it makes all of my alternate forms and inner animals purr with pride.

"Come on. How about you transport us to the

dining room? That's where Saxon says this shindig is being held." He taps his temple, telling me that he asked telepathically.

"Come here then." I wrap my arms around his waist, pulling him into my body so we're pressed tightly together. "Hang on, buttercup, this may be bumpy," I tell him, not entirely comfortable with my teleporting skills, but no one has ever accused me of being scared to try.

CHAPTER SIXTEEN

Link

I wheel Nikos's pod toward the elevators and press the call button. Although he perked up when Lila was around, he's become listless and unresponsive again. I'm worried that until Lila decides to give him a mating bite, he won't fully recover. In this kind of circumstance, the rejected mate has to want to survive, and that isn't always the case—not that Nikos is rejected, she just has other priorities. I'm sure once he gets to the Aquilian pool and can swim and bake in the sun, he will be better. There are also things he can hunt in there. I'm sure getting fresh food will go a long way in making him feel better. The Aquilians wouldn't often join us in the dining room, preparing to eat like they would on their home planet. Occasionally, they cook their food, but they do it in their own little homes. Nixie was really the only one who would socialize with the rest of the crew.

The elevator arrives, and I wheel the pod into it before pressing the button to take us to the right floor, but instead, it goes up to the floor with our living quarters. When the doors open, I find Silac waiting to enter. I move the pod and myself to the side so there is room for his large snake form, but his body shimmers and his tail fades away, leaving him with legs.

He steps in. "Thanks, but I don't think I would have fit," he says as the doors close, and he chooses a floor. I think it's the one where his and Tirrian's quarters are.

"Maybe not," I agree. "What were you doing up there?" I ask, curious but not upset at finding him near our living quarters. I know he is drawn to Lila, and that his Naga would like to mate with her, but there is also something holding him back—something that Xavier has been working on. Maybe now that his parents are here, they can help too.

He chuckles. "The little ones wanted to see me in my snake form. Phew, they are handfuls. They wore me out, so we had a nap together, but now the warlock king and queen are spoiling them, so I will go and find something else to do."

"Do you want to return to your home planet while we deal with all of these issues?" I ask him, unsure if he's been given the choice since we left Rilu. "I'm sure you could take one of the shuttles. It doesn't seem fair to have you hanging around when you could be spending time with your family."

Silac rolls his eyes and scoffs. "I would like to avoid my family as much as possible at the moment."

"Oh?" I ask, unable to help my natural curiosity.

"Yes. You may know that I am betrothed to someone else, which is why I can't give in to my snake's urge to mate with Lila," he says plainly, and I blink with surprise. This is the first time he's said as much out loud to me, though Lila and Xavier both hinted at it. "If I return now, they will move the date of the betrothal forward, and both myself and Kinga, my betrothed, will be forced into a marriage neither of us want. Her family are the Bravalana basilisks, and they are evil and manipulative and think that having her marry me is a way to control my family's company. If I do that, there will be no chance for the warlocks to take care of the problem, so to speak."

"What does your family do?" I ask, unsure that anyone ever told me and not wanting to think about what the warlocks consider as taking care of the problem. Although I know there are bad people, I am a healer at heart, and maiming or death goes against my nature. I'd rather leave that to the warriors in this relationship.

"My family company is Snakebite Logistics."

My eyes widen with surprise. Holy crap, his family owns one of the biggest shipping companies in the galaxy. No wonder the crime family wants in. They would be able to smuggle shit everywhere. Yet again, another super powerful family is being dangled right in front of Lila. His family is on par with wealth with both my and Cas's families.

Silac's eyes drift to Nikos in the pod, who has floated to face us, and his eyes widen. "Holy crap, is the merman pregnant?" he asks, pointing at his belly.

"Yup, turns out that mating dance with Lila had more consequences than we thought."

"What's wrong with him?" Silac steps closer to the pod, his eyes not leaving the listless merman.

"His father was an asshole, and he has not been cared for. I'm taking him down to the Aquilian pool so he can swim and eat properly and bathe in the sunshine on their platform."

"Was an asshole?" Silac looks back at me, and I shrug.

"Apparently Cronus dealt with him, and Tirrian took care of the new crown prince. They have new leadership now."

Silac grins savagely, and I can see he doesn't share the same hesitation I do about killing and maiming.

"Good. Pregnancy is sacred to shifters. We

cherish our partners and young, and those who don't get dealt with swiftly and justly."

"How do Nagas reproduce?" I ask now that we're on the subject. If Xavier is going to help free Silac for Lila, then I'm going to have to know the details eventually. I may as well get ahead for a change.

The elevator comes to a halt in front of the Aquilian pool, and I wheel Nikos's pod out onto the small platform in front of the pool. Silac follows behind.

"Oh, ah, all snake shifters give birth to live young. The female has to be in half form or full shifted form." He rubs his hands against his pants, looking slightly awkward at the subject. It's kind of endearing.

"And do they come out as snakes?" I ask, hoping like hell that Lila doesn't have a snake phobia. She seems to be okay with Silac's half form, but I'm not sure if she's seen his full shifted form yet.

"Yes, they do, and like the kraken babies, it will take them a couple of weeks to shift. All they want to do during that time is eat and lie in the sun. Most snake shifter families have a crib-like containment system with a heat lamp above it where their babies will stay until they shift."

"And how many babies?" I ask, bracing myself for the answer.

Silac shrugs. "Anywhere from one to five, but five is very unusual. Two or three is more likely."

"Fucking multiples. Why do you have so many at a time?" I ask, and he chuckles.

"I'm assuming it's a primal thing. Survival of the fittest or something. Warlocks and Vilaxians don't give birth in multiples," he points out. "What about cyborgs?"

"No. Only single children for us too, thank goodness, but who knows when Lila is ever going to want to have more children. Not that I'm too concerned, I would be happy to just love on the ones we do have." I wouldn't want to give my mother a chance to use a child against me.

I look from the pod to the water, not entirely sure how I'm going to get Nikos from one to the other. Silac must see my dilemma, because he joins me at the pod, and we both search for options, looking for a seam in the bottom of the pod or a latch that might open, but there's nothing.

"How do you think they got him in there?" Silac asks, running his hand through his bright green hair.

"I'm assuming the guards probably tossed him in there. Aquilians can't shift during pregnancy like shifters and lightning cats can," I explain, and Silac looks livid.

They used a net. Scooped me up like the catch of the day

and then dumped me in here. Nikos's voice sounds in my head, and when I look up, his eyes are open and he's staring longingly at the pool.

"Well, we don't have one of those, so do you have any suggestions?" Silac must have heard the words in his mind as well.

Just tip it over, and I'll flow out with the water, Nikos says, sounding desperate now, and I notice he's more alert than he's been since he returned to the ship. Even when he saw Lila, he wasn't this alert.

I step back and look at the pod, assessing it for a way to tip it over, but then I notice there is a hinged section, and when I pull the lever, the pod starts to tip violently. Silac jumps forward and supports it on one side while I do the same on the other, and we gently tip it, and Nikos slides into the water and disappears.

"Shit, should I get Cas down here to check on him?" I ask, worried about him just sinking to the bottom and not having the energy to swim, but Silac shakes his head, going over to the wall and pressing a few buttons, bringing a camera shot up on the screen.

"No, look, he's fine." He points at the image, which shows the depths of the pool and Nikos swimming slowly amongst the reef below. "Brod-erick showed Tirrian, Brannock, and me everything about the security system when we were traveling to

Aquilia in case they decided to board us or whatever, so I kind of figured there were cameras in the pool. They are everywhere but in people's private living quarters."

"Doesn't that count as their living quarters though?" I ask, looking back at the still surface of the pool and remembering that Lila and Cas have used the pool for extracurricular activities. She's going to be horrified if she finds out they've recorded whatever the two of them were doing.

"No. The little houses are classed as their homes," he tells me, pointing to one of the structures in the middle of the pool.

"Hmm, I think maybe we need to have the option to pause this camera. Cas and Lila often come in here to play." Silac's cheeks pinken as what I'm saying registers. "And with her deciding to claim Nikos as her mate, I'm sure they will be doing fun things in the pool as well."

He turns back to the screen and presses a few buttons. "Okay, that stopped the recording. It can only be turned on and off through here, and I routed it to your screen as well so you can continue to monitor Nikos and not have to be in the room to do it."

My eyebrows jump in surprise. "Wow, that's pretty tech savvy of you. You learned how to do all that just from a conversation with the captain?" I ask, and he shakes his head.

"No, tech is kind of my thing. I probably could have hacked into the system, but William gave me full access when he found out. He wanted me to check all of their security protocols to make sure everything was still holding up."

We both watch as Nikos flicks his tail and darts into a school of fish. The fish dash in all directions, but when the bubbles and chaos clear, it shows him with a fish in his mouth. I feel some of the tension and worry I was carrying seep out of my shoulders.

"And is it? I know they were concerned after the Modovian was found on the ship. They didn't want anyone else to slip past their security protocols."

"I've implemented a couple of new background checks and increased the security on certain levels that the Adams brothers wanted me to. Once the circus returns to its tour, and the rest of the performers and staff return, then the only way to access the flight deck, Lila's quarters, and the one below where the Adams brothers are currently staying will be through biometric recognition. There's also a safe in their room that they have asked me to look into more security measures for. They tell me it contains a lot of important and confidential documents. I'm doing some research to combine tech and magic and basically make it inaccessible, but the carevasta bears always pose a problem. Thankfully they haven't ever had their eye on the circus. I think it's too big of a ship for them to raid, but we need one to rescue their wife, so they are worried it will bring the bears' attention to it." Silac rights the pod and clips the lever back into place. "Do you want me to take this to the storage room? You probably want to stay and monitor him, right?"

I wonder if they are trying to increase the protective measures on the orb. Now that we've had a breach, and the Syndicate is looking at the ship as a possible place for it to be, it wouldn't surprise me if that was what they were doing.

"Link?" Silac's voice startles me from my thoughts.

"Oh, ah, yes, that would be great. I want to use their replicator in his shared home with Nixie and make sure he's eating more than just fish. Could you activate the walkway for me?" I ask him, and he goes back to the panel and presses a few buttons again.

The walkway activates, skimming out over the pool until it joins up with all three little houses. I know one of them wasn't occupied, but the bigger one held the rest of the Aquilian performers because they were an established pod. They won't be returning to the show because one of them was pregnant and they wanted to give birth in their home waters. Poor Nikos won't have that option.

"Alright, well, if you need me for anything else, just let me know. I can't help make him better, but if he needs some company later, let me know. I'll come back and sit with him if he needs it. The Aquilian sun isn't as vicious as the sun from Rilu, and I'll enjoy basking under the lights with him, especially if I change to full form."

A wave of appreciation for this man washes over me. It's nice that Nikos has some support from another person. I'm sure all of Lila's mates will be supportive too, but they are all super busy with bonding and children and everything that is going on at the moment. I really hope Silac can sort out his problems and get out of his arranged marriage, because he really would be an asset to our family. He's kind, caring, and gentle, and I think our family needs a little more of that—or Lila does anyway.

"Thank you. I'm sure both Lila and Nikos will appreciate it."

He waves goodbye and wheels the pod back onto the elevator, taking it away and storing it in case we ever need it again.

I use the walkway to cross over to Nixie and Nikos's abode. I am determined to make him a large, well-balanced, nutritious meal. I just have to do a little research on what that will be for him. Their house is open planned with large, open windows with shutters to pull closed if they decide to program the weather in here to be bad. The colors are light and airy, and the furniture is mini-malist. It reminds me of a beach holiday home I stayed at once as a child with my father, but I guess that's not all that surprising. I take a seat on one of the cushioned wicker couches and begin meal planning for a pregnant merman. I mean, how hard can it be?

CHAPTER SEVENTEEN

Echo

When Lila leaves us with that declaration of love, both Maxsim and I are so stunned, neither of us respond in the right way—meaning we don't tell her we're so in love with her it's ridiculous. It's not until a good couple of minutes later that I come to my senses.

"Did she…" I look at my mate, who seems just as flabbergasted as I am.

"Tell us she loves us?" he mumbles, and I nod enthusiastically.

"Yes, that. Did we just let her walk away without telling her we feel the same way?"

"Yes, but in my defense, I didn't think she would feel that way so quickly," he admits, still sounding shocked.

"Pfft," I scoff and roll to my feet, stalking back and forth across our den. "Of course she does. If there is one thing we know about our mate, it's that she goes balls to the wall when she decides to commit. Look at what she told us about Nikos. She's already forgiven him and is now fully in that committed to caring phase. It won't be long before she's telling him she loves him as well, and don't get me started on the dragon and the snake." I feel my tail twitching behind me in agitation. I can't believe she didn't wait so I could tell her I feel the same way. I almost want to hunt her down so I can, but I know she went to finally make the warlock a happy man. He's waited long enough, but as soon as they finish whatever is involved in them completing their bond, I'm going to find her and tell her that I love her as much as I love Maxsim.

"Easy, Omega," Maxsim growls before purring, trying to soothe my agitation.

"She didn't wait, like she was worried we didn't feel the same way. I don't want her to think we don't love her," I tell him, unable to stop the whine in my voice. He gets to his feet and catches me on one of my passes, wrapping his arms around me. The rumbling vibrations in his chest soothe some of my ruffled feathers.

"You know our mate wears her heart on her sleeve. She was probably worried we didn't feel the same way and didn't want to be hurt if we couldn't say it. Remember, Earth people are ridiculously prudish with their feelings. Lila has been on her own for so long that she doesn't realize how loveable she is. Every single one of her mates and a few others are all head over heels for her. Maybe it's time we started showing her. Poor Lila hasn't really had a moment to stop and breathe since she found out about her inheritance. We should plan something special for her." I pull back from my alpha and stare at him in surprise, and he blushes adorably.

"When did you become such a softy?" I ask him, nuzzling his cheek as he shrugs. "That's a fantastic idea. We should throw them a wedding feast. She didn't get it with any of the rest of us. If her matings happened at a normal pace, she would have been subjected to celebrations with her mates' families. Our parents would have welcomed her to our families with open arms."

Maxsim rolls his eyes. "You forget they gifted us to her," he grumbles half-heartedly. I know he doesn't mean it. He is incredibly settled now that we are mated and expecting babies. He's one big ball of furry softness.

"Yes, and I will thank them when I see them next, but they still would have had a party." I look around the room for one of my loincloths. I want to go find our co-mates and make the suggestion.

Maxsim stops my agitated search by grabbing my arm. "Bathe first. You don't want to meet the warlock king and queen for the first time smelling like sex."

"Good thinking." I smack a kiss against his mouth and drag him with me to the central bathroom we all share. When I open the door in the back of our den, steam from the bathroom drifts across the floor. Although I am partial to the snow and cold, I do love a hot bath, and bathing with Maxsim makes the experience even more fun because he's such a sulky pussy cat when he gets wet. If I stroke him the right way and tell him how pretty he is, then he doesn't fight it too much.

An hour later, after I fought my alpha over washing his mane and fur and managed to dry him off with the drying machine, we emerge in the living area wearing Galaxy Circus uniforms. Inside, we find our co-mates and children, the Adams brothers, and the warlock king and queen. The only ones missing are Lila and Xavier—for obvious reasons—and Link.

I ask Saxon where he is after introductions have been made. "Link is observing Nikos. He's very worried about his condition, but he didn't think it was healable through magic. It's just neglect, and only rest and good food and care can fix that."

"Poor silly can of tuna. When Xavier returns,

I'll ask him to spell me so I can go and sit with him and talk babies. He is further along than I am, and I would like to know how it feels," I say, rubbing my hand over my belly.

A flash of dark purple magic washes over me, causing Maxsim to growl and unleash his claws, but when it clears, the warlock king just grins at Maxsim, not scared at all.

"Settle, Alpha. I just gave him the magic he needs to hang out with the mer. There's no way we would hurt our grandbabies he's carrying."

The queen claps her hands and looks at her husband, unable to contain the pure joy in her eyes. "We go from no grandchildren to having almost seven in the blink of an eye. It's wonderful." Aww, isn't that sweet? That's not what I expected of a warlock at all. "The ladies are going to be so jealous. I can't wait to rub it in their faces. This is why our family rules them all." Oh yeah, okay, that was more along the lines of what I'd been expecting. Warlocks are ruthless.

"Thank you, King Cronus. I appreciate you taking care of our omega," Maxsim says gruffly, nodding his head, but the king scoffs and waves a hand.

"None of this king crap, call me Dad or Cronus. You're Xavier's co-mates now, which means you're family."

Maxsim and I stare at the personable king,

unsure if this is a trick or not. He's known throughout the galaxy as someone you don't fuck with.

"Dear, you're scaring them. Tone down the enthusiasm a little," the queen says out of the side of her mouth, bouncing Cordy on her knee. Cronus has both Jack and Cally, and he has them entertained with what looks like a never-ending puzzle toy.

"I'm hungry," Cordy complains. I doubt anyone fed them a snack when they woke up. The snake was here earlier when they were napping, and I wonder where he got to. Same with the dragon and the warrior man, Brannock. They must be awfully lonely on such an empty ship. Maybe they are keeping Captain Broderick company. I know he was showing them how to work the ship just in case it was needed.

"Oh, here, this was Xavier's favorite sweet when he was little, your mama's too. We brought her some every time we came to visit." Cronus pulls something out of the air, and with one look at the packaging, we can tell it's candy.

"No!" everyone shouts in tandem, and the king and queen almost jump out of their skin as Saxon uses his speed and snatches it out of his hands.

"No candy for the shifter babies," he says, crushing it into dust before brushing the remains into the trash compactor.

Cronus pouts as much as the babies do. "Aww, why not?"

"Because it's almost time for dinner, and we don't want to spoil their appetite," Caspian says quickly, and Saxon nods with agreement as I try to hide my amusement. I'm not sure why they aren't telling the warlock king about how the babies react to candy, but I won't go against my co-mates, and Maxsim is also silent beside me. It's not like we were there to witness it anyway.

"Candy rots their teeth," William chimes in, and Eric nods enthusiastically. John stays quiet, but like us, he wasn't there to witness our babies with candy, though Saxon, Link, and Caspian made it very clear that it was never to happen again.

"Anyway," I jump in, changing the subject, "I think we should throw a party to celebrate Lila and Xavier's bonding."

Everyone falls silent and looks at me quizzically, so I hurry along.

"Isn't that normal when someone mates or gets married? Celebrating their happy occasion with family and friends?" I mean, maybe I'm wrong. Maybe what we do on Iceen is different from everyone else.

Xylene claps her hands together in front of Cordy, who thinks it's a game and joins in, giggling. "What a wonderful idea. Of course, with everything that's happening, none of you have had the chance to celebrate."

Now that the idea is out there, people grasp it and run wild.

"We could all dress up and make the dining hall fancy, and we could eat and drink and dance." Eric nods, getting excited about the idea.

"It would be a good distraction from everything," John muses, and I can see the desire to find his wife in his eyes, but we still have a day of travel to the station, and then a few days after that to Husadavia.

"Excellent." Cronus hands the children off to Cas and Saxon. "I just felt them return. They'll probably nap for a while, but we should get a move on. If you show me the way, I can be in charge of decorations."

"I'll dress the babies. The girls can have pretty party dresses," Xylene says.

"Oh, and Jack can have Xavier's warlock robes from when he was small." The king and queen look excited, and I'm pleased everyone likes my idea.

"That would be lovely, and I'm sure Lila and Xavier would appreciate it. Thank you, Echo." Cas nods his head in appreciation, and Maxsim squeezes my knee.

"I'll go find Link and invite the captain and Brannock," Saxon says.

"The merman won't be able to come, but I

want to go check on him before we eat, so how about I tell Link and you tell the other two?" I suggest, and the vampire agrees.

"And I will find the snake and the dragon. They shouldn't miss the happy occasion," Maxsim says, and I beam at him. I'm so proud that he's making an effort to be friendly now that we are mated to Lila.

A hand on my shoulder has me looking over to see whom it belongs to. "Well done, Echo." William nods his appreciation. "I'm afraid Lila has had things thrown at her from the very beginning, so it will be fun to blow off a little steam."

"Yes, but we must do it again when we can have all of your families and friends in attendance as well," John says, looking between us. "Once we have our wife back with us and the circus resumes its tour."

"But this one will do for now. You all have jobs, and if you don't, you need to find something fancy to wear and then head to the dining room and program the replicators with party food. I'll talk to Silac about music. He's the tech wiz." Eric is practically bouncing on his toes. I think this is the distraction everyone needed. We can't make time go faster, so at least we can do what we can to make it feel like it's passing quicker, and we are closer to retrieving their wife.

Everyone takes their leave, and after giving Max

a kiss, I take the elevator down to the Aquilian pool deck. It's quiet when the elevator doors open, and only the sound of water lapping against the side of the pool breaks the stillness. I look around and find that the walkways over to the cute little houses are out. I've never been down here before, but Lila told me that the walkways are usually retracted, so someone who needs them must be here somewhere.

"Hello?" I call out as I make my way to one of the houses. I can smell the electric scent of the cyborg, so I'm assuming he's somewhere in this direction.

"Echo?" Link peers out of one of the large, open windows and waves me forward. "Come on in. What are you doing here?" he asks, sounding surprised. "I would have thought it was too warm in here for you."

"The king gave me protection so I could hang out with Nikos and talk pregnancy with him. Lila suggested it might be good for him."

Link heaves out a relieved breath of air. "Yes! Yes, what a wonderful idea. I just made him a meal, one that is full of everything a pregnant Aquilian needs." He points at a plate on the table. "I was just going to go down to the pool entrance and see if I could call him out of the water and make him eat it. There's also a vitamin drink I want him to have."

"Great. I'll stay and talk to him while he eats, but then he will need to sleep to build up his strength, and you and I have a party to go to." I tell him about the party everyone is planning, and his eyes shine with gratitude.

"That's a great idea. I'm not sure why none of us thought about it," he admits, looking slightly guilty.

"Don't feel bad. It's a perfect time to have one while we still have a day of travel. No one can concentrate on anything else until we have Liliana Adams back with us anyway. Once we have her back and Nikos has his child, we can have another one all of our family and friends can attend. I would like to meet your family," I tell him, and his smile drops, and he shudders.

"My father definitely. My mother won't be getting an invitation," he says with conviction, and I feel a rush of sadness for the cyborg. I guess not everyone's families are as good as mine and Maxsim's. Natalia is proof of that. I'm just sad that someone as kind and caring as Link has this problem.

"I will come back tomorrow, and we can bask in the sun and talk baby names and what it feels like to be pregnant. I'll make sure the can of tuna knows he is wanted and welcome," I assure the cyborg, and he nods, taking the plate and glass of liquid and heading down the stairs to the basement pool entrance. "We will make sure he is in tip top condition for when he has his babies."

"Maybe this situation is going to work. I don't think there's been a mating like ours, and I was worried that with so many strong personalities, we'd end up clashing, but it all seems to be working seamlessly. It's almost like it was meant to be," Link mutters.

"Maybe the gods of creation orchestrated it," I say jokingly, and he stops and turns, looking at me intently.

"Gods of creation?" He sounds confused, and I shrug.

"Yes, you know, the six ancient beings who were said to have created the galaxy. My parents told me stories about them when I was younger." He keeps walking, but I see him shake his head.

"The cyborgs don't believe in those stories, but maybe it's something I need to do some research into." He sounds excited, and I can't help but grin. Only the cyborg would be excited to learn what a lot of us were made to learn in school.

"Ask the warlocks. If anyone knows anything, they will. It's rumored that they aren't even originally from this galaxy. They may be able to shed some light on the legend of the gods. Legends like that usually have a small amount of truth to them."

"I'll do that," he tells me as we step off onto the landing. This one is a cave-like grotto with a pool of water lapping against the side. Before I can ask how we are going to get the merman's attention, a little animal's head pops out and barks at Link.

"Sweetpea, get Nikos for me," he says, and with a splash, the animal disappears.

"Wow. That animal is smart," I say, trying to peer through the water to see where it went, but Link just laughs.

"I'm not sure if it will work, but let's hope it does."

CHAPTER EIGHTEEN

Maxsim

I watch with a small grin as my omega hurries off to check on the Aquilian male who appears to be joining our mating circle. He is so kind and loving and concerned for everyone. I also think he's a little excited to have someone to talk babies and pregnancy with. He's started to complain about little changes in his body. I don't see any of them, but he swears they are there.

I wave goodbye to the others, giving the babies kisses and making them giggle when my fur tickles their faces, and then I go in search of the snake and dragon. The snake was in our rooms earlier, but I'm not sure where he went after that. I'll try their quarters first, and then if he's not there, I'll use the search function to find him.

The elevator takes me down a floor to where the Adams brothers and the captain have their quarters. Silac, Tirrian, and Brannock all have rooms on this level as well for this trip. That may change once the circus is operational again. Most of the flight crew usually stays on this level close to the bridge if they are needed.

I step out of the elevator and start walking down the passageway. It runs through the middle of the ship with the rooms facing outward so they all have views of space. Occupied rooms have a light above them, and the lights are off for rooms that are unoccupied. I pass a few doors that have unlit lights, but as I round one of the bends, I find Brannock, the Aaz'axian, standing in front of one of the doors muttering to himself. I can't make out the words, but he doesn't sound particularly happy. My eyebrows jump in surprise when I reach him and find him standing in front of the Adams brothers' suite. Their name is written next to the touchpad screen next to the door.

He must not have heard or noticed me, because when I stop, he jumps in surprise and yanks his hand off the keypad like he's been burnt.

"What are you doing?" I ask, and he stammers a little before clearing his throat.

"I, ah, was looking for one of the Adams brothers. I wanted to speak to them about a couple of things," he says, and I may not be a living lie detector like some of Lila's mates, but I get the feeling that the spiky man is not telling the whole truth. He has been very helpful with planning the mission to rescue Mrs. Adams, however, so I'm going to give him the benefit of the doubt.

"Why did you want to see them?" I ask. The saying that curiosity killed the cat is perfectly accurate. "They are organizing a party to celebrate Lila and Xavier's mating. Saxon was going to track you down and invite you."

"Uh, I wanted to speak to them about returning to Earth. I have some things I left unfinished. Agent Smith set me up and disrupted my life, and I was perfectly happy minding my own business." His spikes shimmer with agitation as he tells me this, and I feel a pang of sympathy for the guy. Agent Smith sounds like a douchebag.

"We did cut our tour of Earth short. I'm sure we will return sooner rather than later. Dealing with Agent Smith is probably high on their to-do list. Lila tells me she felt like he was hiding something. She said she's worried he has other alien creatures that he's either keeping locked up or experimenting on."

"Yes!" Brannock shouts before rubbing his chin and shaking his head. "I mean, I wouldn't put it past him. I also have a bone to pick with my so-called friend who set me up." I watch in awe as Brannock's skin shifts color, turning a mottled green, and his upper half turns as red as an Earth rose before he shakes himself and returns to normal. Holy fuck, his berserker mode almost activated. I wouldn't want to be his so-called friend when he gets back to Earth.

My fur bristles, and I take a step back. I am a predator, but there's just something about the Aaz'axian that has me feeling fear right now. "Easy, man. I can tell you're upset, but don't take it out on any of us." I hold up my hands, my claws extended, and I'm ready to leap if he tries anything.

I watch as Brannock visibly sags and steps back. "Shit, I'm sorry. Every time I think about what they did to me and what they are doing to others, it makes me mad. Agent Smith is not the right man for that job. He is evil," he says . "I didn't want to raid Madam Aura's house. He said if I didn't help them, then he would make it his mission to harass all the law-abiding aliens he has on file as residing or vacationing on Earth. What was I supposed to do?" He wrings his hands, and his spines bristle again, like they are attuned to his mood.

"You made the right choice. It also helped bring it to the Adams brothers' attention. They have already alerted the Galactic Council. I'm sure something is being done, and if it isn't, when the circus returns to Earth, Lila will get to the bottom of this."

"I only hope they aren't too late," I hear him mutter before he looks wistfully at their suite door.

"Why don't I help you find them?" I suggest, getting a funny feeling about this whole situation. I feel like I should tell Lila about this, but she already has so much on her plate. Maybe I'll talk to Saxon or Xavier. They may be able to help Brannock. The warlock is already helping Silac, so what's one more to add to the list?

"Ah, yeah, okay. That would be great." Brannock doesn't sound so certain but steps away from the door.

"I just need to tell the dragon and snake about the party," I explain and start walking down the corridor toward their rooms.

"Neither of them is here," he says absentmindedly, but then his eyes shoot to mine, and I can see guilt in his gaze. What is going on with this man? Now I'm starting to feel suspicious myself.

"Oh, and you know that because?" I ask, unable to stop the roughness in my demand.

"I saw Silac in the elevator on my way here. He was going to store the pod that carried the merman in one of the prop rooms, and I left Tirrian on the bridge, talking to Captain Broderick. They were monitoring a ship that has been traveling just off our radar for days. Occasionally it pops into view, but then it quickly disappears. They are assuming it's a cargo vessel heading to Z68 for R&R and on the same trajectory as us, but they are monitoring it closely."

My suspicions ease at his perfectly reasonable explanation. I guess I'm just a little jumpy after the altercation with the Aquilians and our upcoming mission to Husadavia, not to mention needing to find a way to survive the planet and the fact that we have to find a carevasta bear for Lila to mimic. I only hope we can find one on the station. Station Z68 is a bit rougher than some of the others. Outlaws and space privateers use it to blow off steam, and it's in a different class than X69. If they can be found anywhere, then that's the place to find them.

"Thank you for telling me. I will try to track them down using the on-board security system. I doubt that Silac will stay in one place long. Saxon was going to find you and Broderick, but you already know now, and if Tirrian is there, he can tell the dragon. That just leaves the snake." I turn and head back toward the elevator, but then I notice Brannock isn't with me. "Are you coming?" I ask him, and he shakes his head. "No, I'll head to my room and freshen up first." He points down the corridor to some doors farther down.

"Alright." I wave a hand and step into the elevator, but when the doors close, I notice he hasn't actually moved. He's a strange one. I guess being on his own and away from space for so long may have made him a little weird. It would certainly do it to me. I'm kind of grateful I can't travel to Earth without a glamour, I am perfectly happy in my fur and staying in the circus pod whenever we are there. Echo would like to be able to look around, but he's a typical curious kitty. Maybe I'll ask the warlock for a charm so he can go shopping with Lila when we are there next.

I use the security system in the elevator to track down the snake, and I find he's already in the dining room. Well, that's handy. I press the button for the right level, and the elevator whisks me down and around to the main doors of the giant dining room. When I step out, I find Eric and Cronus talking with Silac, and they have made a lot of progress in such a short time. There is one large dining table with gorgeous, dark purple table clothes, and it's set with all the fancy things one would need for an elaborate meal. There are purple and silver candles floating on the ceiling, and purple and silver clouds drift amongst the candles, creating an elaborate lighting effect.

"Maxsim, what are you doing here?" Eric asks, looking over my shoulder. "Did you find Tirrian?"

"No. I went looking for them at their quarters and found Brannock near your rooms. He told me that Tirrian is on the bridge, so I left it for Saxon who is telling Broderick," I explain. "So that left Silac." I point at the snake. "But I'm guessing he already knows."

"Yes, he does. We were just talking about his little basilisk problem back on Fluxx. Xylene and I are going to take care of it while you guys travel on to Husadavia." Cronus is practically giddy with excitement. "It's been a long time since we had anything this exciting to do. I'm going to arrange for our personal guards to meet us on Fluxx and request a meeting with Silac's father, citing using their shipping company for royal shipping as the reason."

Silac nods his head. "From what one of my brothers tells me, wherever my father goes, one of the basilisk brothers accompanies him. They aren't willing to let him out of his sight until Kinga and I are married."

"Where is Kinga staying? You said she wasn't involved in any of the family activities," Eric asks, and Silac shakes his head.

"None of the women are. They are all glorified prisoners and blackmail material."

"So not only will we be wiping out a scourge on the galaxy, but we will also be freeing women and children. That is even better. Xylene will be most pleased, but we will search everyone for intent before we kill them. We want to make sure we are getting rid of the right people," he assures Silac, who seems to sigh in relief.

"You have no idea how much this means to me. I will never be able to repay you."

Cronus narrows his eyes and looks between me and the snake before grinning. "Well, now that you will be a free man, maybe that attraction mark on your shoulder will tell you what you should be doing with your time."

The snake's mouth drops open. "You know about that?"

"I know many things," Cronus says cryptically, and Eric scoffs.

"Please, anyone, even people without mystical powers, can see that you and Lila are attracted to each other. At least you will get the opportunity to explore it guilt free now, which is a relief. I can't stand seeing her look all mopey-eyed at you and the dragon."

"The dragon seems to have had a change of heart though," Cronus says, and I feel my eyebrows jump in surprise. This is news to me.

"He has?" I ask, and the king rubs his hands together like a gossipy old woman.

"Yes, he declared her his mate in front of the Aquilians and us. There is no going back from that now. I have already been in contact with his father to congratulate him."

Eric groans. "You didn't. Fuck, you are a meddler."

"I told you I was bored. Xylene was with me too and didn't stop me."

Eric points an accusing finger at the king. "She's as bad as you are."

He shrugs unapologetically.

"Well, fixing Silac's situation will keep you

distracted and help us out immensely. It leaves us to concentrate on getting Liliana back, and when we find out who is responsible for putting her there, I will send you a gold-plated invitation for the fight." Eric's eyes gleam with bloodthirst, and a shiver courses down my back. I wouldn't want to be the person who has kept their wife captive for so many years. She better be in a good condition when we find her, or the Adams brothers will tear down the universe trying to find the culprit.

"I'm sure my mother will offer you some cat warriors to assist with that. They are good trackers if you need those responsible sniffed out. They may need some environmental protection depending on where the trail leads them, but what Cronus did to Echo today should be enough."

"Yes, and Xylene was speaking to the Vilaxian queen a week or so ago, and her elite warriors are bored and doing stupid things to entertain themselves, so I'm sure she will offer some help as well. You have many people on your side, my friend, and we will ensure no harm will come to your family or this circus, and those responsible for your wife's imprisonment will pay."

I feel like there may be some underlying message in those words, but Silac doesn't seem to be any more in the know than I am, so I let it go. If we need to know more, I'm sure they will share it with us.

"Thank you, my friend." Eric nods at the warlock king. "We are blessed with your continued friendship despite the death of our son."

"What do I keep saying? Marcus and Alina were family, and Lila literally is, which means so are you." Cronus slaps Eric on the back. "Now, shall we finish organizing this party? They will be here soon."

They walk toward the replicators to start organizing food. I'm not sure what to do now. Maybe I should go find Echo, but if he's down in the Aquilian pool, I don't really relish getting that close to water voluntarily. I wouldn't even shower if Echo didn't make me, but the silly omega does like a good bubble bath.

I look around at a loss, but the king stops and looks over his shoulder. "Are you coming, cat? I have a few name suggestions for your cubs that I want to share with you." Silac and Eric laugh as I blanch.

"Ah, yup, sure, I would be happy to hear your input," I call back and follow them to the other end of the room where Eric starts programming the replicators. There's a long bank of them to accommodate all of the circus crew and staff, but all of them seem to be in sync at the moment because as one, they produce bottles of sparkling wine from all over the galaxy. Cronus picks one up and waves his hand, and four glasses instantly appear in front of them.

Silac raises an eyebrow, and he shrugs. "We must taste test it. Only the best for our family. If I get the kitty cat drunk, he may be more inclined to name one of his strong, virile cubs after me."

I stare at the crazy warlock in shock. It's no wonder Xavier is the way he is when he's been brought up with this chaotic person, but he seems to be all about family, and that's all that matters to me.

"I'll make you a deal. If you can get the snake man free for my mate to pursue and give my omega a glamour charm so he can go shopping on Earth with our mate, then I will hear your name suggestions," I bargain.

He slaps his empty hand against his leg and shouts, "Ha! You have yourself a deal. Let's toast to that."

I watch on in amusement as he hands out the glasses of sparkling liquid, and we all take a drink. Being in this family is never going to be dull, that's for sure.

CHAPTER NINETEEN

Lila

O ur wedding party was so much fun. All of us forgot about all the issues and problems plaguing us for a short period of time and let our hair down. There was food, drinks, and dancing. Xylene, Cordy, Cally, and I were spun around the dance floor several times. The girls were thrilled, and Jack pouted until he got to dance with all of his fathers. Most of my mates are good dancers, even Maxsim who started off slightly self-conscious, but after a few glasses of bubbly wine and some encouragement from Echo and me, he was soon kicking up his heels and shouting with joy.

The little ones eventually grew tired, as did John, who is still recovering although he is much better than he was. It was like it was a signal for the party to be over. Cronus, Xavier, and Xylene snapped their fingers, and the mess disappeared, then we all retired to our rooms. Broderick hadn't stayed at the party long. He wanted to continue to monitor the space around us and keep us on time for our arrival at the space station. He's been pretty much working nonstop since we left Aquilia. Brannock offered to switch with him to let him rest, so he left the party early so he could sleep before his shift at the helm. The two of them seem to have become good friends over the last few weeks. I'm happy for them, they both seem like they carry sadness with them, and hopefully this will ease some of whatever it is that causes that sadness. I know Broderick misses my dad, but Brannock is still a mystery. I still have those swimming lessons I promised to give him. My to-do list is never-ending.

The following morning, we reach Z68. We're docked and waiting for permission to go aboard the station, but it's taking its sweet-ass time.

"We'll be off. We're meeting our elite guard and taking care of a problem," Cronus says as he gives me a kiss on each cheek. Xylene pushes him out of the way while he's muttering about exterminating vermin.

"We will meet you back on Skarr once you have rescued Liliana, and we can have another big party. That will give us time to invite your friends, Susie and Mark, and everyone's families. It will be the celebration of the year," she says. "I will speak to all your mothers, and we will take care of everything," she says, looking at all my mates.

"Not my mother," Link replies quickly, looking slightly pale. "Please don't invite her."

Xylene purses her lips. "Your mother is rather annoying. Fine, we won't include her, but your father is delightful, and I'm sure he would want to be there for you."

Link sighs with relief and agrees to that.

There's a flurry of goodbyes and kisses and hugs, and then more kisses and hugs for the babies, with Xylene making me promise that they can visit with them on the warlock home world when we have time.

I heave a sigh of relief when they teleport back to their ship, but I don't get a moment to relax, because Bubby sends a message through our communicators saying we've been given permission to go aboard the station.

"How about we take the children back to your quarters while you argue over who is going to go and see Link's contact," John suggests, and my grandpas gather up my babies and take their leave. As much as they want to be involved, they admitted that they aren't in the right headspace to help out with their worry for my grandma. That's fine with me. At least I know my babies are being looked after.

"Echo and I won't be going either. I don't want to put him at risk while he is with child," Maxsim announces, and he's not going to hear any argument from me.

"I'm going to go and see how our can of tuna is doing today. I'll make sure he is eating properly," Echo says with a smile as he assures Link.

"Thanks, that would be helpful. Now we just have to decide who is going to accompany Lila," Saxon says, but Link shakes his head, looking at his own communicator.

"My contact just sent a message saying that Lila must come alone," he announces, sounding dismayed, and my remaining mates explode into an uproar as I just roll my eyes.

"It's not that they don't think you're capable." It's Silac who says this as we watch the rest of them argue with one another.

"They are all control freaks who are used to getting their own way," Tirrian says dryly from my other side, and I raise an eyebrow at him.

"Is that the pot calling the kettle black?" I ask him, and his eyebrows furrow in confusion.

"I didn't call you black, and really, my color is not black, it's more of an iridescent black."

I laugh. Sometimes aliens are so literal. I guess they don't have that saying here in space.

"Settle down. Of course we aren't going to allow her to go on her own." Brannock, for some reason, takes charge, and my mouth drops open in surprise as all of my mates turn to hear what he has to say.

"What the fuck?" I mutter under my breath, and Tirrian leans in.

"Brannock has had some valuable information to share with us. His experience during the war has been invaluable."

I keep forgetting Brannock is that old. Shit, he's as old as Oshan, and he said he was over seven hundred. I have a crush on an old man, but fuck, he looks good for an old man.

"Okay, I think the plan should be to make it look like Lila is on her own, but she really isn't. Xavier and I can both glamour ourselves to look like other beings. I'm sure Xavier can make you all have different faces as well. We know where this meeting is supposed to take place, so why don't you teleport us so we'll already be in the bar when Lila arrives?"

"I can totally do that. I think Tirrian, Silac, and Caspian can be at one table as a group of shifters celebrating something." Xavier quickly jumps on board with the plan. "And I'll glamour Saxon and Link to look like another vamp feeding off his cyborg toy boy." Xavier rubs his hands together with excitement, enthused with the plan. "That just leaves us, and I don't think we should act like we're together. We should be lone people at the bar."

"It's a solid plan," Tirrian agrees, "but we need to look dirty and less kempt than we do now. Z68 is a favorite station for space pirates and criminals. To be honest, no reputable woman would be seen alone. She really should take a bodyguard with her. Is your contact open to negotiation?" He looks at Link, who has been typing furiously on his communicator.

"No, either Lila comes alone, or he won't meet with her."

"Does anyone else not like the sound of that?" Cas says, biting his lip with worry.

"Look, I'm not stupid, I don't even like the sound of it, but I have some pretty badass forms I can use if I need it, and we need this contact, even if it's just for me to mimic them so we can use whatever it is they do to stay alive on Husadavia. I promise if I feel uncomfortable or unsafe, I will let you know." I try to reassure my kraken, but I can see he's still doubtful. Shit, my heart is racing with nerves too. This is the first time I'll be venturing out on my own. I'm sure I'll fuck it up by insulting someone or not knowing the right etiquette.

"How? Do we need a hand signal or a safe word?" Cas sounds so serious, I have to bite my lip to stop myself from grinning.

"I'll tell you telepathically," I promise him.

"Don't you need to be in one of your alternative forms to do that though?" Saxon asks, and I shake my head.

"Nope. I can access it in this form. I guess it must be one of my Skarrian abilities, or maybe it's a whisperer power. Lightning cats can communicate with one another telepathically," I point out, and the males look a little skeptical, but I'm doing that thing where I don't acknowledge I'm a special snowflake who can access my alternate powers in any form.

"Only with images and feelings, not actual words," Maxsim adds helpfully, but I ignore him.

"Right then, shall we get going? I don't want to keep the contact waiting."

"Yes, just let us all get into place," Xavier says and waves a hand, and suddenly, I'm surrounded by unrecognizable men. They all look like they could use a shower and a fresh set of clothes, but I guess that's what's needed to blend in. The only ones who stay the same are me and my two cats. I study what they all look like, trying to fix it in my mind so I'll know who is who when I get to the bar. Thankfully, my mimic powers behave themselves and stay buried deep.

"Can you change their scent?" I ask Xavier, who now has a patch over one eye, a wicked scar across his shirtless non-purple chest, and a robotic arm.

"Why?" He sounds confused.

"Because you all smell too good to be the dregs of the galaxy," Bubby answers, entering the teleportation room. He nods at me with approval. "If you want to get it right, we need you to be authentic. That space station is going to reek of unwashed bodies, blood, and sex, and you will stand out like a sore thumb even in those outfits. Don't be polite, and maybe when you see Lila, catcall and proposition her. She isn't the kind of clientele they will be used to. You have to make this performance authentic, or the person waiting for her will know it's a setup."

Instantly, the room is filled with a gag worthy stench. I wave my hand in front of my nose, and my eyes water, but Bubby just nods with approval.

"Yes, that's perfect."

Both of my cats look a little green and start backing toward the door. "Good luck. We'll see you when you get back," Maxsim calls while Echo dry heaves, holding his belly. As soon as the door opens, they hurry through it and down the hall.

I want to go with them, but I'm sure the station is going to smell even worse, so I have to tough it out. "I'll give you all twenty minutes to get organized. We don't know if the contact is already waiting for us, so be careful," I warn them, and with a wave of his hand, Xavier transports them all to the station, taking the smell with them.

I breathe a sigh of relief, and Bubby and I walk back down the hall to the bridge. I take a seat to give them the time they need to get situated.

"Now that we're alone, I wanted to talk to you about a few things," Bubby says, going over to the replicator and programming something into the machine. When he returns, he has two steaming cups of coffee—his is black and mine is white—and when he hands it over, it's perfectly sweet.

"Yes, this is just what I needed." I take a large sip and sigh. "Actually, I need like a whole fucking month with no drama, but that isn't going to happen anytime soon, so I will take this. What did you want to talk about?"

"Brannock mostly. I've gotten to know him rather well over the last few weeks, and he is adamant about returning to Earth. I can't say for sure, but I have a feeling there is something there that's important to him."

"Are you sure he doesn't just want revenge on Agent Smith? If I were in his shoes, I'd want to go postal on the asshole, especially after he stuck a dog collar around his neck and controlled him like a slave."

He nods thoughtfully. "That may be it, but I can't help thinking there's something more. You know I have access to all the ship's security, and one of the programs shows movement of the performers and crew around the ship. Now, I haven't really looked at it since everyone else is still on holiday, but I accidentally pulled it up yesterday. That ship that shadowed us all the way to the station made me nervous, and I wanted to make sure there were no unauthorized people on the vessel."

"I'm assuming there aren't because you haven't said anything."

"No, but it shows the movements of people who are over the last few days. Most of the movement has been between this floor and the next and everyone's suites. It shows you and the warlocks in Xavier's old suite, Link's clinic, and movement in the Aquilian pool, which is expected. It also shows Silac returning Nikos's pod to the equipment room, but what surprised me the most was Brannock's movement. He has been all over the ship at weird times, mostly in the middle of the night when I thought he was taking his turn at the helm while I was asleep."

I purse my lips and frown, my stomach rolling with nerves, and Bubby continues. "The ship was on autopilot, so it was just a matter of watching the screens for any anomalies, but he seems to be making a systematic search of the ship, like he's looking for something specific."

"Fuck. Is Brannock looking for the orb? Has he lulled us into a sense of trust, and he's really going to fuck us over? But how would he know it's on the ship?" My grandpas decided Bubby was trustworthy enough to be brought in on the secret, and we were just going to need more help if the Syndicate was after it. It helped that Xavier has spelled him to never be able to talk about it. I still haven't told the cats about it, and Silac, Tirrian, and Brannock also don't know about it either—or I didn't think they did.

"I don't know. It could be that he's restless and just wanted to explore the ship and get to know it. He has been super grateful to you and your grandpas for offering him somewhere to live and giving him something to do until he can get back to Earth. If he settled anywhere else, he would have had to continue to wear his glamour, but everyone here just accepts him despite the Aaz'axian's fearsome reputation."

I shrug. "I judge people individually, not as a race. If I did, I certainly wouldn't have a warlock husband. They are kind of assholes. Okay, let's keep an eye on him. Silac just increased the security on the ship, specifically my grandpas' new room and the safe inside it. I'm assuming that's where they hide the orb. They've actually never even told me. If he seems to be showing too much interest in that room, we will confront him."

"It will be disappointing if he's been scamming us this whole time. I like him," Bubby says over the top of his coffee before taking another sip.

I sigh. "Yeah, I do too."

CHAPTER TWENTY

Lila

I debated what to wear but decided to go with my Galaxy Circus uniform. You can't hide that big of a ship docked at the station, and the cloth is supposed to be pretty resistant to weapons. If only I had known that when I had been practicing the cat whip, I would have worn it then.

Unlike the others who Xavier teleported where they need to be, I have to disembark the traditional way. There's an alien waiting at the end of the walkway, and he demands that I sign a waiver before I go any farther. I was already nervous to begin with, but when I read that it's a waiver that says they can't be held liable for the injury, dismemberment, or sudden death, my nerves really kick into overdrive. I quickly sign it, but my hand hovers over my laser gun in my holster. I didn't have to hand it over, but the alien did say I was responsible for any damage to the space station caused by me firing my weapon.

He then moved on to the next waiting ship, and I went on my way. Once I leave the space port and walk down a narrow hallway, the sounds and smells get louder and more offensive the farther I go.

When I step out onto the main platform, I stop and stare in surprise. I'm not sure why I'm surprised. I was warned, but there is a brawl going on in front of me, and it seems to involve anyone in the vicinity. I shuffle backward and put my back to the wall, protecting it as I watch on in wide-eyed horror as people stab, shoot, punch, and kick, not caring at all about the bodies littering the floor. I'm not sure if they are dead or just bleeding except for the four-armed being that is missing a head. I'm almost certain he's seen his last fight, but then again, I could be wrong. Maybe his head can regrow.

My stomach rolls, and I fight to keep my recently drank coffee from reappearing. Suddenly, an alarm blares and short, barrel-chested blue security officers appear from another hallway. They seem to have stun weapons, because they point them at all the participants, and they drop to the ground and start to twitch. I watch in awe as they then proceed to grab a foot in each hand and drag them all away.

"Are you okay, miss?" one of them asks me through a mouthful of gnarly teeth. His face is bumpy with ridges and dips, but despite his terrifying appearance, his eyes are kind.

"Ah, yeah, I just arrived and kind of walked into it."

"You weren't hurt?" he asks, looking me up and down, and his eyes widen when they stop on the Galaxy Circus logo on my uniform. "The circus is here? We're not your usual stop," he says, starting to look a little suspicious.

"Oh, no, the circus is on hiatus. I'm here on personal business. The uniform has protective qualities, so that's why I wore it."

The suspicion clears. "Good thinking. You can't be too careful of the rascals and rogues on this station. Well, my name's Glup. If you need any help, just ask for me at the security phones located at any of the establishments. I know any of us would be happy to escort you in exchange for a couple of tickets to the show."

I chuckle under my breath. Of course he's not being altruistic. "Thank you, I'm fine. I'm meeting someone at the Poison Hideaway," I tell him. "But if you could show me how to get there, then I'm sure I can have a few tickets made available to the hard-working security of Z68."

He beams at me, his yellow teeth sharp, but I don't feel particularly threatened. "Right this way, madam. Oh, wait until I tell the boys. They will be so excited. The Galaxy Circus is always sold out, and it's pretty expensive for a guard."

"Really? I've only just joined, so I don't really know anything about the pricing. I'll talk to my grandpas about it. It might be something we need to look at so we can help the average space person be able to go too. Maybe we can have discount nights."

He stops and looks at me. "What did you say your name was?"

"Oh, sorry, Glup, I'm Lila Adams," I tell him, holding out my hand.

He stares at it in surprise before his eyes narrow slightly, and I can practically see the wheels turning in his mind. Fuck, did I do something wrong?

Instead of shaking it, he kind of does this bow curtsy thing. "The Adams brothers' granddaughter and a mimic. It is my honor to meet you," he murmurs before straightening. "I have heard so many things about you. The galaxy is riddled with gossip regarding the new Skarrian mimic that has appeared. If you'll just follow me, I will personally escort you to the Poison Hideaway."

Shit, maybe I should have lied about who I was, but I hadn't expected any rumors or knowledge of my existence, let alone my powers, would have traveled this far so fast.

"Why don't you have an escort? This is no place for a lone woman, a beautiful and powerful one at that. Someone with your powers is worth a gold mine to the wrong people."

I grimace and shrug. "I'm not actually that powerful. I can only take a couple of extra forms. Every time I try another, I get sick. I guess being a whisperer as well has canceled out the mimic abilities," I lie out of my ass as we make our way through the station. It's not as chaotic as the original brawl I stumbled upon, but still eye-opening. We pass a group of men gathered at some sort of cage and watch as they place bets on the animals fighting inside it. When pink, viscous liquid flies in an arc, I avert my eyes.

"Really? Even more reason for someone to escort you."

"Well, between you and me…" I lean in like I'm confiding in him, and his eyes sparkle with excitement. "I'm meeting someone, and I was told that I had to come alone, or the meeting would be off. I need the information this being has."

He tuts and shakes his head. "Still, you make sure you're careful. How about I stay just outside the establishment and watch your back from there? I'm station security, so I could just say I was doing my job," he offers, and I smile, but I'm guessing he has ulterior motives, so I'm going to beat him to the punch, even though I don't need him because my guys are undercover, and I can quite easily defend myself. He doesn't know that, though, and not accepting his help may seem suspicious.

"Would you? That would be wonderful," I gush, patting the little man on the shoulder. "I'm sure I could arrange for you to receive a lifetime ticket to the circus." I don't even know if there is such a thing, but the greedy little man seems convinced as he rubs his hands together.

"Oh yes, make it a double pass, and you have a deal," he counters, and I almost roll my eyes. What an idiot. He was the one who offered in the first place.

The rest of our trek through the station is spent dodging fights and ignoring catcalls and propositions, each one more disgusting than the last. I feel dirty and gross when we finally make it to my destination. "This is one of the better establishments, but it's still not great. You should be able to have a drink without getting ill, but I would avoid the food," he tells me, waving an arm. "I'll just be out here if you need me. Once you're done, I can escort you back to your ship," he promises and moves to the side, making himself comfortable against the wall.

"Thank you, Glup. Hopefully I won't be too long," I tell him as I walk into the bar. Some of the bars and restaurants we passed on the way were gross and kind of scary. I didn't regret having Glup with me because people seemed to take one look at him and avert their gazes. No matter Glup's motivations, I'm kind of grateful to have him with me.

This place looks like a little old English pub with low lighting and wooden decor. I stop just inside the entrance and look around. There's a rowdy group of shifters in the corner, whom I recognize as my guys in glamour. I let my eyes slide past them, not wanting to look too suspicious. There is a hooded individual in another booth on the opposite side of the bar from where my guys are. I can't make out any features, but he looks to be quite tall and bulky if the shape of the hooded cape lends any clue. Nope, that isn't one of my guys. I wonder if it's my contact. Link didn't give me any clues. I see the head lift to look at me, but when he shows no movement in my direction, I dismiss him. If he was waiting for me, I'm sure he would call out or wave.

I move on to a couple snuggling in a booth just past the entrance, but when I peer a little closer through the dark, it's not actually a couple, but a vampire with his fangs in his partner. The partner's head is tossed back in ecstasy, and I can see the vamp stroking him through his pants. Holy shit, Saxon and Link are really selling their disguise. I kind of want to hurry over to the booth and sink my own fangs into the other side of Link's neck, or better yet, ride him to completion while Saxon continues to feed.

A customer entering behind me gives me a

shove, shaking me from lust-filled stupor. "Out of the way," they growl and take a seat at the bar, calling for the bartender's attention. I think that was Brannock, but I didn't get a good look as he went past. Someone at a table in the back stands up and shouts, waving his hand. I start to move toward him, but the man who shoved me out of the way calls back and gestures that he's just getting a drink. "Bring the pretty lady with you. I bet she smells like sunshine." The leering man at the table has an eye patch and a scar, and he waggles his forked tongue at me. Xavier is such a freaking ham.

I smile wanly and shake my head. There are a few more occupied tables, but nobody is paying any attention to me or giving any sign that they are waiting for someone. Crap. I'm going to sit at a table and wait. Maybe my contact is running late, and he'll find me. I can't even consider the possibility that I've been stood up. Brannock claims we need the halla harvester or at least know what they do to survive. If not, we're as good as dead on that planet.

I take a seat in the back corner, not far from the lone hooded man. Here, I'm equal distance from all my bodyguards if things go pear-shaped. I scan the menu screen, looking for something to order, and find a Coke. Who would have thought I'd find an Earth item this far into space? When I look at the price, though, I nearly swallow my tongue. Holy shit. One thousand galactic credits. The rest of the galaxy works on galactic credits, which makes things a lot easier. I use my wrist communicator to order the Coke. It's ridiculous, but I have the money, and I hope it's fairly safe for me. I can't really look to the guys for advice.

Once that's done, I take another look around the room, hoping maybe I missed someone, but everyone seems to be occupied except for the large, hooded figure across from me. I study him for a moment. I don't think they are looking at me, but it's hard to tell because there's just a dark space beneath the hood. I don't know if this being doesn't actually have a head or if they are just shrouded in the darkness of the hood. Movement behind him has my eyes jolting up. The whole back of his cape is wiggling and moving in agitation, a little like my cat's tail does, but this is a whole lot more. I choose to look away, not willing to find out if it's my staring agitating the being or something else.

A chime sounds, a small gap opens in the table, and my drink pops up. I chuckle with pleasant surprise. It looks exactly like a glass bottle of Coke I'd get on Earth. The color is right, and it is sparkling with carbonation out of the top of the open bottle. Hopefully nobody spiked it with anything, but the guys are all here, so I have to trust them to get to me if anything happens. As I reach for it, there's a flurry of movement at the entrance to the bar. I stop what I'm doing and look up, hoping it may be the person I'm here for.

I stop and stare in shock, unable to help myself. I've seen a lot of interesting creatures, but none of them have made me say, "What the fuck?" quite like this one. He looks like a corn cob grew a face and started moving around. Seriously, his arms and legs are shaped like the elegant leaves of a corn husk, and when he moves, it's in a rambling gait. There is no discerning between body and head, he's just one piece, but it's segmented like kernels of corn, just more round than square. His coloring is unusual. His arms and legs are the dark green of an avocado skin, but the rest of his body is a mottled green, like a brussels sprout. If this is one of the halla harvesters, he must be well camouflaged on Husadavia. Maybe that's the trick to surviving.

I don't want to stand up and wave in case I'm not who he's looking for and I embarrass myself, so I finally take a sip of my Coke and wait. A wide smile crosses my lips at the familiar taste, and a sense of rightness flows through me. Things can't be all bad if they have Coke.

When I look up again, the corn man is heading in my direction. My heartbeat increases, and I sit up straighter in my chair. Here we go.

"Lila Adams?" The voice that comes out of him almost has me bursting with laughter. It's high-pitched and kind of girlie, but I manage to keep my shit together and nod, gesturing to the chair in front of me.

"Yes. Would you like a drink?" I ask him, and he shakes his… body, looking around with nerves. Suddenly, his body shudders, and one of his kernels bursts, and I shit you not, an honest to goodness piece of green popcorn-like substance drops to the ground. I blink in shock before peering under the table. "Do you need that?" I ask, pointing to the bit that just exploded and fell off him.

"No. Did you bring the money?" He ignores my question, still not taking a seat, and he's casing the joint like a junky coming off a three-day bender.

"Money?" I ask him just as a message appears on my communication screen. It's from Link. I don't look up to where he and Saxon are, but instead, I read what it says.

We're paying him a hundred thousand credits for the information.

"We're what?" I shout, but the creature in front of me jumps and starts to back away. Shit. "Ah, yup, I do. I just have to transfer it to your selected account," I tell him quickly, not wanting him to bolt. He twitches a little more, and another kernel explodes, this time off of his back, and drops to the floor.

"Fine." He holds out his long green limb, and I notice there's a communication device much like mine on the end of his wrist.

"Information first," I argue, not completely stupid and naïve. I don't have any doubt the minute I pay this guy, he will disappear.

I can sense him fighting with himself on whether he's going to tell me anything or cut his losses and leave. This is no calm and collected person here to share information with me, but someone who looks like they are terrified of whatever he is about to tell me.

"Okay, how about I ask questions, and you answer them? How do you harvest the halla fruit without dying?"

I mean, it's why I'm here, right?

He glances around once more, and I do the same. What is he looking for? The room's occupants are either here for me or fairly innocuous. I frown in surprise as I notice the table across from me is now empty. I didn't even see the large, hooded being leave. Aw man, I really wanted to see what he looked like under that hood. But how did I miss it? There's only one entrance.

"Zeygan has some power I've never seen before," he mutters under his breath.

"Zeygan?" I ask.

"Our boss. He just stands there, and nothing approaches us while we harvest the fruit."

My heart sinks as he imparts this knowledge.

"I thought you were the leader of the halla

harvesters. That's what we were told. That you were the one who could give us information."

He sneers, "I gave you information. I didn't promise you any success." He slams his hand against mine, and I hear a beep as the funds transfer. Quicker than I can react, he tries to leave the bar, but of course my guys are prepared. Saxon uses his speed and stops the being in his tracks, and Xavier appears, still wearing his glamour, and freezes him on the spot. I don't doubt all of them overheard the disappointing conversation. I don't think they are going to have any luck, since he doesn't seem to know anything, but maybe we can get more information about this mysterious Zeygan.

"I'll take him back to the ship and see if we can't extract more information from him," Xavier tells me.

"Try to find out when he has to be at work next. If I have to, I can mimic him and take his place. I guess that's the next best possible solution." I'm trying not to panic. Our rescue mission just took a step in the wrong direction, but we've got this. Between me and my guys, I'm sure we will come up with a solution.

CHAPTER TWENTY-ONE

Lila

Sighing with disappointment, I make my way out of the Poison Hideaway feeling defeated. Xavier teleported everyone back to the ship, since technically none of them have permission to be on the station.

"Ah, Lila, there you are." I startle slightly, having forgotten about the security guard who was watching my back. "I hope your meeting was successful?" he asks politely.

"Unfortunately, it wasn't as successful as I hoped," I tell him, sounding defeated.

"Oh no, is there anything I can help you with?" he asks, concern shining in his eyes, and I shake my head.

"Unless you know the secret to surviving on Husadavia, then there's nothing you can do."

His eyes widen comically, and he shakes his head emphatically. "You're not thinking of going on the planet, are you? That's a death sentence. Nobody goes there and survives unless it's the halla harvesters."

"Unfortunately, I have no other option. That guy was one of the harvesters, and I was hoping he could tell me what they do to survive. Oh well, I need to get back to my ship so we can figure something else out." I start to walk back in the direction we came from, and he shakes his head.

"Let's go this way, and you can tell me what the harvester had to say." Glup points in the opposite direction, and I stop.

"But the ship's back that way." I point, and he smiles and winks.

"Yes, but I know a shortcut through some security guard tunnels." He takes off, and I decide to follow him. He's been super helpful so far. "So, what did the harvester say to you? I've heard all sorts of rumors about Husadavia. They say it's one of the first planets the old gods created, and it's been around for so long, that's why the plants and animals have become sentient and aggressive."

"Old gods?" I ask him as he opens a panel in the wall that I hadn't noticed and steps through. This tunnel is a lot narrower, and the lighting is dim. I hesitate for a moment but then step through. Glup has been helpful, and I want to hear about the old gods. He starts moving forward. The tunnel isn't wide enough for us to walk abreast, so I stay behind him, but his voice carries back to me.

"Yes, the galaxy is said to be created by six original gods—life, death, fire, water, earth, and air. They had names, but they seem to have been forgotten over the years and are known by their element. Each of them began with one planet for themselves, but then it became a bit of a competition to see who could create the most interesting planets. Then, they added life-forms who worshiped them, and all was right in the galaxy. Everyone existed in peace for thousands of years, each planet growing at their own pace, influenced by the gods who were happy to watch their creations evolve and grow, but one day, they just disappeared. Nobody knows what happened, they were just gone. Whether the six beings had a falling out and went their separate ways, or they moved on to a new galaxy to start the process all over again, no one knows, but over the years, the planets kept evolving and their memory became legends and stories. Husadavia is supposed to be the home realm for the earth god. The plants and animals were his companions, and that's why they are sentient. They are aggressive because he left them, but they are keeping his world safe for his eventual return."

Wow, Glup just gave me more information than the halla harvester did. "How come this information isn't anywhere? We've been doing as much research as we can on Husadavia, and this didn't come up anywhere."

Glup turns back to me and rolls his eyes. "The Galactic Council doesn't like rumors of the old gods. They control the galaxy now, and if the old gods were to return, they would lose their grip on everything. They believe if the old gods are mentioned, it will turn their attention back to this galaxy from wherever they are, so over the years, they have slowly withdrawn all mention of them from any records. Only stories, which are passed down from family members, keep the legends going."

He keeps moving down the tunnel, his short legs covering the distance quickly, I almost have to jog to keep up with him. "Does the name Zeygan mean anything to you?" I ask, and he stumbles, pressing a hand to the wall to right himself, and he turns back, wide-eyed and jittery.

"Zeygan is the original name of the earth god. Husadavia was his home planet."

Holy fuck. Could the person the halla harvester was talking about be one of the old gods? He said he just stood there, and the inhabitants would stay away. That certainly points to the old god. Or is he just named for the old god and has some repellent type powers? None of this speculation is going to help us rescue my grandmother, and I don't think my grandpas are going to wait much longer. We may be making an attempt without any assistance.

All of this has been running through my head as I follow Glup. He gets to the end of the tunnel and pushes open another hidden door. Glup steps out, and I follow him, still distracted by everything I learned. I hear voices but don't pay any attention until I realize Glup has stopped. I look around, and my mouth drops open in shock. Everything I was thinking about disappears as I take in the creatures surrounding us.

I can't believe my eyes. These are life-sized motherfucking Care Bears. They are shaggy, brightly colored bears with round bellies exaggerated by the circular white patch in the middle of it. All that's missing is the symbol in the middle of the white circle. The one talking to Glup is unlike the others in that he isn't a solid color, but a kaleidoscope of colors, almost like the limited-edition tie-dye Care Bear I wanted when I was a kid. Instead of pastel colors, though, he's bright, but when I tune into the conversation, it's nothing like my Saturday morning cartoons.

"Is this the bitch we can fuck girl babies into?" The lead bear is handing something that looks suspiciously like cash over to Glup, who rubs his greedy motherfucking little hands together before taking it.

"Yes, this is the mimic. Rumor is she can take

on any form. She should be able to be a female carevasta bear and give you girl babies."

"Glup, you asshole," I snarl and try to take my warlock form, but one of the bears quickly leaps forward and snaps a bracelet onto my wrist. My power disappears, and I stagger, my body suddenly feeling drained. He wraps his arms around me and holds me upright. His blue fur is soft, and I just want to snuggle into it and breathe him in. My mind struggles with my reaction. I should be fighting him, but all I want to do is get closer. As I go to rest my head back and lean into him, his hands come up, and he gropes my breasts.

"Her tits feel amazing," he growls. He thrusts his hips into mine, and a wave of desire rushes over me. I squeeze my legs together to try and ease the ache that's now there.

"That's my bitch. Take your fucking hands off her before I blow your fucking head off." The bear who handed over the cash stomps over to the one who holds me and yanks me out of his arms and into his, pointing his gun at the bear who was fondling me. I stumble and find myself pressed firmly up against his body. Despite the round belly, the rest of his body feels solid, and his fur feels amazing against my exposed skin. I bury my face into his chest. "When I'm finished with her, you can all have your turn. She's going to keep us very happy for years to come. Good work, Glup."

"You better leave. The circus ship is here. I don't know who else is on it, but I heard she has a Vilaxian and a warlock mate. You don't want to fuck with the warlocks or the Vilaxians. I'll try to detain their ship for a few hours so you can get away, but I can't promise longer than that."

The bear scoops me up bridal style and starts to move. I can hear the others follow behind us, but I can't bring myself to lift my face out of his fur. I'm squirming, trying to get some kind of friction where I need it, and a whimper comes out of my mouth.

"Ah, my bitch needs my cock. You are all the same, easy conquests for me and my boys. Just wait until we get to our ship. I will stuff your pussy full of my cock and cum, and you will love it." Oh yes, I really like the sound of that.

"Why don't you finger fuck her while we walk, Ghosie? Bitches love that. I always make mine come on my fingers when we catch them, and then her cunt will be ready for your cock when we get back to the ship," the blue bear suggests.

I look up into the eyes of the one who has me. Holy crap, his irises are multicolored like his fur, but I see his eyes narrow in annoyance before a growl rips from his mouth, making me shudder.

"Fuck off, Lizis. This is my bitch, and I will do what I want with her. I want to strip her down and suck on her pretty titties to get her ready for my cock and then maybe shove my tongue into her cunt and drink up all the delicious juice first, and only then, when she is begging for my cock, will I bend her over and fuck her hard."

"Yes please," I whimper, because I really like the sound of that, but I guess everyone behind us hears me, because they all laugh loudly.

"You've got your bitch begging from just your words. She wants your cock now. How about we stop, and you can fuck her here and now." That's Lizis again, and I have to admit, I like his suggestion, but Ghosie obviously doesn't, to my disappointment.

He whirls and steps up to the blue bear. "Lizis, you fucking idiot. Her people will realize she's gone soon, and we want to be on the other side of the galaxy when they do. Her Vilaxian and warlock mate are probably enough to destroy our small crew in moments. We need to get back to the main ship. I can wait a few more moments until we get to our ship before I get my cock wet."

Lizis is leering at me with greed, but he takes a step back. "I want a turn too. You're going to knock her up and keep her to yourself while she carries your baby. I want a turn before you do."

The other five bears in the group exchange glances before quickly agreeing with the blue bear, but Ghosie just holds me closer to his chest, emitting a continuous growl.

"You're all fucking morons. How will I know it's

my baby if you spill your cum in her cunt?" He whirls around and starts moving a little faster, but I can't take my eyes off his face. Unlike the cute, rounded features of a Care Bear, this guy has sharp cheekbones with the cutest button nose, and plump lips that I want to sink my teeth into.

"Hey, this was my idea. You didn't even know about her until I heard about her from one of those last whores we picked up from X69. While I was fucking her, she told me all about the mimic who could give us girl children. I rewarded her well by fucking her extra hard and often until she was full of my cum. She's a warlock, they always produce extra strong sons for us, but I should get first dibs. I want a daughter for my son to play with."

"Fuck off. I'm the leader, and it's my right to have first dibs on any bitch we get. You know that. If you don't shut up now, I will skip right over you and give her to someone else once she has my child. Unless you'd like to challenge me for leadership?"

We come to a sudden stop. I look around and find no ship or door or tunnel leading anywhere. We're just facing a random wall.

"Are you so eager to die before you can feel this one's pussy wrapped around your cock?" Ghosie raises an eyebrow at Lizis, who seems to be considering it.

"Don't be an idiot, Lizis. You know it's a fight to the death and no one has beaten Ghosie in years.

Be patient, you'll get sloppy seconds, and you should be grateful. The rest of us have to wait our turn." Another of the bears punches Lizis's arm.

"Bah, you don't have any other children, so you're probably shooting blanks. None of the women you've fucked have ended up pregnant. If it doesn't happen in a month, I want the next go. I'll have her knocked up in no time. My fifteen sons prove I have the goods."

I feel Ghosie tighten his arms around me. "Fine. Why don't you all go find a bitch to ease the ache? But be quick, we are leaving in ten minutes."

This seems to mollify the rest of the crew who disappear before my eyes, leaving me and Ghosie still facing a blank wall. I feel his body relax minutely, and he mutters, "Fuck," before I feel his body start to vibrate, which in turn vibrates me in his arms as well, and then he just moves through the wall, taking me with him.

It's creepy as fuck but over in seconds. I look around, and we seem to be in a vessel of some sort. Ghosie doesn't say anything, just starts moving quickly through the ship. He gets to another group of five bears who are sitting around a table, playing dice or cards or something. They all seem to have a bottle of alcohol in their hands. Shouts and jeers sound out as they continue to play the game. I see movement under the table and discover one of them has a woman at his feet, and although I can't make out details through the fur, I think she's giving him a blow job.

"Pack this shit in. We need to be ready to leave in ten minutes. There will be a ship riding our ass across the galaxy if we're not careful. I want you to plot a course to the Tarllion Asteroid belt. Our smaller ship should be able to lose them in there."

"Is that the mimic bitch?" One of the bears, this one a sickly shade of green, looks at me with wide-eyed amazement. "Why haven't you made her mimic you yet? I want to see what a female carev-asta looks like."

"Fuck off. We haven't had time. I'll make sure to parade her around as soon as we get far enough away. Now get to your fucking jobs and leave me in peace. I'm going to have her riding my cock in no time."

The rest of the bears cheer and start to move, taking their bottles of spirits with them. The one getting a blow job yanks his female up by her hair before kissing her soundly on the mouth.

"That's a good bitch. Go back to our room, and I'll be there shortly," he promises her, and she simpers and totters away drunkenly.

"Don't let her out of your sight for too long. I hate it when the fog clears and they start scream-ing," Ghosie warns him. "It's enough to make a cock go soft."

"Aye, Captain. I'll make sure she's good and

fogged as soon as I program the coordinates for the course."

"Excellent. Don't disturb me until we get to the asteroid field," he demands, and the bear leers and winks.

"Good luck, Captain. May her pussy be wet and tight."

CHAPTER TWENTY-TWO

Lila

My brain is foggy, and my body aches with need as Ghosie carries me farther into the ship. I rub my body against his. His silky fur is deliciously soft, and I can't wait to rub my naked body against him.

He enters his room and gently lowers me to my feet before stepping back against the door. I start to chase after him, but he holds his hand up. "Wait, just give it a moment."

I'm confused. What is he talking about? Doesn't he want me? I feel a tear trickle down my cheek, the ache in my body acute. My hands come up to cup my breasts, trying to ease the heaviness I feel.

"Please," I beg and start to step toward him.

"No," he shouts, and that seems to have some effect. "Just stay over there." He's almost pleading with me at this stage, so I stay where I am.

Now that I'm no longer in his arms, it doesn't

take long for the foggy feeling to fade and the ache to dissipate until I'm clear-headed again and fucking mad.

"What the fuck?" I look around the room and find I'm in a bedroom. The bed is neatly made, and the room is tidy, which is a big difference from the room we just left. It was filthy and messy with dirty plates and cups and trash everywhere.

"I'm sorry. It was the best I could do with short notice."

"What the hell are you talking about?" I am so fucking confused.

"You are Lila Adams, the new Skarrian mimic, aren't you?" Gone is the foul-mouthed asshole, and in his place is a quiet, softly spoken, polite male.

"Yes, but you already knew that because that traitorous weasel Glup told you."

"Yes, Glup contacted Lizis. They have a trans-actional agreement. Glup tells him when there are interesting females on the station, and Lizis pays him to turn a blind eye when we arrive and procure them."

"Procure them? You mean you steal them," I retort, and he has the grace to blush but doesn't argue.

There are so many questions running through my head. I start pacing back and forth, avoiding the bear who watches me with bright eyes.

"What was that?" I ask, pointing to my body,

and he sighs, knowing exactly what I mean. "I wanted you to bend me over and show me your one-eyed Care Bear stare." He frowns, and I know my words have confused him. "Your cock," I clarify, and he nods with understanding.

"Our fur has aphrodisiac pheromones, and as long as you are touching it, you will feel needy."

"So you just take women and roofie them with that soft as fuck fur and then keep them?"

He sighs, running agitated hands down his body, trying to smooth his fur, but he's having no luck, and it continues to stand up like it has a mind of its own. It's actually freaking adorable, but I refuse to smile while I'm so fucking angry.

"Yeah, it's our way," he says, shrugging. He leans his body against the door, which makes his round belly stick out a little bit more. "It's always been our way for as long as I can remember. Some say we were cursed by a vindictive goddess. Once upon a time, we had females of our species, and long ago, one of our rulers got arrogant and used his fur to seduce this goddess away from her mate. She insulted him, and he wanted revenge. When she came out of her fog, she placed a curse on all of us. The only way we would ever be able to find mates was to coerce them. We would never know the feeling of true love. The pheromones, which were once voluntary, became something we had no control over, and our female population slowly dwindled until there were none. We had no other options. A lot of us don't like our way, but without it, our species will die out." He sounds so sad, and I find my anger waning. "You can't change a whole society overnight, and as you saw, there are many who embrace our ways now."

"And you're hoping I will be able to fix that for you?"

He closes his eyes, and I see his body stiffen as his fur sticks out even more. "There are many of us who believe you are the answer to our prayers. We have been searching the galaxy far and wide for a mimic to help us, but until now, we haven't been able to find one. I didn't want this. I wanted to find another way, but I was overruled. If I hadn't claimed you as mine, they would have passed you around without a care."

"They can't force me to mimic them," I argue, and he just looks at me, shaking his head sadly.

"Did you feel what touching me did to you? You would do anything to please me, and all I would have done is ask you to mimic me, and you would have done it."

I shudder because he's not wrong. "So why did you let the fog wear off?" I ask, and now it's his turn to start pacing.

"Because I don't want this. I don't want to force you. I want you to contact your mates and tell them where you are. We have a few more minutes because I sent them off to steal more women. They are occupied."

"Why?" I question, still so confused.

"Because you don't deserve this. None of the women who get stolen by us do."

"But you keep doing it," I point out, and he throws his hands up in agitation.

"I've never fucked any of them. I've always let the fog wear off, and in exchange, they agree to pretend."

"That's what the douchebag blue bear meant by you shooting blanks?" I ask, trying to make sense of everything I heard while I was foggy.

"Yes. Now stop asking questions and call your mates to you."

I hold out the hand that has the power dampening bracelet on it. "But how? I can't with this thing on me."

Ghosie stares at the offending piece of metal in dismay. "I can't let you use the ship's communication because they will know what happened. Fuck."

"Don't panic, we can think of something," I tell the stressed bear who has started to pluck his fur with distress.

"How can I not panic? If you aren't off this ship before it leaves port, then all is lost. They are not going to be satisfied with trusting me. Lizis has been eyeing my leadership position for a long time now. If any of them have reason to doubt my loyalty or question my allegiance, I'm as good as dead. They will want to see you in your carevasta form. They may even demand to watch me fuck you."

"It's fine. We can work something out. I just need to work on getting this bracelet off." Then something occurs to me. "I can't mimic."

"What do you mean?" he asks, and I wave my hand with the bracelet on. "I can't mimic your form without you removing the bracelet or at least deactivating it."

His eyes widen, and a smile creeps across his lips, and holy shit, the bear is handsome. His dad bod just makes me want to snuggle into him and wind my legs around his waist and... Nope. What the actual fuck, Lila? There must be something wrong with me. I can't be thinking that way about the life-sized version of my favorite stuffed toy. No, it must be some weird, repressed shit that occurred when I lost my parents and ended up in the foster home, bouncing from family to family with only my friendship bear for company. Yeah, we're not even going to touch that.

"Okay, yes, we can work with this. Straun has the controller for that. When they arrive, I will demand it from him. Then, as soon as I deactivate it, you can call your mates here or teleport out or whatever it is you can do to get away from us." He sounds happy now, and I notice as he turns away from me to pace in the other direction that he has a short, stumpy little tail, and it's wagging furiously with this information. Oh my god, it's fucking adorable. I just want to scratch his big belly and watch it wag for me.

Fucking focus, Lila. "I can probably telepathically tell my warlock mate to come and get me, but what's going to happen to you?" I ask him.

His tail stops wagging, and he turns back to face me. "You're going to have to knock me out, and I can say your warlock got the drop on me."

"Do you think they will believe that?" I ask him, and he shrugs.

"It won't matter as long as you're safe." Fuck, now he's being sweet too.

"What will happen to you?"

"Lizis will probably challenge me for leadership. It's a death match, but I've been challenged before, and hopefully I will live to be challenged again. The big issue is if there is mutiny because I lost the first real chance we had at fixing our society. I wouldn't survive that. Then again, I was surprised they were so insistent in trying to capture you. I thought most of them liked our ways. I'm not sure if they realize things will change if they actually have female bears to mate with, but then with how our pheromones work, I doubt things will be different except we can mate with our own species. I'm sure most of them will still take away their choices. There is a large portion of our society who really takes advantage of it. Most of our males will only use their gifts occasionally when they want to have children. Some of us have never used it." He won't look me in the eye when he says this and busies himself at the communication panel of his room when it suddenly lights up.

Shut the front door. Is he saying what I think he's saying? "Are you saying you've never used your gift to have sex?"

"That would be dishonorable," he says without looking back at me. "I want a woman to see the real me, not the foggy version my fur would cause her to see and feel and want."

"Are you saying you've never had sex?"

He scoffs and shakes his head before turning back to face me. "I'm a romantic but not stupid. I've had my share of male lovers."

"Ah, okay, but never had sex with a female? How do you know you'd even want one? That you aren't gay?"

"Because when my hormones are fogging those women I've struck deals with, and they've rubbed themselves all over my body, my dick gets very happy," he says somewhat dryly, and I guess he has a point. "They are back, and they are demanding to see you. Are you ready for this? You'll be under the influence of my pheromones, and I'll try to move away from you once they remove the bracelet."

"It's fine. I'll be okay," I assure him.

"I apologize for everything that comes out of my mouth, but I have a role to play if we're going to make this work."

I wave my hand at him. "Don't worry about me. I will play my part, and if, for some reason, I can't get away, you do what you have to do to keep us both safe. I won't be upset if you have to cop a feel or if you have to do something to reassure your crew that you're serious about this. Just don't let me be passed around."

"What if they demand a demonstration?" he asks, looking me in the eye.

"If we can get the bracelet deactivated, we won't even need to worry about it." I sigh and think about what he's really asking. Would this be considered cheating? I find myself incredibly attracted to this bear. I can still feel my kraken inside of me even though I can't shift into her form, and she is fully on board with helping the bear in whatever capacity he requires. My whisperer form is quiet, but that's no surprise—she is a two-cat woman—and I can feel that my mimic is intrigued. It wouldn't take much to convince my body to mimic Ghosie's form.

I think my mates would be okay with whatever happens, especially if it helped me escape. What they wouldn't be okay with is him taking my choice away from me, but he's not doing that, and I am grateful for that and happy to play along in any way.

"You do what you have to do to keep us safe. I am okay with that," I assure him, and he holds my eyes for a moment longer, really looking to see that I'm being honest.

"Okay, Lila. Let's go and put on a show. My life and your sanity depend on it."

"Wait." I hold up my hand as he steps toward me, and he freezes. I look down at the floor, a little nervous to ask for what I want. "Um, would you maybe kiss me before we go out there? I kind of feel like I need that before I can face all of them."

He inhales sharply. "You want me to kiss you?" he asks, the words flowing out in a hurry.

"Yeah, so we can, you know, get all the awkwardness out of the way, and we can perform authentically." Fuck, that excuse sounds lame even to my own ears. I kind of just want to feel his lips on mine. His sweet gentleness is attractive, and the fact that he's a virgin for females is a temptation.

He steps toward me, one side of his mouth quirking up slightly. "Just so we're not awkward, even though you'll be in a pheromone induced fog, right?" he asks, calling me out. Meh, I guess I kind of asked for it.

"Yeah, exactly." I'm not admitting anything.

"Okay, well, don't touch me. Just close your eyes and stand there with your hands behind your back," he demands, and I want to squirm on the spot, because his voice just got all growly and commanding, and I am so here for it, but I need to remember what's about to happen. I do as he asks, puckering my lips and closing my eyes with my hands firmly clasped behind my back. I want to be fog free for this.

I feel him lean in, his breath against my face, as he gives me little Eskimo kisses with his cute button nose. My lips tip up in joy. Just as I feel his lips ghost across mine, a buzzer sounds throughout his room.

"What the fuck are you doing in there? Pull your cock out of her cunt and get out here. We want to see what she looks like." The voice comes through speakers set somewhere.

My eyes snap open, and I see Ghosie glare at the door before sighing loudly. "Are you ready for this?" he asks, stepping back, and my heart sinks a little in disappointment, but I nod and pull the zipper down on my top, tossing it to one side of his room, before toeing my shoes off. I unfasten the button on my pants and shimmy them down my legs. Ghosie's eyes widen when I pull my hair out of my ponytail and shake it around, giving it that well fucked look.

"What are you doing?" he asks, almost sounding panicked, and I hold up a hand.

"Relax, dude, they think we've been fucking. I'm just setting the scene, and I didn't want you to feel bad for having to do it when I'm fogged." The panic clears, and I have just enough time to lean in and steal a kiss, my fingers burying into his fur before the door slides open. Ghosie is quick and drags me in, lifting me to wrap my legs around his body before turning with an annoyed glare aimed at the intruder as I feel the needy fog descend on my body.

"Oh God, you feel so good," I say as I rub my face on his furry chest. "Please stick that big cock in my pussy."

CHAPTER TWENTY-THREE

Ghosie

"Why hasn't she mimicked you yet?" Lizis demands, and it's all I can do to drag my attention off the little mimic rubbing herself against my body. Her delicious curves feel amazing under my paws.

"Because, you fucking idiot, we slapped a power dampening bracelet on her, and she can't access her powers. I've barely even had any time to have her suck my cock either. Fuck off so I can get to the fun part." It's all I can do to stop my cock from pushing out of its sheath.

Lizis narrows his eyes in suspicion. I'm pretty sure he was expecting me to be balls deep in Lila— he certainly would be, which is why I used my power as captain to overrule him. "I want to see the bitch become a carevasta bear. Glup says she claims she's low powered. I want proof before we start a chase across the galaxy."

"What the fuck?" I roar, pushing Lila away. I lunge at the blue idiot and shake him. "She can't even change forms? You've invited trouble, and you don't even know for sure that she can do what you said she can!" The rest of my crew have gathered in the hallway now, and they start muttering. I can hear the worry in their tones.

Lizis pushes me away. "Glup said he was sure she was lying." The stupid fuck defends himself to the rest of the crew, but I can see the worry on his face.

"You better fucking hope she was, or we instigated a fight we are unlikely to win." I point my finger at his chest before going back and grabbing Lila by the arm, dragging her out of my room and down the hallway to the filthy common area. She never mentioned anything about not being able to change forms, so I'm assuming what she told Glup was a lie, otherwise, she would have argued with me when she first became cognizant.

"Holy shit, look at the ass on that bitch. I bet you could bounce a galactic coin off that," I hear one of my bears say.

"I just want to rub my face against those delicious tits. That's a pair of tits a man could drown in," another one says wistfully, and neither of them are wrong. Lila's body is fucking incredible—all round curves and soft lines with an ass and breasts that are perfect handfuls of lushness. She's rubbing against me for all the wrong reasons, and I won't be despicable like a lot of my comrades and take her against her will.

We arrive in the common room, and the rest of my crew surrounds us. I point my finger at Straun. "Deactivate the power dampener," I order him, but he frowns, and I feel a moment of panic. He was always smarter than ninety percent of the rest of my crew.

"What's to stop her from teleporting away then?" he asks.

"Do we even know if she has teleporting abilities?" one of the others asks, eyeing the woman who is still pressed against me with need.

She's trying to climb my body, and I am having trouble focusing on the conversation. I've never allowed a woman to be fogged around me for long, only long enough to make sure the rest of the crew doesn't grow suspicious, and once I get to my room, I step back. Thankfully the rooms are sound-proofed, and I usually lock my fucking door—something I forgot to do this time in my haste.

"Do we want to risk it?" Straun looks at Lizis who is completely mesmerized by Lila. She is now on her knees, rubbing against my lower half, which I think is going to work to our advantage.

"Who cares? I want to see her take our form. We've been searching all our lives for a solution, and this is it. Now turn off the power dampening bracelet and force her to shift," he demands, not taking his eyes off the prize.

"How are we going to force her to shift? What's your big plan?" I grind out between clenched teeth. Lila's hands have started wandering, and she found my cock pocket. She's trying to reach into it, and my cock is trying to leap out and greet her. My pleasure nub is wriggling around, and I come on the spot as she swipes a finger through the sheath, brushing against it for the first time.

I watch on as Lizis holds out a hand and one of the other crew members puts a gun in it. He points it at Lila's head and puts his finger on the trigger. "I'm pretty sure she will cooperate now."

Fuck! Seeing him hold a gun to her head makes me want to go berserk and tear him to shreds. Why do I feel attached to this pretty little human? But maybe this is the opportunity we need. If we force her to shift, that may give her the time she needs to contact her mates.

I step back and grab hold of her hair, not allowing her to touch me. I watch as her gaze starts to clear and she looks around the room, her expression turning calculating before I see her eyes fill with fear.

"What do you want from me?" she whimpers, cowering away from me and eyeing the gun pointed at her head with fear. I'm almost certain it's an act, but all I want to do is reassure her that everything is going to be okay.

"Mimic my form," Lizis demands.

A roar escapes my lips, and I feel my hands tighten in Lila's pretty colored hair. "Not his, mine. This is my bitch, and she will mimic me," I tell him, my voice leaving no room for argument. A burning sensation on my back has me flinching for a moment, but I ignore it.

He sneers, "Fuck it, fine. I'll close my eyes when I fuck her. I don't want to see a multicolored mutt."

This has been a bone of contention all my life. I am the only bear I have ever seen with multicolored fur. All the other bears are a single color. Their shades vary, but the color is solid. It's why I'm such a good fighter. I had to learn to defend myself when I was a cub, and I learned quickly early on that in a species of all males, being bigger, badder, and willing to swing fists got me a lot further than being polite and kind.

"Do you understand what you need to do?" I ask Lila, who winces when I tug on her hair, but she nods.

"I can pull this trigger faster than you can assume any of your forms, so don't fuck around, and do as he says." Lizis waves his gun erratically. "If you even look to be something other than a carevasta, I will put a bullet in your brain, and we will shove you out to rot in space."

He's not fucking around. I just hope Lila is able to communicate with her mates over the short distance, because with everything that's happened, we haven't started moving yet. That is going to work in our favor. She didn't seem to think it would be a problem, so I just have to trust her.

Straun uses the little remote to deactivate the band around Lila's wrist. I can see the moment her power comes flooding back into her. Her entire body shudders, and she closes her eyes, looking like she's fighting an internal battle. Lizis pokes the gun against her temple, and when she opens her eyes and growls at him, they are pitch black, and she has fangs in her mouth.

"I am doing everything I can to stop my kraken from coming out to kill you, so have some fucking patience." Her eyes flash from black to red and back to black again, and her body shudders once more before she takes a long, deep breath, and when she opens her eyes this time, they are green again. "Okay, that battle is won for now. I sent the right message to my creatures," she says slowly as she looks at me, and I understand what she's saying. She sent an SOS to her mates, so hopefully they will be here shortly.

"I'll count to three, and you better fucking mimic Ghosie, or you'll be sorry." Lizis pushes against her head again.

She nods, and mist covers her body. When it

clears, she has changed completely. Gone are the soft, round curves of a human, and in their place is a female version of me, except her color is the same as her hair—pearlescent orange, pink, blue, and purple shimmer through her silver fur. She's fucking gorgeous.

"Stand up," Lizis demands, eyeing her and licking his lips.

She gets to her feet, and none of us can take our eyes away from the lush, chunky body standing before us. Her form is very similar to my own, but her belly is smaller and her chest region is bigger. She looks like she may have breasts, but all her fur is covering it. My eyes scan down her body, and I stop when I get to the white patch on her belly and stare in surprise. Sitting there is an image of a hand holding up a middle finger.

"What is that?" Lizis asks just as a haze starts to appear behind him. The rest of my crew sees it and steps backward as Lila starts to laugh.

"Sayonara, motherfucker." She lifts her middle finger to mirror the one on her belly as two figures appear behind Lizis. The one with the purple skin throws up his arms, and suddenly, I can't move. He's frozen us all. The other one with fangs similar to Lila's and flashing red eyes lifts his clawed hand and quickly draws it across Lizis's throat. Pale pink blood splatters across my and Lila's faces, and I see her grimace before licking her lips, her eyes lighting up.

"Holy shit, it tastes like strawberry candy." She steps forward and swipes a finger across the throat of a now gurgling Lizis before holding it out to the man who did it. "Taste, it's fucking amazing."

His eyes burn with intensity as he leans forward and sucks her finger into his mouth before licking it clean. He's not saying anything, but I can hear a menacing growl rumbling in his chest.

"Well, what kind of trouble have you gotten into now, *phoeall*?" The man who I can now tell is a warlock is laughing as he looks around the room before his eyes settle on Lila. "What the fuck is that?" he asks, pointing at the same thing Lizis had.

"It's my belly badge."

The two men exchange confused looks, and she throws up her arms in frustration. "Did you know we have cartoon characters on Earth that are very much like these?" She points at all of us, and again, the two figures exchange a glance.

"That's because we allowed them to do an Earth visit, and they drank too much and dropped their glamour charm. Thankfully the circus was able to play it off as a mass hallucination, but one of the victims used it for his own gain. That was before our time, but it's a cautionary tale to any other creatures who want to visit Earth," the warlock explains with a shrug.

"Well, those cartoons have symbols on their tummies—nice ones mostly, but I thought this was more fitting."

The warlock chuckles and moves over to Lila, waving his hand and cleaning the blood off her before giving her a hug. "You look like you've been busy." His eyes run the length of her, and I don't see any disgust, just heat, but she pulls away from him.

"Careful," she warns, "the fur has aphrodisiac qualities."

His eyes widen with surprise, and he looks impressed. "So that's how they coerced all those women. That's going to be fun to play with."

"Can I kill them all now?" the Vilaxian asks, dropping Lizis now that there is a puddle of pale pink blood on the ground. If I could move, I would probably clap him on the back in thanks. He has been a thorn in my backside for years.

"I think we're going to have to." The warlock nods at his friend, and my heart rate starts to race. I guess I knew there was always a chance I would end up dead whichever way I played this. I'm happy with my decision, because it means that Lila is safe, and none of my brethren will have knowledge of her. Luckily my crew was made up of greedy bastards, because we hadn't shared the knowledge with anyone yet, so as I make peace with my fate, Lila jumps in front of me.

"All but Ghosie. He was the one who was trying

to help me escape. It was his plan to get the power dampening bracelet off so I could contact you. He also could have taken advantage of me when I was in his arms, but he didn't," Lila explains, and the two of them regard me with different expressions. The Vilaxian still looks like he wants to eviscerate me, but the warlock looks intrigued. He waves a hand, and I'm unfrozen.

"Well, Ghosie, would you like to plead your case?" the warlock asks. "Why didn't you take advantage of Lila when you had a chance? Don't you think she's sexy?"

What the fuck? Did he want me to take advantage of her? I'm so fucking confused, and I stare at him in shock as I wipe Lizis's blood off my fur, but all that does is spread it around. Fuck, I'm going to need a shower.

"Xavier," Lila scolds and moves toward me, and I feel her fur brush against mine. Both of us shiver in unison. "Holy fuck. Did you feel that?" she asks, staring at me in shock.

My cock instantly turns rock-hard and tries to push out of its sheath. I put my paws in front of it to hide my reaction, but I don't think I'm fooling anyone.

"My guess is yes, he did." Xavier smirks, looking at my hands.

"Fuck, I almost orgasmed on the spot. Okay, maybe let's not touch while we want to have a coherent conversation." She sounds breathless, but not upset, as she takes a small step away from me. "Ghosie says there is a faction of bears who hate how they have to coerce women."

"Oh really?" The Vilaxian sounds skeptical, and I know I'm going to have to explain.

"Yes, but none of the bears on this ship are part of that faction. Would it make you feel better to kill them all first, and I can tell you my story after? Then, if you still don't trust me, I won't fight your decision." I'm risking my life here, but having Lila on my side is huge, and I am never going to be able to repay her for supporting me. I'm also having trouble keeping my eyes off her in front of her mates, because she's my version of a wet dream. "Maybe you should change back too," I suggest, and she smirks at me but does as I ask, except now she's naked, and that doesn't help my cock situation at all.

"Lila, you are such an exhibitionist," Xavier teases before waving a hand, clothing her in a Galaxy Circus uniform again. "Why don't you head back to the ship while we take out the trash?" he suggests, his teasing tone turning menacing as he turns his attention to the rest of my former crew. The Vilaxian's claws flex, and he bounces up and down on his toes.

"Actually, there are women somewhere on this ship whose minds are going to have to be wiped before they are returned to the station. Ghosie can help me with that while you take care of all this." Lila gestures to my crew.

"This way." My cock has settled slightly and is no longer trying to push out, so I can remove my hands and point in the direction we need to go. I would like to hold her hand, but I know that's just going to fog her up again, and I don't want to do that to her.

As we turn our backs to them and walk away, the warlock calls after her. "Oh, and Lila, don't think I didn't see those marks on both your backs."

She ignores him and flips him the finger without even stopping. Both men chuckle, but I'm confused. I felt my back burn when I declared Lila was my bitch. I'm going to have to find a mirror and have a look at my back, but later, once everything has been settled.

"Ignore them, Ghosie. They are assholes," she tells me as screams echo down the corridor from the room we just left. "They'll play with their food for a little while and then take care of them. Let's go save some women."

CHAPTER TWENTY-FOUR

Saxon
Half an hour earlier

We arrive back at the circus ship, the vegetable man firmly in my grasp and unable to escape. My body is buzzing with energy after drinking from Link. I've never drunk from a cyborg before, but it's like a bolt of lightning has infused my blood, and I feel like I can fly across the galaxy. Xavier is eyeing me suspiciously.

"What is wrong with you?" he asks as I bounce up and down on the spot.

"Fuck, man. Link's blood is like a shot of pure energy," I tell him, and the cyborg rolls his eyes at me, but I know he enjoyed me drinking from him as much as I did. The wet spot on his pants tells the truth.

"Keep it together while we question this guy, and then I'm sure our mate will let you use up all your excess energy on her when she returns," he promises me.

"I'm going to go change if you have everything in hand here," Link says, grimacing and pulling his pants away from his skin. The rest of the guys chuckle but don't stop him.

"As much as I want to watch, I'll go give the grandpas a reprieve from watching the babies. Echo was going to hang with Nikos, and I'm sure Maxsim is helping them, but our babies are hard work," Caspian says affectionately and leaves with Link.

That leaves Xavier, Tirrian, Silac, Brannock, and me to intimidate the vegetable man, and I would say from the way his body keeps exploding and leaving debris all around him, it's not going to take much.

There isn't anywhere to interrogate beings on the ship, so we have brought him straight to the containment cells Brannock was kept in when he first arrived. Xavier conjures up a chair that has restraints, and Brannock assists me in manhandling him into them. He dropped his glamour, and the vegetable man just about peed his pants when he saw the Aaz'axian looming over him. Having him here certainly makes our job easier. I wouldn't be opposed to Lila adding Brannock to our family. No one will ever fuck with us once they realize she has him as a mate.

"Agh, please, what do you want with me? I told

the girl everything I know." He's blubbering like a baby, and it's all I can do to not backhand him just to get him to shut up. Pathetic.

Tirrian scoffs. "He's useless. Let me shift, my dragons want to eat him." He flexes his wings, and smoke drifts out of his nostrils. The minute we returned to the ship, Xavier dropped our glamours.

"Maybe he just needs a little help?" Silac flares his cobra hood and hisses, and it proves to be too much, because the asshole faints.

"Fuck." I punch the wall of the cell, and my hand goes straight through it. Xavier just tuts and rolls his eyes before waving a hand and fixing the mess I made.

"Lila's going to be pissed you hurt yourself," he scolds me, and I shake my hand and hold it out, and we all watch as it repairs itself in front of our eyes. "Huh, that's a handy trick."

"Yes, all that blood from Link has made my regeneration even faster," I tell them as the skin knits itself back together. "It's even better than yours," I tease the warlock who flips me off, not even taking the bait.

"Are you going to search his memories?" Brannock asks Xavier.

"Yeah. I'll wait until he's conscious and we can question him. People can't help but think about their answers, even if lies come out of their mouths."

"What are we going to do if he is telling the truth and knows nothing?" Silac asks. It's the question that has been rolling around in my mind. We need the answer to be able to rescue Liliana Adams.

"Lila will have to mimic him and go in his place when the crew is recalled. It might add some time onto the mission, but..." Tirrian shrugs, leaning against the cell wall. "Without that information, it's basically a suicide mission.

"But what about a forcefield around us?" Xavier suggests, and I can hear his frustration. He doesn't want to drag this out any longer, and none of us want to put our mate in even more danger. It's hard enough as it is, even though we know she is fully capable of defending herself with all her powers.

Brannock shakes his head. "No, we tried that, both magical and mechanical, and neither of them worked. One of the creatures has acid spit, and it could eat through either of them."

"Fuck," I growl and pace back and forth, unable to stand still. "I really don't like the idea of Lila going on her own," I announce to my friends.

We're all silent for a moment, and Xavier shakes his head. "She won't have to. Link told me that the doctor friend of his who found this guy" — he gestures to the unconscious vegetable man— "mentioned that the job has a high turnover rate, and the company who hires them is always looking for new harvesters. How about I mimic this idiot, and I can say I have two friends who want to become halla harvesters. Lila can take her earth elemental form, and Brannock, you can either glamour yourself the same or just go as you are. We can use the excuse that nobody wants to give an Aaz'axian a job."

Brannock nods slowly. "That could work. Then we can get a good look at this leader. Either Lila will have eyes on him to mimic, or we can force him to take us to the death forest and rescue Liliana."

Tirrian scoffs. "Sounds like a long shot, but it's the best we've got so far. I can come and watch from the air," he suggests.

"I don't remember there being any flying creatures big enough to take out a dragon, but I can't guarantee things haven't changed since I've been there," Brannock tells the dragon.

"Sounds a little risky to me," Silac remarks, and Xavier nods.

"Seven hundred years is a long time for something new to evolve. Let's just play it by ear. Both of you can always teleport down from the ship if needed," he tells Silac and Tirrian, who reluctantly agree.

"Alright, let's see what we can do to wake this guy up." Xavier waves a hand, and a bucket of water appears in mine. "Want to do the honors?" he asks me, smirking.

I shake my head at his ridiculousness. He could

have just nudged his mind. I think he can tell how edgy I am, and he's trying to distract me.

I throw the contents of the bucket over our detainee, who jolts to consciousness. Xavier doesn't even wait for him to talk, he just lets him splutter slightly before he drives into his mind. The man's eyes roll back in his head, and his body twitches violently.

"How do you survive on Husadavia?" Brannock demands, bringing the memories we need to the front. We're quiet as we watch Xavier sift through them, his eyebrows jumping in surprise at what he sees. It doesn't take him long, maybe five minutes, before he releases the captive who slumps, unconscious once more.

"Well?" Tirrian asks, unable to be patient.

"He wasn't lying. This being who they call Zeygan really does just stand there and everything stays away. They walk through the bushes, picking everything they can, and move onto the next section. It looks like he can control maybe a couple of hundred yards. Anything that steps out of that area gets attacked, quickly and violently I might add, and he doesn't warn them, he just moves. He doesn't speak, and he wears a long, cowled cape, and I couldn't make out any details according to what this man has seen. Once they finish, it looks like he teleports them all off the planet to a ship that hovers in orbit. They usually have at least one hundred harvesters, but regularly lose four or five a trip on average because he doesn't wait for them. If they don't keep up, it's too bad."

"That doesn't seem like good staff management," Silac jokes nervously, and Xavier shrugs.

"From his memories and conversations with his fellow harvesters, I got the feeling that the being doesn't care. They call him a sociopath. They think he lets people get eaten on purpose. This guy has only been twice, but there are some who are seasoned veterans who gave him tips to survive. Don't draw attention to yourself is the main one. It's the ones who do stand out who end up dead."

"That's actually good to know," Brannock comments, but suddenly Xavier freezes. His eyes turn white, and his body crackles with power. He snarls, and when his eyes open, I can see the fury in them.

"Lila has been taken. Care to have some fun?" he asks me, but he doesn't wait for an answer. He reaches over and puts his hand on my shoulder, and I feel that telltale tingle of teleporting, and then we are somewhere else.

It only takes me a second to assess the room. Xavier freezes everyone in place, but the bear with his gun pointed at my blood rose must die. I unsheathe my claws and rip out his throat, splattering blood across my blood rose and the bear next to her, but she just grins and tells me how tasty the blood is, offering me a sample from her finger.

I suck the blood off her finger, noting that while delicious, it's not as tasty as my blood rose's. I can't stop the rumbling growl that comes from my chest as Xavier and Lila discuss what's going on.

"Can I kill them now?" I manage to grind out when there is a lull in the conversation.

Lila gives her consent, except for the brightly colored one next to her. Apparently, he's been protecting her, and she's grown attached. As they walk away, Xavier and I can see how attached they are. Lila's top doesn't have much of a back, since Xavier loves seeing all our marks on her—but there's a new one that wasn't there previously. My eyes shift to the bear's back, and sure enough, Lila's mark is on his fur. She flips us off as he calls some teasing remark, but he quickly unfreezes the rest of the bears, and then he and I make sure that none of them live to tell anyone else about our Lila, who now has the carevasta bear in her repertoire.

Using fangs and claws, I tear the bears to shreds with Xavier's help. He doesn't use magic, instead conjuring a wicked pair of sickle blades and going about beheading any of the bears I haven't gotten to yet. Pale pink blood is splattered across the whole entire room by the time we finish, and I'm barely breathing hard.

"Well, that was fun," he says as I lick the blood

off my claws. Lila was right, it does taste good, so there's no point in wasting it.

"Bah," I scoff. "They barely put up a fight."

Xavier starts to chuckle. "I see what you did there."

I frown, confused. Did he get hit on the head when I wasn't looking? As I scan his body, he doesn't seem to be injured.

"Barely. Get it? They are bears?" he explains, and I just shake my head. My bloodlust and need to maim and injure still ride me hard, and he can tell, so he saunters over to me and kisses me hard.

"You want to fuck it out, or should we pop over to the station and start another fight?"

"No time for fucking or fighting," Lila announces, appearing with a group of whimpering women who whimper even harder when they catch sight of all the dead bears, but it's the one whose attraction mark is on her shoulder that I watch carefully. I want to see if there is any outward display of emotion for his former crew, but all I see is grim satisfaction, so I relax a little more.

One of the women is a little feistier than the others, and she hurries over to the original bear whose throat I tore out and kicks him in the crotch before spitting on him.

"I hope you rot in hell," she says. Xavier's eyes widen comically when he sees who it is.

"Nambra?" He sounds confused as his eyes scan

her, noticing the obvious pregnant bump she's now sporting. "But we just saw you a little while ago on X69."

She turns to face him and flutters her eyelashes, her hands cupping her obviously pregnant belly. "Yes, we were taken from the brothel the next day. That asshole knocked me up before I could even blink, and I couldn't fight back because I liked what he was doing to me," she sobs, and her eyes are shadowed with memories.

"You had your powers back, so why didn't you fight them?" Lila asks, not giving the redheaded warlock any sympathy. Nambra sneers at her and holds up the hand which has the same bracelet as Lila.

"Were you able to fight back?" she asks, and Lila shakes her head, looking slightly sympathetic.

"Okay, we need to make sure the rest of them aren't pregnant, mind wipe them, and send them home," Lila announces, getting back on track.

"Please don't send me home," Nambra begs. "I have nothing and no one. My parents will disown me."

"Most of these girls were from here or X69," Ghosie says. "You shouldn't have to mind wipe these five. There was no time for any of them to have anything done to them." The girls quickly agree with his assessment, so Xavier waves a hand,

and those five disappear. That leaves four remaining women—Nambra and three others.

"Here, this will scan for pregnancy." Ghosie picks up a small handheld device from a nearby shelf, wiping it free of the splattered blood before handing it to Lila.

Xavier raises a questioning eyebrow, and Ghosie looks suitably ashamed but doesn't give any excuses.

"Okay, so these three aren't pregnant," she announces, and all three of them burst into tears of relief. "Xavier will wipe your minds, and we will arrange transport home for you."

"They are just whores from my brothel too," Nambra informs us.

"That's why we're not pregnant. Thankfully, our mandated birth control worked. What's your excuse?" one of the girls sneers, looking at the redheaded warlock with disgust.

"I heard her talking with her friend. They both got rid of their birth control in the hopes they can get knocked up by someone rich," one of the other women says, and Lila just shakes her head.

"Of course she did. Always the opportunist."

"She's also the one who told Lizis about you," Ghosie announces, and if it wasn't for the fact that she has a living being in her belly, I would have ripped her throat out. As it is, Xavier crackles with power.

"Be thankful for that child, because it is the only reason you will continue to exist."

"Wipe her mind this time. I don't need her sharing my existence with anyone else either. Knowing her, she would go in search of someone to get rid of me," Lila suggests, picking at her fingernails. She's acting nonchalant, but I know she's feeling as bloodthirsty as I am.

Xavier nods, and I can see the moment he takes control of all of their minds, removing all knowledge of Lila and the fact she is a mimic. He then puts them in a state of unconsciousness and sends them away.

"Where did you send them?" I ask.

"To Link's clinic. We need to find a way to get them back to X69. They will be fine in his clinic until we finish on Husadavia."

"What do you want to do to this ship?" I ask the bear who looks satisfied at what Xavier did to the women. He's going to fit in well, I think.

"Can we make it look like a space accident? Maybe blow it up or something? Then people will assume I died as well," he asks.

"Is that what you want? Don't you have family or friends who will miss you?" Lila asks, and he nods.

"I do, but for now, I think it would be safer for them to think we died, especially if word of your abilities got out. They will assume you were killed as well."

"Good thinking." Xavier claps the bear on the shoulder. "How about you and I navigate this ship into open space and then teleport us back to the circus ship, and Saxon can take his bloodlust out on it with the laser cannons."

I feel a grin cross my lips. "You do know how to spoil a friend," I say to him, and he winks.

"Well, I reward those who suck my cock nicely."

Ghosie looks back and forth between us with confusion, and Lila waves a hand at him.

"Ignore them, I do. Okay, I'll let Bubby know we'll follow your ship." She looks between the warlock and the bear. "Play nicely," she cautions the warlock who rolls his eyes and grins, but he agrees.

"Come on then, lover. I can at least do something to take care of that." Lila points at my hard cock behind my pants and puts her hand on me, teleporting us back to the ship.

When we arrive, she's quick to use Xavier's trick, divesting us of our clothes with the snap of her fingers. Before I can blink, she's in my arms with her legs wrapped around my waist, impaling herself on my cock.

"Fuck yes," she cries as she fully seats herself. "I have been so horny since that bear got his hands on me," she admits, wide-eyed and a little sheepish. "Take care of both our aches, but be quick, because we need to get underway." She's bossing me around, but I'm not complaining. My dick is wrapped in hot, wet heat, and I'm about to get my fangs in her neck. Nope, no complaining here, and I proceed to give her exactly what she needs.

CHAPTER TWENTY-FIVE

Lila

F eeling refreshed after my quickie with Saxon, I hurry to the bridge to tell Bubby the plans. He pulls away from the space station, and I watch the viewing screen as a much smaller vessel moves in front of us.

"That's the vessel that followed us from Aquilia," Bubby shouts, stabbing a finger at it.

"Well, your concerns were well-founded. That ship was full of carevasta bears hell-bent on making me the salvation of their race," I tell him, and he gapes at me in shock.

"What?"

"Or it was. All but one are dead now, and the one left alive was trying to help me escape, so we're keeping him."

"What's this about keeping a bear?" Link joins us on the bridge, as does Silac, Tirrian, and Brannock, all demanding to know what happened.

The noise creeps higher, and questions are being thrown left and right. I eventually have enough and freeze them all on the spot.

"Ugh, stop it. We can have a family meeting in a minute and debrief, but first, we need to blow something up. If you guys can be quiet, I'll unfreeze you so you can watch."

"Ah, Lila. They can't answer you when they are frozen," Bubby says.

"Hmm, you're right. Let's leave them frozen for a little while. The peace is actually really nice. Now, Xavier and Ghosie are on that ship. We're going to follow them away from the station, far enough away so when we blow up that ship, the debris won't impact anything. Then Saxon is going to use the laser cannon to destroy it once Xavier and Ghosie have teleported back to the ship. Okay?"

"Yes, ma'am." Bubby salutes me, giving me a wink, and he presses a few buttons before using the throttle to get us moving. I take a seat next to him, fully aware of the stares I'm getting.

"I'll unfreeze you, but I just need five minutes, okay? I'm bummed about not getting the information we need about Husadavia, and I'm really not looking forward to telling my grandpas that the mission will be delayed and that I got sold by a weaselly little security guard. Fuck, I forgot to make him pay. We need to make a note to return to the station and fuck up Glup. So yeah, I just need a moment to decompress, then Saxon can blow that fucking ship up, and only then will I be willing to talk. Okay?"

I give it a moment for my words to sink in before unfreezing them, and surprisingly, they all listen. Saxon and Link both give me a kiss on the forehead before each one of them takes a seat at one of the empty bridge positions, and then they watch in silence as we move farther into space. I think we travel for a good hour before Xavier and Ghosie appear in the bridge.

"How are you doing there, *phoeall?*" Xavier asks, coming up to stand next to me, and I lean my head against him. Ghosie just looks around the bridge with wide-eyed amazement and concern when he sees everyone here, but nobody moves. They know if he's with Xavier, then he is okay. I'm sure they all have questions, but they are doing a good job of respecting my wishes for now.

"It's all a bit much," I admit. "I need some downtime, and I don't see that happening anytime soon."

"No, probably not," he agrees, and the small amount of hope I had fades, and I sigh.

"How about you fire the lasers at that ship?" Saxon approaches and rests his hand on my other shoulder, giving me a squeeze. "Trust me, you'll feel heaps better."

"Yeah, okay. What do I need to do?" I ask him, and it's Brannock who waves his hand.

"Come over here. This is the weapons station you need."

I stand up and stretch my arms into the air, groaning at the aches in my muscles, before going over and taking a seat next to him.

"Some of our weapons' systems are manually operated, and they are on a different level, but the laser cannon can also be fired from here," he explains as the screen in front of us shows an up close version of the carevasta ship. "All you have to do is line them up in the crosshairs and press this button here," he tells me, showing me a joystick with a big red button. It kind of looks like an old-fashioned computer game, and I feel a rush of excitement. He moves out of the way, allowing me to slip into the hot seat.

As I take the controller, he leans over and wraps both arms around me, placing his hands on top of mine, and shows me exactly how to move it. I can't help but breathe in his scent. Surprisingly, he has this light fruity smell that reminds me of summer and eating watermelon in my foster family's back-yard. His arms are warm, and the ridges and bumps along the length of them tickle my bare skin. I bite my lip to stop from giggling, but I lean back into his embrace. I hear him suck in a surprised breath and can't help the small smile that creeps across my lips.

He shows me what I need to do, and then he drops his arms, allowing me to operate it by myself. I feel a momentary pang of loss, but I'm determined that it won't be the last time we have our hands on each other. After all, I can't teach him to swim without manhandling him.

The screen starts to beep and flashes red once I get the ship lined up how I want it, and I take that as my cue to shoot. "Fire in the hole," I call out loudly and press the button. I can't take my eyes away as two bright beams of light shoot from somewhere below us and hit the carevasta ship dead-on. I whoop with delight as it explodes into a million pieces.

"Good shot," Bubby calls as he maneuvers the circus ship away from the floating debris. I watch on for a few more moments as the debris gets smaller as we move farther away from it.

"Okay, what now?" I turn to appeal to the men behind me, because I'm kind of at a loss.

"Good job, sweetheart. How about we gather everyone, and we can have a family meeting? Then we won't have to tell what we've learned five different times," Xavier suggests, pressing a kiss to my head.

"That sounds like a good idea." My eyes drift to the bear, who looks a little lost, leaning against a far wall. "That's Ghosie," I tell the others. "He's the one who helped me get away. Be nice to him, please. He's now homeless and displaced because of it."

"Hey, man, thanks for taking care of our girl." Tirrian nods, and my eyebrows just about jump off my face in surprise. One, he called me his girl, and two, holy hell, he's being nice. "Come on, after the meeting, we'll find you a room, but how about we find you a drink and something to eat? Are we meeting in the dining hall?" he asks me, and I nod.

"Yeah, it's probably the place where we'll be most comfortable."

"Okay, you go get your grandpas and the babies and the others, and I'll show Ghosie where to go," he tells me, standing up and stretching out his wings before coming over and giving me a kiss on the cheek. My mouth drops open in surprise, and he and Ghosie leave the room with Silac following behind with a wave in my direction.

"What the fuck was that?" I ask, pointing after the dragon, and Xavier and Saxon chuckle.

"Looks like the dragon is stepping up," Saxon says.

"But why?" I ask, and it's Brannock who answers.

"Sometimes it takes a kick in the ass to realize what you have right in front of you. I'll meet you in the dining room. I have something I need to do first," he says absently, and then he hurries out as well.

Bubby and I exchange a glance, and I watch as he casually pulls up the tracking screen. "I'll let you know," he assures me, and I sigh. I really hope he's not scamming us. I really like him.

"Okay, let's do this. I need some baby snuggles before I can face the rest of this," I tell Link, Saxon, and Xavier.

"They will be happy to see you. They were asking for you when I went and changed my pants."

"Bubby, I'll let you know what's going on after the meeting. Maybe just hover around for the moment until I have a destination for you. What time is it? I seem to have lost track with everything that's going on," I ask as I wave goodbye to Bubby and head toward our suite. Thankfully it isn't far. I'm exhausted. After this meeting, I need a few hours of sleep.

"It's past dinner time. The babies have eaten, but they are tired and cranky and ready for bed. They refused to go without cuddles and kisses from their mom and all their fathers," Link says, and I wince.

"My poor grandpas must be exhausted too."

"I think they are anxious to see what you got from the halla harvester. They asked me, but I couldn't tell them anything."

"Crap, that was a bust. They are going to be so disappointed."

"Not necessarily," Xavier says as we approach our door. "While you were busy rubbing all over your bear, we came up with a plan."

I flip him off at the bear comment, but then I hear the rest of what he said. "You did?"

"Yeah, don't worry, babe, we've got this. I assure you, your grandma will be back on the ship and reunited with your grandpas before you know it."

"Have I told you that you're my favorite mate right this very moment?" I joke as we walk into our suite.

"What's this? I thought I was your favorite mate," Cas says, bouncing Jack on his hip.

"Mama!" all three children shout. Jack throws himself out of Cas's arms in a move that always makes my heart race, but Xavier catches him telekinetically and floats him across the room to me. Jack giggles the whole way.

"How many times have I told you not to do that, you rascal?" I scold him as I pluck him out of the air. The two girls get up from the pile of blocks on the floor and hurry over on their own two feet. I get down to their level so I can smother all three babies with kisses. Maxsim, who is in cat form on the floor as well, stretches his limbs out before rolling over onto his belly, wanting a scratch as well. I reach out and give it to him, giggling.

"Oh, I missed you, but isn't it way past your bedtime?" I ask them, and Cordy sticks a thumb into her mouth and shakes her head, but Cally looks at me with teary eyes.

"We missed you, Mama."

"Aw, baby, I missed you too," I say, rubbing my nose on her cheek before kissing it. "I'm super busy with work at the moment, but I promise once we have Grandma Lilly back, we will have plenty of time together." I wince internally. I hope we will.

"We're going to have a family meeting. I think that we'll put you in your pj's and clean your teeth. Daddy X will conjure some beds down in the dining room for you, and you can all go to sleep while the adults talk. Then he can move you back to your beds when we're done," I say, looking at my warlock, and he quickly agrees. Come on, Mama, will help you." I stand up, and Cas and Link bring Cally and Cordy for me as we go to the children's room and change them.

Everyone is in the dining room when we finally arrive, babies in tow. Echo gives me a kiss and assures me that Nikos is healing slowly and is in much better spirits. That's one less thing I have to worry about, but I will need to schedule a visit.

I try to get the kids to settle on the big bed that Xavier conjured for them in the corner, but then they catch sight of Ghosie.

"Teddy!" Cally screams and hurries over to him. I am quick to stop her before she can get to him. I pick her up, and she starts to scream her lungs off. "Want to cuddle the teddy."

"Aww, baby, no. That's not the kind of teddy you can cuddle," I tell her, feeling awful that she can't have what she wants, but his fur kind of makes it impossible.

Ghosie's eyes are comically wide as he looks at all three of my children. "You have babies," he says, sounding surprised.

"Yup, my kraken knocked me up before we even got to exchanging surnames." I laugh and look affectionately at the culprit who blushes a little. It's so freaking cute.

"May I?" Ghosie holds his arms out for Cally, looking at her with wide-eyed wonder.

"What about your fur?" I remind him, and he smiles, shaking his head.

"It doesn't affect children. Otherwise, none of us would ever be able to be around kids. It doesn't seem to have any effect until they reach the age of maturity. It's why some of us like to keep our children in our lives. It's the only time we get this kind of nonsexual love."

Fuck, imagine not being able to give someone a comforting hug. That would suck. I pass Cally over to Ghosie, who seems to melt before my eyes. Great, one more man my children have managed to corrupt. Jack and Cordy are quick to get in on the action and hurry over to hug his legs. He is soon sitting with all three kids giving him cuddles, telling him how pretty his fur is, and I can see tears stream down his face from happiness. Fuck, that's not fair.

"Tell us more," Link says, going over to the replicator and pressing a few buttons. I take a seat at a table with my grandpas as I watch the giant bear playfully wrestle with my children. Everyone else is in the process of getting food or drinks. I lean over and give all of them an absent kiss on the cheek as Ghosie starts to talk.

"There are very different factions of carevasta bears. The ones who enjoy the lifestyle we must live to be able to continue our species are happy to steal and use their fur to coerce women, and they are also happy to turn those women away once they've given birth. They keep the male children, who are always bears, and discard the female children. The male children are handed over to a nursery facility to be raised, and these males have very little to do with their offspring—and they have many of them. Our reproduction rate is actually quite extreme considering we have no females. Gestation is three months."

"That sounds awful," Silac says, looking horrified, but shifters revere their children, so it's no surprise.

"Yes, and that's the opinion of the other faction. Males like my dad choose to be completely involved in the children's upbringing. It's mostly the older generation. They remember what it was like when we did have females. My father remembers his grandmother, but the goddess curse turned all our females to males, and there haven't been any since then. There are a few women who are part of our lives, other species who were asked to bear our children and fell in love with their partners. At the colony I grew up in, there were quite a few, but again, none of these women could have female bears. Our only hope is to find the goddess and beg her forgiveness and hope she has had enough time to cool off since being offended."

"That's so freaking sad." Cas, my big softy, has tears in his eyes and a gentle smile on his face.

While Ghosie told his story, our babies curled up against him and went to sleep. Ghosie looks at them with complete wonder. He strokes a huge paw over Jack's forehead, pushing his hair back from his face. "So you can see why Lila would be such a temptation and why it was imperative that none of the others survived to share her existence."

"But what about you?" William has his arms crossed and is staring at Ghosie with suspicious eyes. "Don't you have a responsibility to your species to let them know about Lila?"

Ghosie shrugs. "Why? It's not going to fix the problem. Not really, unless we keep Lila knocked up for the rest of her life, not to mention we would then have to wait for all her children to mature before they could even be considered potential mates. It's just enslaving more people. I'd rather keep searching for another solution."

"Have you consulted reproductive specialists? Maybe we can manipulate DNA in a test tube to create girl babies." Link sounds excited about the opportunity, but Ghosie shrugs.

"We did seek the help of a cyborg doctor once, since your species is so advanced technologically. They were able to create a female embryo, but by the time it was ready to be implanted, it changed to male. The curse is buried in the male sperm, and nothing has been able to counteract it."

"Look, as sorry as I am for Ghosie's plight—and I appreciate the fact that you rescued my grand-daughter, so you are welcome to stay with us for as long as you wish—what I really want to know is how do we rescue my wife?" Eric can no longer be patient, and I really don't blame him.

Now I just have to break his heart, and I'm not sure if any of them will recover from it.

CHAPTER TWENTY-SIX

Lila

"I'm sorry, the harvester was a bust. He couldn't tell us anything," I admit, and my heart breaks as my grandfathers look crestfallen. "He was just a worker, he wasn't the leader or anything, and what he did have to tell us was kind of weird." I look at my mates. "Did you guys get any more information out of him?"

"I was able to confirm that he didn't lie to you. This Zeygan does exist, and I could see in his memories that he does exactly as he told you. He just stands there as the halla harvesters do their thing. His presence is what keeps the flora and fauna away," Xavier says, confirming what the scam artist told me.

"Fuck!" William picks up a chair and throws it. Thankfully Xavier catches it in the air and stops it from crashing to the ground and waking the children. "Shit, sorry." William scrubs his hand through his hair. It's grown out since I met him, and he is in desperate need of a haircut. It doesn't help that he keeps tugging on it when he gets frustrated, which has been a lot recently.

"But what we did learn was that they are being picked up tomorrow for another run, and we have a plan." Saxon grabs William's shoulder and squeezes. "Be calm, my friend. We will find a way to get to your wife."

"We were thinking that I could glamour myself to look like our vegetable friend, and I will take Lila in her earth elemental form and Brannock, and they can pose as new harvesters. They need new ones every time because this Zeygan isn't very cautious with the crew. Then Lila can either mimic Zeygan and use his abilities or we can force him to help us," Xavier explains, and I feel a dash of hope.

"Sounds a little weak," John says, but he can't hide the yearning in his eyes.

"But what about the bear? We were specifically told by Zamala that we would need a carevasta bear to retrieve her from her stasis," Tirrian reminds us.

"The circus ship can hover in orbit, and when you have the right location, we will teleport him to where he needs to be." Saxon doesn't sound worried at all. I mean, I could use my own bear form now, but I won't have time to practice how to use their special matter manipulation powers, not to mention if I accidentally brush against one of my mates, we may end up having an orgy amongst the man-eating flora and fauna, which is not my idea of a good time. I like to be eaten, but I prefer to keep all my body parts when it happens.

"Do you know anything about my wife?" William demands, scowling at the bear. "It had to have been one of you who went into the cave on Rilu and retrieved her for whoever holds her captive. It's the only thing that makes sense. No other creature could get into the cave."

"Actually, a powerful warlock could teleport into it if they had a picture of the place in mind."

"Yes, but neither Zamala nor Zilla, who are the only people before Lila who could get into that cave, had ever been in there," Silac replies.

Ghosie frowns, deep in thought. "I remember a job coming up on Rilu, but it wasn't my crew who took that one. I know it paid well and had to be kept quiet."

"Do you know which of the carevasta crews took the job?" Link sounds excited. "If we can find out who did, then maybe we can find out who paid them to move Liliana."

"Yes, a captain by the name of Osid, but I heard through the grapevine that his crew perished on that job."

"That actually makes sense. Zamala said the crew who situated Liliana on Husadavia hadn't survived," Silac reminds us.

"Well, there goes that idea," Cas grumbles.

"But if their ship is still orbiting Husadavia, I could probably get the information out of its communication logs," Ghosie offers.

"It sounds like we have a solid plan then." I'm feeling more hopeful by the moment.

"Excellent. We are a little bit closer to figuring out who is behind her disappearance." Eric rubs his hands together before turning his gaze to Silac. "Unfortunately, we have some bad news for you."

And there it is, my hope disappears as I see the worry on Silac's face. "What is it? Is my family okay? Did Cronus and Xylene succeed?"

"They contacted us while you were all over on the station. They hit a snag. When they arrived for the meeting, they found that Sissoik, who is the head of the Bravalana basilisks, turned your father to stone. They can't make a move on him until they reverse it, and he won't reverse it until you return and marry his daughter. He is sick of waiting, and he was suspicious of the warlocks."

"Fuck! When will it stop?" I can't help the words that burst from my mouth. "It seems like the whole fucking world is against us, and I've had enough."

"Cronus thinks that someone tipped off the Bravalanas," John tells us.

"I bet it was their fucking private secretary. He

was such a fucking weasel." I look at Saxon who nods.

"Yeah, you could be right. He didn't like you one little bit."

"Eryan?" Xavier's eyebrows jump. "When did you speak to him? And no, he wouldn't have liked her one bit. He is Elyan's brother, and I'm sure my parents have informed her family what has become of her. I'm almost certain he would have jumped at the chance to get rid of my parents. His father has been gunning to replace them for years."

"When I called them to arrange for them to meet us at Aquilia," I tell him. "Why would they keep him as their private secretary then?"

Xavier snorts with amusement. "Because they are sick and twisted individuals who enjoy mind games. They love that saying, keep your friends close but your enemies closer. They've been feeding false information to his family for years."

"I need to go." Silac is on his feet, his cobra hood flared and his tongue flicking in and out in agitation.

"Whoa, hang on." Tirrian puts his hands up in a calming manner. "I don't think we should separate. You most certainly shouldn't go on your own. The minute you marry the girl, they could freeze you as well."

"Tirrian is right. We shouldn't separate," Maxsim says gruffly. "We are a family, a team, and we take care of everyone's problems together. We will rescue Liliana Adams, and once she is safely on board, we will rescue your family."

Echo snuggles into our alpha's side and nods his head in agreement. "We need to stick together." He rubs his hand across his belly. "We are stronger as a team."

"But what if that makes it worse?" Silac hisses the last word.

"Cronus said they were fine at the moment, that they were being wined and dined, and still pretending they want to negotiate a contract with them. They are pretending to go along with everything," William assures Silac.

"We told them the circus was on the far side of the galaxy, auditioning for new acts, and that it would take us at least a couple of weeks to return. They indicated that they were happy to wait three weeks but no longer. If you don't return by then, they will make sure the stoning is irreversible."

Silac heaves out a huge sigh, and his hood flares up and down in agitation. "Fine, but as soon as we get Mrs. Adams, we need to go." I can't stand seeing him this worked up any longer, so although I've been cautious about showing any affection for this engaged man, I can't help but go over and give him a hug.

It's the right thing to do. His entire body shudders, and he sinks into the hug. "Thank you," he says gratefully. "I know this has been hard, but if you wait for me, someday, we can be together," he whispers so only I can hear, and I feel a thrill of excitement. I was worried he would give me up to save his parents, which makes me feel guilty because how fucking selfish am I, especially with how many mates I already have? But the heart wants what the heart wants, or the mimic powers do, and thankfully, it seems like he is still interested.

"It's fine. We will get through all of this, and one day, we will look back and laugh."

He pulls away, but I drag him over and make him sit down before taking a seat on his lap, making myself comfortable.

"Okay, well, I need to share something I learned from that fucking little troll, Glup," I announce. I'm not sure how helpful his information is, but we need to make use of everything available to us.

"Who is Glup?" Cas asks, his face adorably confused. "Was that one of the bears?"

"No, that was one of the security guards on the space station—the one who fooled me into thinking he was helping me, but in reality, he was just trying to make a quick buck."

"Glup is a Gurko," Ghosie announces to the rest of my family, and the confusion clears.

"Fucking weaselly parasites. They would sell their own mother if the price was right," Tirrian spits.

"That's why the station employs them as security guards. They aren't afraid to get their hands dirty for the right amount of money. It's why it was so easy for Lizis to strike a deal with him." Ghosie looks apologetic, but I don't hold him responsible for someone else's actions.

I tell them what he told me, and although Link and my grandpas look a little like this is the first time they've heard this, none of the other men do.

"Origin gods are still worshiped on a lot of planets," Saxon tells me, seeing my confusion. "Not by the masses, but there are small pockets of believers here and there. The Galactic Council hasn't managed to stamp them all out."

"Does anyone else know a species who has the ability to repel like Zeygan does, or do we think we might be dealing with a god?" Cas asks the question that had been playing over and over in my mind. Is it a coincidence that he can keep everything away, or is it because he created it all?

Everyone is strangely silent, and I feel the tension rise.

"Can I even mimic a god?" I ask, hearing the panic in my voice.

"We won't know until we get there. Let's not worry about it. The old gods haven't been seen for many years. There are a few species that have repelling powers. I'm going to spend the night researching and will have a list of possibilities by the morning." Link sounds hopeful and positive, and I relax a little now that I know my cleverest mate is on the job.

"Okay, well, it seems like we have a plan then. Tomorrow, we will go back to Z68 and join up with the halla harvesters, and then when we get to Husadavia, either I'll mimic this being or we will force him to help us. One way or another, we are getting to Grandma."

Brannock has been quiet through this whole entire conversation, which is weird, because he is usually involved in planning. I must not be the only one who notices.

"Brannock, is there anything you would like to add?" Xavier asks, and when the Aaz'axian looks up, nobody can miss the anguish in his eyes.

"I have a confession, and if it means that you'll kill me because of it, that's okay, but before you do, I beg you to hear my story."

"Hey, I'm sure nothing you have to say to us is too bad. Shit, Ghosie kidnapped me, and I forgave him. Tirrian was a raging dick, and we're getting past that."

Tirrian rolls his eyes but doesn't deny the truth.

"I wouldn't be too sure. I haven't been honest with any of you, and I can't go on lying to all of you anymore, especially since you've been so kind, and you took me in and gave me a home despite me being one of the most feared races in the galaxy."

"We don't judge a race, only individual actions," Link reminds him.

"Except Madovians. They are all evil." Silac shudders beneath me, and I have to admit, the reaction is not unwarranted.

"And the Seiomann. They are a nasty race too," Xavier adds helpfully.

"Okay, fine, we judge some races, but you are not one of them." Link sounds exasperated at my other mates.

His gaze meets mine, and I can see the agony and anguish in his eyes. "I wouldn't be so sure. I was deliberately deported from Earth to the circus ship so I could search for the orb. The Syndicate believes it's here, and as one of its members, I was tasked with the job of retrieving it."

I'm speechless, and the man who I've come to think of as a friend and maybe someday something more drops an atomic bomb sized announcement on me and my family.

The dining room erupts into loud noise, and the babies wake and start crying in fright, but I just stare at the man who I hoped to add to my mates one day in disappointment. I'm sure he probably has good reasons for his actions, but at the moment, I can't think of any.

When I look around, I find Xavier has had to freeze Saxon and Tirrian both of them started to leap at Brannock. Thankfully, he is being a little more rational. Cas and Link just look disappointed, as do my grandpas.

"I'm sure you have an explanation," William says, but I can tell it's costing him to be calm.

Brannock nods quickly. "Yes, and if you would allow me to explain, I'm sure you will understand why I had to do it."

"But why?" My question silences everyone as we wait for him to answer. He walks over to me and gets down on his knees in front of me. I'm still sitting in Silac's lap, so his head is almost in line with mine.

"Smith is a part of the Syndicate, and he is the one who ordered me to find the orb."

"But why?" I repeat, not really able to form a different question.

"Because Smith has my child locked up behind a door at Area 51 with a whole heap of other aliens. He threatened to experiment on her because she shouldn't be possible, and he wants to find out why. He promised me if I found the orb and returned it to the Syndicate, she could go free."

To Be Continued

AFTERWORD

Hey! So I hope you all enjoyed that. I know you probably all thought Grandma would get rescued in this book. Heck I thought Grandma would be rescued in this book, but my characters decided differently. But we are on the down hill slide. I can now confirm there will be two more Galaxy books, because that's how many I'm going to need to wrap up all the open threads.

But first I have some other series to wrap up. I'll be back to working on Galaxy at the beginning of next year so I expect you will have at least one of them in the first half.

I hope you enjoyed the book. It would be super awesome if you could leave a review wherever you bought it, because I love to hear what you thought of the story.

Keep an eye out for any news on Galaxy or anything Lexie Winston by following me on all my social media.

In the mean time why don't you check out one of my other series. You can find everything you need to know here.

www.lexiewinston.com

To my cover designer Jessica, of Raven Ink Covers. Thank you for making the covers exactly what I envisioned, you nailed it and all of them.

Thank you to Jess at Elemental Editing. My book is pretty and readable thanks to you. As always you are the best and I appreciate you being flexible this year with all my delays.

My ever reliable and faithful beta reader Kerry…

You da bomb xxx

And lastly to you guys the readers. I love what I do, and probably would do it regardless if anyone read them or not, but you guys make it that much sweeter so thank you.

Until next time, happy reading

Lexie

www.ingramcontent.com/pod-product-compliance
Lightning Source LLC
Chambersburg PA
CBHW020247120726
47904CB00001B/113

HANNAH
PENFOLD

SIGNED BY THE
AUTHOR

CONTENT WARNINGS

This book contains material that may be triggering for some readers. Reader discretion is advised. For a complete list of content warnings please scan the below:

Copyright © 2022 by Hannah Penfold.
All rights reserved. No part of this book may be reproduced or transmitted, copied, stored, distributed or otherwise made available by any person or entity (including Google, Amazon or similar organisations), in any form, electronic or mechanical, including photocopying, recording, scanning or by any information storage and retrieval system, without prior written permission from the publisher, except in the case of brief quotations embodied in critical reviews and certain other noncommercial uses permitted by copyright law.

This book is a work of fiction. All names, characters, locations and incidents are products of the author's imagination or are used fictitiously. Any resemblance to actual places, things, living or dead, locales, or events is entirely coincidental.

No part of this publication is to be used to train generative AI technologies and machine learning language models.

THE CRIMSON SCAR
Editing by Leonora Bulbeck
Cover Design by Miblart, www.miblart.com
Character Art by Ekaterina Vasilevna
Map by Danielle Greaves
Ebook ISBN #978-0-6455270-0-1
Paperback ISBN #978-0-6455270-1-8
Hardback ISBN #978-0-6455270-2-5